ANNA JACOBS is the author of over seventy novels and is addicted to storytelling. She grew up in Lancashire, emigrated to Australia in the 1970s and writes stories set in both countries. She loves to return to England regularly to visit her family and soak up the history. She has two grown-up daughters and a grandson, and lives with her husband in a spacious waterfront home. Often as she writes, dolphins frolic outside the window of her study. Inside, the house is crammed with thousands of books.

annajacobs.com

By Anna Jacobs

The Honeyfield Series

The Honeyfield Bequest
A Stranger in Honeyfield

The Hope Trilogy

A Place of Hope
In Search of Hope
A Time for Hope

The Greyladies Series

Heir to Greyladies
Mistress of Greyladies
Legacy of Greyladies

The Wiltshire Girls Series

Cherry Tree Lane
Elm Tree Road
Yew Tree Gardens

The Peppercorn Street Series

Peppercorn Street
Cinnamon Gardens
Saffron Lane

Winds of Change

a&b

A Stranger in Honeyfield

ANNA JACOBS

Allison & Busby Limited
12 Fitzroy Mews
London W1T 6DW
allisonandbusby.com

First published in Great Britain by Allison & Busby in 2017.
This paperback edition published by Allison & Busby in 2017.

*All characters and events in this publication,
other than those clearly in the public domain,
are fictitious and any resemblance to actual persons,
living or dead, is purely coincidental.*

A CIP catalogue record for this book is available from
the British Library.

10 9 8 7 6 5 4 3 2 1

ISBN 978-0-7490-2025-5

Typeset in 10.5/15.5 pt Sabon by
Allison & Busby Ltd.

The paper used for this Allison & Busby publication
has been produced from trees that have been legally sourced
from well-managed and credibly certified forests.

Printed and bound by
CPI Group (UK) Ltd, Croydon, CR0 4YY

Part One

Chapter One

April 1916, Wiltshire

Isabella Jones, better known to her friends and fellow VADs as Bella, put on her best clothes ready to meet her fiancé's family for the first time. She had been working as an ambulance driver in the Voluntary Aid Detachment for the past year, attached to this convalescent hospital near Swindon, playing her part in the war effort.

Matron had given her the weekend off for such an important visit and was standing at the front door taking a breath of fresh air as Bella went out to wait for Philip.

'Enjoy yourself, Jones. You don't often ask for time off and you did an excellent job of cheering up Captain Cotterell while he was recovering here. Congratulations on your engagement.'

'Thank you, Matron.' She couldn't hold back a sigh.

'What's wrong?'

'It's the right thing to go and meet his family, but I don't think they will be at all pleased to meet me.'

'Toffee-nosed, eh?'

'Yes.' Bella knew Matron understood how she felt because the older woman also came from a humble background, unlike most of the nurses in the VAD. Bella had only been accepted into the organisation as a cleaner at first, but later she'd applied to train as a driver and had discovered how much she loved driving.

'What does your mother say about the engagement?'

'She's not best pleased either. She says no good ever comes of marrying outside your own class.' Her mother had grown very sour since she'd been widowed and nothing seemed to please her these days. And since her daughter had turned twenty-five without getting married, she'd begun to hint that as Isabella was turning into an old maid, it was her duty to care for her mother in her old age.

Bella missed her father dreadfully. She'd tried to get on with her life, which she knew he'd have wanted, but she could never go back to live with her mother again, not now she'd tasted independence.

'I think after the war that sort of class snobbery will change,' Matron said. 'I don't suppose we'll get rid of it entirely, but it won't matter as much, not after the men have fought together and the women worked together here on the home front. Anyway, enjoy yourself today. You've worked hard and earned your little holiday.' She turned and went back into the hospital.

Would it feel like a holiday? Bella wondered. It felt more like an ordeal to her.

Philip's car drew up in front of the convalescent hospital just then and she ran across to greet him. They'd known each other such a short time, and yet it felt as if she'd known him for ever.

He got out of the car to give her a hug and twirl her

round, as he always did when they met. When he put her down he studied her face. 'Nervous?'

'I'm afraid so.'

'Me too. But I won't have them insulting you, so if necessary we'll leave.'

'We couldn't do that!'

'Oh, yes, we could. But let's hope it isn't necessary.'

Just over an hour later he stopped for a moment outside the gateway of a country house. It wasn't a stately home, but it was large and beautiful, like a picture in a magazine, which only made her feel worse.

'Westcott,' Philip said in fond tones, taking one hand off the steering wheel of his Ford Model T to gesture towards it.

'It's a lot bigger than I'd expected.'

'Too big. It costs the earth to maintain. Never mind that. Remember what I said: it's me you're marrying not my family and certainly not the house. It's not as if I'll be inheriting it. My parents and my elder brother are snobs. They don't approve of me, let alone you. When I became an engineer, they were horrified because it's not a *gentleman's* profession.'

He still didn't set off again and she waited patiently.

'My father won't be there. He never is. He left a message at the barracks to tell me he'd have to stay up in London today to attend a meeting but he wishes us well.'

'But you sound to have plenty of other relatives.'

'I doubt we'll have much to do with any of them after the war, Bella my darling. But when a Cotterell gets engaged, there's always a family gathering and I want to give them the chance to do the right thing by you – publicly, at least. If they don't, well, I'll know where we stand and I won't be coming back here again. I have some wonderful friends, people I was at boarding school with, like Tez, who'll make you welcome into our circle.'

She couldn't think what to say, so made a murmuring noise to show she was listening.

'At least you'll like my sister, I can guarantee that. Georgie and I have always been close. Well, we're twins, aren't we? Spencer is ten years older than us, so we two always stuck together because he was a bit of a bully.'

The door opened and an elderly maid greeted Philip fondly, gave Bella a perfunctory smile and took her coat and hat before showing them into the drawing room.

'Mother's over by the fire,' he whispered. 'The one standing up talking to her is Spencer.'

Adeline Cotterell was seated in a huge armchair chatting to her older son and about a dozen people were clustered in pairs and trios round the edges of the room, with two much older women sitting on a sofa. All of them looked stiff and unfriendly; no one smiled at the newcomer.

Philip's usually smiling face had turned into a stone-like mask.

Mrs Cotterell made no effort to greet Bella with more than a brief nod accompanied by, 'Miss, um, Jones.'

The older woman had spoken in terms of icy disdain. Bella had read the phrase in books but she'd never encountered such an attitude in real life before. She didn't flinch but stared calmly back at Mrs Cotterell. She was as good as any of them!

Philip reminded his mother that he and Bella had got engaged and were there so that she could be introduced to his family, but Mrs Cotterell said only, 'Hmm'.

He seemed to be waiting for her to do something, but she stayed silent. 'I'll take her round to meet everyone, then.'

He introduced Bella first to his elder brother. Spencer was standing at the other side of the fireplace and he too stared at her scornfully. He looked like a haggard, much older version of Philip, but without the kindness and *joie de vivre* usually there in her fiancé's eyes. She already knew that Spencer had failed his medical for the army, though not why. He merely nodded at her before turning his head away.

Looking angrier by the minute Philip went on to introduce her to the two elderly cousins on the sofa. Both women followed Mrs Cotterell's lead and greeted her as 'Miss, um, Jones'.

No member of his family addressed any remarks to her, other than repeating her name.

By now, Bella was just as angry as Philip, but she too kept control of her feelings. These people could be as uncivil as they liked but she had vowed to behave impeccably, whatever happened. Her father would have been horrified by these people's bad manners. He'd always told her a pauper could be as courteous as a king and she would prove that today.

She'd hoped to win over Philip's family by good manners and pleasant behaviour, so that she would at least be tolerated by them, if not liked. It was already obvious that this wasn't going to happen. They had decided in advance to dislike her.

Philip gave her arm a quick squeeze of sympathy as he took her across to meet his sister, who said, 'I'm really happy to meet you,' in a low voice.

He left her there in the bay window in response to his mother's beckoning forefinger. 'Look after my Bella for a moment, Georgie, there's a dear.'

His sister looked suddenly terrified, which puzzled Bella. But Philip had already left them to return to his mother's side.

Georgie said in a low voice, 'I wish I could get to know you properly, Bella, because I can see how much you and Philip love one another.' She hesitated then added in a rush, 'I'm not trying to be nasty, but someone needs to warn you: they won't let him marry you, whatever he says or does. And Mother always gets her own way. That's how I came to be engaged to Francis Filmore, the one standing behind Mother. She threatened to throw me out without a penny if I didn't do as she told me and I don't come into my annuity till I'm thirty so I'd have nothing.'

She glanced quickly across the room at the tall, older man who had been introduced as Francis Filmore and it wasn't a loving look, then turned back to Bella. 'Stay away from this miserable place and keep Philip away too. He deserves a happy life after all he's been through during the war.'

There was silence for a few moments as Bella tried to take this in, then a voice said, 'Georgina, your aunt wishes to speak to you.'

Georgie froze, then took her fiancé's arm and walked across the room like a marionette whose strings were being pulled by someone else. She didn't offer a word of farewell. The man stared right past Bella as if she didn't exist.

Which left her standing on her own, surrounded by people who had either turned their backs on her or were staring at her as if she was some new species of wild animal.

After a few minutes' low-voiced argument with his mother and elder brother, Philip strode back across the room to Bella, looking furious. He took her arm and tugged her towards the door, saying loudly, 'You won't wish to stay with such ill-mannered people, my dear, any more than I do.'

In the hall he asked the maid for their coats and waited, foot tapping impatiently, until these were brought.

'Your sister said—' Bella began.

'Shh.' He waited till they were outside to say, 'I thought I could rely on Georgie to be polite.'

'She was. She even said she was sorry she couldn't get to know me. And she warned me that your family wouldn't allow us to marry.'

'Georgie meant that my mother will try to stop it. Mother made that very plain to me just now. She feels entitled to rule her children's lives, but I've told her I'll choose my own wife. They're all terrified of her, even poor Georgie, because she can be very nasty. Were you afraid?'

Bella considered this for a moment or two, then shook her head. 'No. I was angry more than anything else, darling. Besides, I shall probably never speak to her again, and she has no say in what I do with my life.'

'That's what I've told her. Several times. So let's plan to get married on my next leave, eh? To hell with the lot of them. I shall be proud to have you as my wife.'

'Are you sure? I don't want to come between you and your family.'

He helped her into his car. 'You behaved perfectly. I was so proud of you and how dignified you looked. My family don't matter any more to me, my darling. There's only Georgie I really care about and once she marries that vicious brute, I won't be allowed to see her. I know she doesn't love him. She should break off the engagement and run away, and so I've told her several times.'

'Maybe she can't afford to.'

'I haven't mentioned it before but strangely, my twin sister and I were left a little money by our grandmother and Spencer wasn't. Her choice who to leave it to, I suppose. It's just a few hundred pounds a year, not a fortune.' He grinned. 'My mother resents the independence it gives us and the fact that Spencer got nothing! Georgie got our grandmother's jewels as well. They must be worth a packet but won't be given to her till she marries. They're just sitting in the bank till then and she has to ask the lawyer if she wants to "borrow" them for a party.'

'She said the money doesn't come to her till she's thirty.'

He looked at her in surprise. 'That's not so. It's like mine, came to her at twenty-five.'

'She seemed very sure it was thirty.'

'I'll have to have a word with her next time I come back

on leave. If you see her before then, tell her to check that with the lawyer.'

'Perhaps Georgie doesn't want to break off relations with her family.'

'Ha! Strange sort of family we are. I'm not sure Georgie and I have relations with our mother, really. She didn't bring us up, but left that to Nanny. I always feel as if Mother is a stranger whose face I recognise. If Nanny were still alive, I'd take you to meet her and she'd give you a great big hug. You'd have liked her and she'd have liked you.'

He went to crank-start the car and drove away, sending gravel scattering as he turned on to the main road.

It was a while before he spoke again, so Bella waited, giving him time to calm down.

Eventually he turned to her and smiled more normally. 'I'm jolly glad I met you, my darling. Let's find somewhere to buy luncheon, then go back to your lodgings and make mad, passionate love.'

She smiled back at him. 'Let's.' Thank goodness for an understanding landlady, and lodgings so close to the hospital. If she hadn't found Mrs Sibley, Matron would have squeezed her into the crowded dormitory shared by the other VAD drivers. She'd been in a place like that before and didn't enjoy being treated like a schoolgirl.

Things seemed so different in wartime. How could you deny the comfort of your body to a man who was not only your fiancé but who might be killed at any time once he went back to France? Besides, she enjoyed making love and feeling close to him.

As she waved him goodbye, she forced herself to smile. Philip had survived more than two years of war, having been one of the first waves of volunteers. A lot of those brave lads were dead now, or maimed.

How many more young men must give their lives for their country?

A few weeks later, Bella watched through the window for the postman and ran out to meet him when he stopped at the house where she had lodgings. Thank goodness she was on a late shift today.

'Is there a letter for me?'

He smiled. 'Yes, Miss Jones. He's written to you again.'

She sighed in relief. Philip usually wrote every day, but occasionally had to miss a day or two when his regiment was in action. This time there hadn't been any letters from him for three whole days. To make matters worse, she'd had a strong feeling that something was wrong, the sort of feeling you got sometimes when the man you loved was in danger.

But it was Philip's own handwriting on the front of the usual army envelope, not that of a stranger. Oh, thank goodness! Her heart gave a great lurch of relief and she plopped a quick kiss on the smudged address.

The minute she was back in the house she tore the envelope open and froze in sheer terror because the single sheet inside it wasn't from Philip!

She knew then, oh yes, she knew what the feeling of doom had meant! She had to take a few deep breaths before she could face reading the letter.

Dear Miss Jones,

I regret to inform you that your fiancé, Captain Philip Cotterell, was killed yesterday. He was shot in the head and died instantly, so he could have felt no pain.

Philip and I were at school together and have served in the same regiment ever since we enlisted. He asked me to let you know personally if anything happened to him, because of course, the official letter will go to his family, as next of kin.

Philip was buried with comrades who fell and I'm sure he will lie at peace here in France.

My sincerest condolences

Aaron Tesworth, Captain

Bella let out a wail of anguish and burst into sobs so loud her landlady came running. It was a few moments before she could weep more quietly and try to explain what was wrong.

In the end Mrs Sibley took the piece of paper from her hand and read it, then put her arms round Bella, rocking her to and fro and letting her sob into the flour-stained pinafore, murmuring 'There, there' as if she was a little child in need of comforting.

But there was no comfort to be found.

After that Bella waited in vain to hear from Philip's family. Why hadn't they written to her about his death? There might not be a funeral, because the new regulations followed those of Marshall Joffre of 1915 forbidding repatriation of bodies. The soldiers had fought together, often becoming as close as brothers, and they were to lie together in death, no longer separated into officers and other ranks.

Given the lack of body, many families held some sort of memorial service and even placed a marker in their family cemetery plot to remember the dead person.

Surely the Cotterells would know that she'd want – no, *need* to attend anything of that sort? How far were they prepared to carry their rudeness and hostility?

In the end she booked a phone call at the local post office and rang them. 'May I please speak to Mrs Cotterell?'

'May I have your name, please?'

'Miss Jones.'

'Ah. Sorry, miss. I'm afraid madam is not accepting calls at this sad time. May I take a message?'

'Perhaps I could speak to Mr Cotterell, then?'

'I'm afraid the master is in London.'

'Miss Georgina, then.'

'Miss Cotterell is not taking any phone calls either.'

'Is there to be a memorial service?'

After a hesitation the maid said yes.

'Could *you* tell me when it is to be held, then?'

'I'm sorry. I couldn't take it on myself to do that, miss. Invitations have already been sent out to those who are involved.' She put the phone down.

Bella stared at the earpiece in shock, then hung it back on the 'candlestick'. It had been four days since the letter from Captain Tesworth arrived and she hadn't received an invitation. Surely they wouldn't – they *couldn't* be so cruel as to exclude her?

When she sat down and thought about it, she grew angry. Which was better than weeping.

But only just.

Chapter Two

Aaron Tesworth, better known as Tez, let out a long, shuddering sigh as he stared down at the bandaged hand, feeling dizzy at the speed with which it had happened. Two of his fingers gone, just like that. He looked up at the doctor, noting the lines of weariness on the poor man's face.

'What will happen to me next?' he asked.

'We'll send you back to England and they'll assess the damage.'

'And what do you think they'll say?'

'It's not for me to—' He broke off. 'Unless you're left-handed, you may have a chance of getting a desk job in the army.'

'I am left-handed. Very much so. The teachers were unable to eradicate the fault.'

'Ah. Then you'll very likely be given a medical discharge – an honourable discharge, of course. If you ask me, you're one of the lucky ones. How long have you been serving?'

'Almost since the beginning.'

'Then you've definitely done your bit. Go home, Tesworth. Find a nice woman to marry and get on with your life.'

A voice called, 'Doctor! Come quickly!'

'Good luck.' And he was gone.

Tez sat staring down at the heavily bandaged hand.

When he looked up, a nurse was standing beside him.

'Let me find you a bed, Captain.' She gently eased him to his feet. 'Lean on me.'

'I can walk by myself, thank you.' But he did feel light-headed and distant as he followed her to a small tent with INJURED OFFICERS written on the canvas in wobbly capitals.

An orderly came forward to take over from the nurse. With impersonal efficiency, he showed Tez which bed to use. 'They'll probably ship you out in the morning, sir,' he said as he helped Tez to bed. 'If you give me directions to your tent, I'll retrieve your belongings and make you more comfortable. Tomorrow, once we're sure of the time, I'll help you get ready to leave.'

And that was it. As suddenly as that, Tez's war had ended. And he was never, ever coming back to Verdun. He'd lost too many friends here, as well as his two smallest fingers on his left hand.

Unlike poor Philip, he would be able to carry on with his life. If he could think what to do with it. To lose two fingers was fairly minor, but the doctors weren't sure yet how well that hand would function, whether it might have nerve damage and be fairly useless. He might have to train his stupidly clumsy right hand to take over.

In the middle of the night, delayed pain woke him abruptly and it took all his willpower not to cry out. As it began to ebb, it occurred to him that he might, with a bit of luck, be back in time for Philip's memorial service.

It would be good to say a last farewell to his best friend.

Bella hastily wiped away the tears as Matron came into the storeroom. 'Sorry.'

'What are you sorry for, Jones? Grieving? You have a right to do that.'

'I was crying because I can't find out when Philip's memorial service is to be held.'

The older woman grew still. 'Hasn't his family invited you?'

'No. And they must be deliberately keeping it quiet. There are no notices in the papers that I can find. They haven't answered my phone calls, though I've got through to a maid each time, so they must know I've called.'

'Leave it to me. I know a few useful people.'

It was kind of Matron to try to help, Bella thought listlessly. But what was the point? She'd still have to get to Upper Westcott and the village wasn't on a railway line, so was difficult to reach without a car.

She went off for her lunch break, but couldn't force any food down, just sat stirring it about on the plate.

One of her fellow drivers peered into the room, then came rushing across to her. 'Matron wants to see you straight away, Jones. You're to hurry.'

Bella ran across the rear yard to Matron's office, expecting to have to drive an emergency patient to a London hospital for life-saving surgery. It wouldn't be the first time.

Matron looked up from her desk. 'Ah! There you are.

I've found out that your fiancé's memorial service is to be held this afternoon.'

'Today! Then I've no hope of getting there in time.'

'On the contrary. I've got you a lift there and back. One of our newly arrived injured officers is a friend of your Philip and is going to the service, representing his mother, who knows the Cotterells. Her chauffeur is coming down from London to drive him there and back. They live in Gloucestershire, near Malmesbury, don't they? He'll be happy to take you as well.'

'Who is it?'

'A Captain Tesworth.'

'He's here? Philip spoke of him often, called him Tez, said they'd been friends since school. What sort of injury has he suffered? Wouldn't he be better in an ambulance?'

'No need for that. He's lost two fingers but is otherwise all right. He's just come here so that we can keep an eye on the hand. They can save the rest of his fingers as long as the hand doesn't get infected. The doctor prefers to have someone who knows first aid with him, says he's still in shock about his injury.'

'I'd better go back to my lodgings and change quickly into more suitable clothes.'

'I think you should go as you are, proudly wearing the uniform of someone serving her country. An ambulance driver's blue uniform and cap may not look as pretty as a nurse's uniform, but you ask the men whose lives you've helped save what they think of your work.'

Bella's confidence was boosted by these bracing words and she managed a misty smile. 'Thank you, Matron.'

'Good girl. Remember, you can hold your head up in that uniform whoever you're facing, however snootily they behave. Go and tidy yourself up, then wait at the front of the building for the car. It'll do you good to get a bit of sun on your face.'

It was only after Matron had gone back inside that it really sank in that she would be facing a hostile group of Cotterells again. She wasn't looking forward to that.

Bella had been sitting on the wall waiting for only ten minutes when a car drew up. An orderly came to the front door to see who it was.

The chauffeur got out and called, 'Captain Tesworth's car.'

'I'll bring him out,' the orderly called back.

In other circumstances she'd have been happy to meet Philip's best friend and thank him for writing to her. Was his injury enough to keep him out of the war? For his sake, she hoped so.

'Captain Tesworth is giving me a lift,' she called.

'Miss Jones, is it? Right you are.' The chauffeur hurried round to open the rear door for her just as the captain appeared at the top of the steps.

'Help the captain in first. I can get in on my own.' Bella opened the other door and took her place on the rear seat behind the driver. Her companion nodded to her as he was helped in. He looked white and weary, poor man, and his left hand was heavily bandaged and in a sling.

'Thank you for letting me share the car, Captain.'

'My pleasure.' He leant against the seat back, his head slightly turned towards her. 'I'm Aaron Tesworth.'

'Yes. But everyone calls you Tez.'

'Did Philip tell you that about me?'

'Yes. He thought a great deal of you.'

'And I of him. So you're Bella. You made him very happy.'

'He was a wonderful man. He made me happy too.'

They both fell silent as the car pulled away, remembering Philip.

'I'm glad I could help you get to the service today. I hope you won't hold it against me that I had to send you the bad news.'

'I was grateful that you did. His family hasn't been in touch with me at all.'

He looked at her in shock. 'You mean – they didn't even let you know about him being killed?'

'No. Philip must have told you they don't approve of me.' When he nodded, she added, 'That was putting it mildly. They were openly hostile at the family gathering, presumably to put me in my place.'

'I'm so sorry.'

'Thank you. I'd better warn you that when I telephoned the maid told me the service is by invitation only . . . and I haven't been invited. So there may be a fuss when I turn up. But if you let me out of the car in the village, I can walk the rest of the way, so that you're not involved when I push my way in, and then you can pick me up on the way back.'

'I wouldn't dream of it. We'll walk into the village church together, though I'm more likely to need to lean on you than to be able to offer you the support of my arm.

But I can offer you my moral support, if needed. That at least I can do.'

'I don't want to damage your relations with your family's friends.'

'The Cotterells aren't close friends of ours, never have been, which is why Mother is sending me in her place. It was Philip and I who had the close friendship.'

The captain sighed and leant his head back against the seat. 'Sorry. I'm still a bit woozy. This injury only happened a couple of days ago, or was it three?'

'Well, I'm not in the mood to chat, so why don't you rest quietly for a while?'

'I think I will.'

As he fell asleep, his head settled gently on her shoulder and she left it there.

Philip had done that a few times, so tired when he came home on leave that with the best will in the world, he hadn't managed to stay awake all night and enjoy every minute of being with her, as he'd intended.

She had to fight to hold back the tears those memories brought, but she'd promised herself to show no weakness in front of the Cotterells, so she blinked furiously and refused to give in to the raw anguish of her grief.

As the two of them entered the church an usher moved forward with a list in his hand. 'May I have your name, sir?'

'Tesworth.'

He crossed it off and turned to Bella.

She was proud of how calmly she said it. 'Miss Jones, Captain Cotterell's fiancée.'

His look of horror was unmistakable. 'But . . . but . . .'

Captain Tesworth grasped her arm firmly with his good hand. 'Miss Jones is with me.'

'I'm afraid Miss Jones hasn't been invited to the service today.'

Just then three other officers joined them in the vestry.

Tez turned to greet them. 'Just in time, chaps. Did you know, they're trying to turn away Philip's fiancée, who is, apart from her relationship with him, also serving in the VADs as an ambulance driver?'

They stopped short and gaped at her and then at the usher, who was bright scarlet now.

'Is there some problem?' A tall, thin man came across the back of the church to join them.

Francis Filmore, Bella remembered, Georgie's fiancé. He looked even more snooty today. And was his breathing always a bit raspy?

It took him a minute to recognise her, then he said harshly, '*You* were not invited to the service, Miss Jones. Kindly leave at once.'

The four officers glanced at one another then at Filmore. Their scornful glances seemed to ask why he was not in uniform.

'Are you really trying to turn her away?' one demanded.

'She hasn't been invited.'

'She shouldn't need a formal invitation. She's his fiancée, dammit.'

'His mother doesn't recognise that relationship, especially now.'

More glances and the four of them moved to form a protective circle round Bella.

'Come and sit with us,' one of them said. He turned to move to the front of the church, but Filmore continued to bar the way.

It happened so quickly that Bella could never afterwards quite work out how it'd been done, but suddenly Filmore was lying on the floor and the four officers were shepherding her past him.

There was a gasp of outrage from the front of the church and Adeline Cotterell stood up. Georgie remained seated beside her mother, tugging at her arm and looking unhappy.

'You! Jones woman! You were not invited!' Mrs Cotterell shouted.

A gasp ran through the congregation.

'*I* have invited her,' Tez said loudly.

'But she isn't—'

Mrs Cotterell broke off, flinching as the four officers reached a pew three rows behind hers and stood glaring at her.

'If she leaves, so do we,' Captain Tesworth said loudly. 'But I'll make sure people know about your petty and spiteful behaviour.'

After a few more moments of silence, Mrs Cotterell turned her back on them and sat down without another word.

'This pew suit you, Miss Jones?' one of the officers asked.

Bella nodded, concentrating on holding up her head and

not betraying how humiliated she felt by this reception.

The red-haired officer followed one of the men into the pew, speaking loudly as he gestured to Bella to join him. 'Miss Jones should really be sitting at the front with the rest of the family. Still, we're not responsible for other people's bad manners, are we?'

She slid along the pew after the two officers, leaving Tez to take the aisle seat. Philip would have wanted her to be with him for the final farewell, she told herself. That was what mattered.

Mrs Cotterell's voice rang out equally loudly. 'The impudence of it! Such a vulgar young female! We can all guess how she trapped my son.'

The other guests had been murmuring to one another, but none of them had made any effort to intervene.

Georgie mouthed 'Sorry' to the newcomers before turning back to her mother. There was the sound of a low-voiced argument between the two women.

Where was Philip's father? Bella wondered. Surely he ought to be here today? Philip had said his father was engaged in important war work, but in London, not in France, so surely he could have come here for a short time.

'Are you all right, Miss Jones?' Tez asked gently.

'Yes. And thank you, Tez. I mean Captain Tesworth.' Bella heard her voice wobble and couldn't go on with her apology.

'I prefer my friends to call me Tez, and I hope I can count you among them now.'

She smiled and nodded, then turned to the other side to say, 'I'm more grateful than I can say for your help today, gentlemen.'

'I can't believe they'd insult someone who's serving her country!' The red-haired officer was still speaking so loudly he must have wanted to be heard.

A few people turned from the other side at the front to stare at her and the whispering began again. From the staccato nature of some sounds, more arguments were taking place.

'Ah! There are the others.' Tez got up and beckoned to two men in uniform who'd just entered the church. Before they sat down in the pew behind his, he quickly told them what had been happening.

With looks of outrage towards the front of the church, they each turned to Bella and loudly offered her their condolences on her sad loss.

'Bit of luck that enough of us are on leave at the moment to attend,' one of the newcomers said. He had a livid scar across one cheek and looked exhausted, but when there came the sound of someone else arriving from the rear of the church, he turned round then got to his feet. 'I'll go and have a quick word. You stay there, Tez, old chap.'

By the time the service began, eight men were sitting around and behind Bella, which was a great comfort. She bowed her head and prayed for Philip's soul, then, as the service ended, she prepared to listen to the eulogies.

Spencer Cotterell moved to the lectern at the front, speaking woodenly, mouthing platitudes but not offering any anecdotes or expressions of affection for his brother.

'And now—' the minister began, moving towards the front again.

But Georgina Cotterell got up and moved to stand at the lectern before anyone could stop her. 'I want to share my own thoughts about my dear brother with you all this one last time. Being a twin is something very special, and no one knew Philip as well as I did. He would have been glad to see you all here today, especially his fiancée, Miss Jones, who made him so happy in the months before he died.'

Her mother rapped a silver-headed walking stick on the wooden floor to gain her attention. 'Georgina, come back here this minute. You've said more than enough.'

She shook her head and continued, 'I'm proud of his military service, but I shall miss Philip all the years of my life. We were—'

Filmore stood up and moved purposefully towards her, one arm outstretched. 'Come along, Georgina, there's no need for this. You've said your piece. Do as your mother asks.'

For a moment she stared at her fiancé and you could have heard a mouse breathe in the church, so quiet had it become. Then she held up one hand, palm outwards to stop him going on. 'I haven't finished.'

He glared at her, looking questioningly towards Mrs Cotterell.

'Come and sit down, Georgina,' she called. 'Stop making a spectacle of your grief. Leave that to those who know no better.'

Georgina clutched the lectern as Filmore once again tried to pull her away. 'Sometimes you have to stand up and be heard.'

She had to kick him in the shins to make him let go of her and she shouted the next words at the congregation. 'What I've seen today, the shocking way Miss Jones has been treated, has made my mind up for me. It is an insult to my dear, brave brother not to have invited his fiancée to his memorial service. And I can be no less brave than he was, so I'm about to take an important step, to which you can all bear witness.'

Now she turned to face Filmore, who was still standing by her side. She edged quickly to the other side of the lectern and continued loudly, 'I shall not be marrying a man who has treated me unkindly today and not respected my grief.' Taking off her engagement ring, she hurled it at Filmore's face.

As he ducked instinctively the silence was still so absolute that the ring could be heard tinkling as it hit the floor and rolled on.

He reached out and grabbed her arm. 'You are not yourself, Georgina.'

She tried to shake him off, but he was holding her more firmly this time. She was looking afraid of him now. 'You're hurting me. Let me go!'

Two of the officers stood up. 'Can't resist rescuing a damsel in distress,' one of them said loudly.

They marched to the front, saluted briskly and the same man said, 'Do you wish to go with this chap, Miss Cotterell?'

Again she tried to free herself, but in vain. 'No. I do not.'

'Let her go, you.'

'She's my fiancée and I will thank you not to interfere.'

'She just gave you your ring back, so she's not your concern now, what?'

There was quite a hubbub from the congregation, but Mrs Cotterell said nothing more. She continued to sit stiffly upright with a look of outrage on her face and the way she was looking at her daughter was a threat in itself.

The two officers moved to either side of Georgie and with a nod of thanks, she went with them to the second pew full of military.

Filmore bent to pick up the ring and returned to his place next to Mrs Cotterell.

What on earth was going to happen now? Bella wondered. But she was glad Georgina had broken with that man. Philip had hated him, hated the idea of the marriage, blamed it all on his mother's nagging.

Chapter Three

The service ended and Georgina sobbed openly as a cloth-covered board bearing bouquets of flowers and a stone plaque were lifted and carried out. Four of the officers moved forward to help perform this final service and the minister looked at them uncertainly, then gestured to them to take their places.

Hearing the other woman's agonised weeping for her twin made Bella weep too. This time she didn't attempt to stop the tears rolling down her cheeks, couldn't have done.

As the pall-bearers paused for a moment just beyond their pew, Georgina moved sideways to grab Bella's arm. 'Walk with me. Please.'

As they fell into place behind Mrs Cotterell and her son, Tez and another officer also slipped out of the pew to walk behind them. Was it really necessary to form a protective barrier between them and Spencer? Bella wondered. But the others knew so much more than she did about the people here today that she simply did as Tez and Georgina wanted.

Mrs Cotterell ignored the two younger women completely and continued to move slowly forward on the arm of her son. Her face was like a pale shadow beneath the heavy black veil which she'd pulled down from the crown of her hat.

Bella found it impossible to hold back more tears as the minister spoke the final words at the graveside and the plaque was lowered to a place that had been prepared for it among the family headstones. She waited till the others had sprinkled earth on the ground in front of it to pick up a handful as her own token.

'Stop her! Don't let her defile his grave!' Mrs Cotterell cried suddenly from the other side of the hole. 'She's nothing but a whore!'

Bella made no attempt to respond to this gratuitous insult but tossed down her own handful of earth in tribute to the man she'd loved. This ceremony seemed unreal, like the worst of nightmares, but she wasn't going to be drawn into an argument, whatever they said or did. Not now, not with poor Philip's body lying in France and this plaque the only sign of his life left to his family in England.

As people began to move away, Georgina clutched Bella's arm again. 'What am I going to do? Where can I go? Mother will make my life unbearable if I go home.'

'I'm sure my landlady will let you stay with me for a few days. You can share my room and I can lend you some money, if you need it.'

'Thanks, but I drew some money out of the bank yesterday. I had a feeling I'd need it. My main worry is to find somewhere to live, a place where my mother can't get to me. I daren't even go back to the house for my clothes.'

Bella didn't know what to suggest, but if Philip's sister needed help she'd do anything she could.

* * *

The red-haired young officer who had been standing nearby moved closer. 'Couldn't help overhearing. Don't know if you remember me, Georgina?'

'Philip always called me Georgie and so should his friends. I hate being called Georgina. Only my family and Francis do it.'

'I'm Harry Lewison. You and my sister were at school together and you stayed at our house a couple of times. Penny's married now but her husband is away a lot, serving in the navy. She's staying in the depths of the country in a cottage belonging to a distant relative who has a farm. She's finding it very quiet and I'm sure she'd welcome some company.'

'You're Penny's brother. Of course. That's why you looked familiar.' She stood there indecisively. 'What do you think, Bella? Should I see if Penny can take me in for a while?'

'You're absolutely sure you want to be done with your engagement, Georgie?'

'Oh, yes! More sure of that than anything else.'

'Then from what Philip said about your mother, you definitely can't stay at home any longer. And staying with your old school friend will be better than staying with me, where there isn't a spare bedroom and I can be transferred at any time.'

'You're right.' Georgie blinked furiously. 'I don't know why I've grown so timid. I used to think for myself. Thank you for helping me today.'

Bella got out her notebook, scribbled her present address down and tore the page out. 'This will always find me. My landlady, Mrs Sibley, is a darling and even if I'm transferred, she'll forward any letters.'

Georgie took the paper and shoved it in her handbag. 'Thanks.' She hesitated, then gave Bella a hug. 'Thanks for everything today. Please stay in touch.'

'I'm glad to help.' Bella turned to Tez. 'Is there any chance you could take Georgie to see if this Penny can give her a bed for a few nights?'

Harry intervened again. 'No need. I'm going to spend the night with my sister and can drive you there, Georgie. But we'd better leave straight away. Looks like that Filmore fellow is bringing in reinforcements.'

'Mother's lawyer is away in London. That's his partner, Mr Marley. I've not had much to do with him but he's probably just as much on her side as Mr Polbrook. Let's go quickly.' Georgie turned to flee.

Bella grabbed her arm. 'Wait. It'd be better to face them now and make sure the lawyer realises you're leaving of your own free will.'

'I never thought of that.' But Georgie still looked terrified.

And Philip's mother looked icily furious.

Mrs Cotterell came up to them, accompanied by Spencer and a silver-haired man in an old-fashioned high-collared shirt. Filmore followed them and stood slightly to one side, the scowl still painted on his face.

'I'm making allowances for how upset you are today, Georgina,' Mrs Cotterell said. 'You don't realise what you're doing. You must come home and lie down till you feel better. We'll get the doctor to give you something to calm you.'

Spencer said nothing, but the look he gave Georgie promised retribution not support. Bella was surprised to see the lawyer looking from him to his mother in faint puzzlement. Wasn't he part of this?

Her mother's remarks seemed to stiffen Georgie's spine. 'I am upset, very, at the loss of my twin. But I know perfectly well what I'm doing today. I didn't want to get engaged to Francis in the first place, but you persuaded me, Mother, and he seemed kind. However, as soon as I had his ring on my finger, he changed and started ordering me around as if I was nothing. Telling me not to speak at my twin's funeral was the final straw. I do not wish to marry Francis and nothing you say or do will make me change my mind.'

Filmore stepped forward. 'Don't say anything you'll regret, Georgina. We can discuss everything later. Your mother needs your support today of all days.'

Georgie scowled at him. 'There's nothing to discuss. I *won't* marry you. As for my mother, she has Spencer to support her. He's always been her favourite. He doesn't even have to go away to fight, because of his poor health. I'm going to make a new life for myself from now on and maybe I'll join the VADs too.'

'You'll never manage on your own,' her mother said scornfully. 'You'll dither around and get into debt because you'll need to find a job. And with your lack of skills, you'll only earn a pittance. You've always had an unstable temperament and you need your family's support.'

For a moment Georgie seemed to hesitate, then she shook her head again. 'That's not true. And I have enough money to go into lodgings. One room will be paradise as long as I have it to myself.'

'You've been persuaded to act foolishly by these people who turned up today. Poor Philip made some very dubious friends in the army and—'

'I haven't been persuaded by anyone. Philip's friends never came near me, didn't speak to me till *I* asked for their help today.' She turned to the lawyer. 'Mr Marley, I've been dealing with your partner until now, but since Mr Polbrook handles my mother's affairs, I think I should get a lawyer of my own. I'll let you have his name. Once I'm over thirty, I'll gain control of my annuity, will I not? So it's just a question of surviving for four more years.'

He looked at her in puzzlement. 'You gained control of your money when you turned twenty-five, actually, as did your brother.'

Georgie gaped at him, then stared reproachfully at her mother. 'But Mother, you said it was thirty!'

Mrs Cotterell was looking flustered.

The lawyer took over. 'I handled your grandmother's affairs and therefore her bequests to you and your brother Philip. Arrangements were the same for both of you. You could have taken control of your money once you turned twenty-five, Miss Cotterell, but you wrote to tell my partner that you had no head for business and wished your mother to handle things until you married Mr Filmore, after which he would take over. Have you changed your mind about that?'

'I didn't write any such letter!'

'You're sure you didn't assign management of your money to your mother?'

'No. Definitely not!'

'See how forgetful you've become,' Mrs Cotterell said quickly.

Georgie ignored her mother. 'Mr Marley, I am *not* forgetful and I didn't want my mother to handle my money. I'd like to take back control as of today.'

Mrs Cotterell opened her mouth, but her son nudged her and shook his head, so she said nothing, but the look she gave her daughter spoke more of hatred than of love.

There was a pregnant silence till Mr Marley said, 'Once my partner recovers from his illness, I'll inform him of the changes you wish to make. In the meantime I'll make sure your new instructions go on record. It will help if you put your exact wishes into writing, with two witnesses, and send that to me as soon as possible.'

Bella saw Filmore and Spencer exchange glances. They looked as if they were plotting something so she said quickly, 'Why don't we do that now? I have a notebook and it'll only take five minutes to write a short letter. Is that all right with you, Mr Marley?'

He nodded. 'Certainly. A bit unorthodox but I can quickly draw up a document that will hold firm, if you'll allow me to borrow your notebook. I have my fountain pen with me.'

She passed him her notebook, he took out his pen and leant on the top edge of a tombstone, writing rapidly.

This took only a few minutes and after he'd showed it to Georgie and gained her approval, he made a copy.

Bella and Mr Lewison witnessed Georgie's signature on both papers then the lawyer gave one copy to Georgie and put the other safely in his breast pocket. 'Good. That's done. Now, I'll also need your bank account details, Miss Cotterell. I gather you have recently set up a new account at the Midland Bank but there are no details on record for it at our rooms.'

She looked at him blankly. 'I haven't opened a new bank account. I still have the same account as previously and it's at Barclays Bank.'

If anything he became even more glassy-eyed but it was obvious he was shocked. 'Quite a muddle, then. If you will contact both banks, I'll make sure the details are sorted out *completely* to your satisfaction. And I can assure you that your affairs will be dealt with exactly as you instruct from then on. I was your brother's lawyer and he trusted me. I hope you'll do the same, but if you wish to find another lawyer, I'll understand.'

She studied him, then nodded. 'If Philip trusted you, so will I. But please keep my information carefully locked away from . . . other people.'

'Oh, I will, believe me.' The look he gave Mrs Cotterell and the two men standing on either side of her was a warning as much as anything.

'And please don't pay any of my annuity money into this Midland Bank account, which has nothing to do with me. In fact, please don't take money out of my Barclays account, either.'

He couldn't hide his surprise. 'It's not for me to take money out, Miss Cotterell. It's *your* bank account.'

'Well, Mr Filmore took money out of the Barclays account two days ago, apparently authorised by my mother, the manager told me. I only found out about it when I went into the bank yesterday. I was going to ask about it when we got home today.'

Filmore cleared his throat to get their attention. 'We needed new financial arrangements since I'll be handling your money after we're married and—'

'We are *not* getting married,' Georgie said again, this time loudly enough for the mourners still lingering in the churchyard to hear her. 'There is no way I'm going to change my mind about that.'

'I'm sure Mr Filmore will pay back the money straight away, then, given the new circumstances,' Mr Marley said. 'Please check your bank account tomorrow afternoon to make sure that's been done and let me know if it hasn't.'

'I will. Um, can I ask? How do you know all this?'

The lawyer's expression slipped a little and he threw a quick disapproving glance at Mr Filmore. 'Since my partner will take a while to recover from the pneumonia, I will have to take charge of his clients' affairs. I decided to take a quick glance at your details this morning and I found some of what had been happening rather . . . let us say, puzzling. So I went through the recent paperwork for the annuities rather more carefully than I would have done.'

'I see. Thank you for doing that.'

'I also discovered a list of the jewellery you inherited from your grandmother, Miss Cotterell. There are some valuable pieces and most of them are stored in our safe, though they really should be in the bank vault. What do you wish to do about them?'

'I'd be grateful if you'd check that every item is there, because I have none of them in my possession and I know my mother has borrowed pieces from time to time.'

A faint look of surprise again escaped the lawyer's control. 'I shall attend to that for you.'

'And there are my clothes and personal possessions.'

Mrs Cotterell intervened. 'Surely you can leave them where they are till you calm down and come home again, Georgina?'

'I'm never coming back to Westcott.' Again Georgie appealed to the lawyer, 'Surely I have a right to my possessions?'

'Of course. But can you not pack them yourself?'

'I daren't go back home.'

'Ah. Then I'll send someone to do it for you. That will be all right, will it not, Mrs Cotterell?'

She gave him a sour look and inclined her head.

'I'll have to let you know where I am later,' Georgie added.

'If you like, they can be sent to my mother at our London address. I think you'll be staying with Penny, so Mother can send them on to you.' Mr Lewison waited for her nod and when the lawyer asked for the address, he pulled out his card and held it out.

Mr Lewison turned to Georgie. 'If that's all, could we leave now, do you think? Penny's expecting me and she worries if I'm late.'

* * *

Once the others had left, Tez touched Bella's arm. 'I'm not feeling well now, I'm afraid. Would you mind if we left straight away, Miss Jones?' He stared down at his hand. 'I may be missing two fingers, but they still feel as if they're there, and very painful they are, too.'

'I've heard before of that happening,' she said. 'I'm happy to leave at once.' She tried to scrub away the dampness from her tears surreptitiously.

Tez turned to Mr Marley while she was doing that and said quickly in a low voice, 'I'm sure Miss Jones will be safe in your hands for any other business matters, but if there's ever anything I can do to help, don't hesitate to call on me. Or my mother.'

'I won't hesitate. If I may say so, Mr Tesworth, you've helped greatly already today. I'm sure your friend, were he still with us, would be most grateful that you've helped his fiancée. I hope your hand recovers quickly.'

Mrs Cotterell had been moving to intercept her daughter and Georgie muttered a quick farewell to Bella and avoided her mother by walking out with Mr Lewison through the graves.

The older woman stood scowling while her son and Filmore continued to mutter together.

Wooden-faced again, the lawyer offered his arm to Mrs Cotterell. 'Shall I escort you back to the car now, ma'am? Your guests will be waiting for you at the house. I can wait and collect your daughter's clothes while we're at it. And any pieces of jewellery that are hers.'

She didn't take his arm, nor did she look towards her

daughter again, just turned to her son and clutched his arm as she left.

Filmore looked thoughtfully in the direction his former fiancée had taken before following them.

Harry put an arm round Georgie who was weeping again. 'I'll see you're all right.'

She nodded and let him take her to his car.

As he helped her in, he said, 'You stood your ground bravely, old girl. You're stronger than you think.'

'I was pretty feeble at first and look at me now, crying like a baby.'

'You aren't used to standing up to your mother. She's a fearsome old witch. I can just imagine her riding a broomstick.'

That brought a genuine if brief smile to her face.

'I'll drive you to my sister's now. I shall have to go back to France soon, so can't always guarantee to be available.'

Tez watched them leave. 'Harry's had a thing about Georgie for years. Maybe now he stands a chance. When he asked permission to court her, the old witch sent him off with a sharp refusal. He wasn't, apparently, wealthy enough. And anyway, she said Georgie already had a chap courting her. She wouldn't tell him who and you can see why.'

'I don't know anything about Mr Filmore, except that Philip detested him.'

'He isn't well thought of, however good his birth and breeding are supposed to be. He's scrabbling a bit for money these day, from what I hear. I can't imagine why Mrs Cotterell approved of him as a suitor.'

'Maybe she's scrabbling for money too and they're going to divide Georgie's money between them.'

He stopped walking for a moment to stare at her and say thoughtfully, 'You may just be right about that.'

Within minutes, Mrs Tesworth's chauffeur was driving her son and Bella back to the hospital. Tez slumped against the seat, closed his eyes and sighed. 'Sorry. I'm not usually so useless.'

'You've done amazingly well, Mr Tesworth, and—'

'Do call me Tez. Philip always referred to you as Bella, but I think Isabella is a lovely name, too lovely to shorten, so if I may, I'll call you that.'

'I gather no one calls you by your real name.'

He grinned. 'No. Definitely not. It means "exalted or on high", you know, which is not what I feel like at any time, I can tell you.'

'I'll call you Tez, then. I can't thank you enough for all your help today. I'd like to thank the other men, too, but I don't even know their names, except for Mr Lewison.'

'I'll thank them for you. They were glad to come to your aid, I know. What you're doing, driving ambulances, is really important and to see you treated so badly upset us all.'

They didn't talk much during the rest of the journey. Bella had said a final goodbye to Philip, which she'd wanted to do, and that eased some of the pain. But she'd made enemies today, she was sure.

Well, she need have nothing more to do with the

Cotterells except for Georgie, who was just as nice as Philip had said, and who looked so like him, even to having some of the same gestures, that it hurt.

Bella managed to have two more chats with Tez at the hospital while his case was being sorted out. She was able to speak to him about Philip more easily than to other people, because they had both loved her fiancé and because he was such a nice chap.

To her amusement he continued to call her Isabella and she found that she liked it. It seemed like a symbol of the new phase in her life.

When she went into the ward one day, however, she found only a stripped bed and no sign of Tez.

She went to see the ward sister and was told that he'd been sent to his mother's home in London to finish recovering under the supervision of a London specialist.

'Did he leave a message for me?'

'Not that I've seen. Sorry, dear. I've only just come on duty. If I find any note from him I'll give it to you, don't worry.'

It seemed strange that he'd leave without a word, but Bella knew how abruptly patients could be moved from one place to another. At least after their first chat he had given her his card and told her, 'If you ever need help, any kind of help, don't hesitate to contact me. Or my mother, since you don't seem to get on with your own. Mine is a great person. She's been organising a lot of war work. She'd help you.'

'I'll be all right, I'm sure. After all, I've still got a job, haven't I? But thank you for the offer.'

He'd studied her, head on one side. 'You aren't looking well.'

'I'm a bit tired.'

'More than a bit, I think.'

She shrugged.

She'd keep the card but she hoped not to need any help. She could go on working and supporting herself, as she had done since she left school at fourteen. She would prefer to stay here because she'd made friends among the staff, had a kindly landlady and found the nearby countryside beautiful for long walks. But a VAD could be transferred at a moment's notice, and as long as there was a war going on, she would always do her duty.

It surprised her when she continued to feel tired, though, more tired than she could ever remember. She even fell asleep sometimes during her breaks. And her stomach was upset, just a little. She'd been sick a few times.

If that had been happening in the mornings she'd have worried, because everyone knew what that meant. But it was in the evenings she felt nauseous, so it must be something else. If it didn't clear up, she'd ask Matron if she could see a doctor.

It took Georgie a while to stop crying as Harry Lewison drove her away. Her whole world seemed to have fallen apart. She'd said a final goodbye to her twin, broken off her engagement and completely alienated her mother, who would hold a grudge about that unless she apologised and agreed to marry Filmore – which she'd never, ever do.

She'd alienated her elder brother too, but she and

Spencer had never had much to do with one another, so that didn't worry her. She and Philip had puzzled over his behaviour all their lives. It was as if he'd hated the two of them from birth, though why he should do that when he was the eldest and he would inherit Westcott not them, they'd never been able to work out.

It seemed terrible to have no close family to turn to. Terrifying.

Harry pulled over to the side of the road and reached out to hold her hand. 'Chin up. I'm quite sure Penny will take you in.'

'Your sister always was kind. It's not that. I just don't know what I'm going to do with my life now. I'm going to need some sort of home of my own, aren't I? You can't live with other people for ever. Only I've never lived on my own, can't imagine what I'd do with myself all day.'

She tried but failed to sound amused as she confessed, 'I don't even know how much houses and flats cost, let alone how to do housework. The maids have always seen to that. Once I left school, my mother kept me dancing attendance on her and doing – you know, the social stuff, making calls and entertaining visitors, fetching and carrying for her.'

'Penny will help you adjust, I'm sure. M'sister's a capable woman.'

'We were quite friendly at school, but I've only seen her a few times since then and not at all lately. When I think about it, that was my mother's fault. Why didn't I realise what she was doing, separating me from my real friends, pushing me at Francis when I got lonely?'

'Philip used to worry about you and her. He said distance

and listening to other chaps talk about their families had made him realise the tricks she played for getting people to do as she wished, especially you. She can be quite charming when she wants to, he said.'

'Yes. And I've always been told it's a daughter's duty to obey her parents. I wonder what my father will say about all this? If I ever see him again, that is. He may take her side.'

'I doubt it, from what Philip said. I heard he's doing some rather important war work for the War Office.'

'It's not that which is keeping him away. He's hardly had anything to do with us and he hardly ever comes home. I bet it's been less than a dozen times that we've seen him. And on the rare occasions when he does return, he sleeps in a separate bedroom to Mother and goes out for most of the day. He never talks about his work, either, so I haven't the faintest idea what he does.'

'He's quite an important person.'

'Other people have told me that. But Mother doesn't go to see him in London. In fact . . . she speaks of him as if she hates him. Do you think he hates her? And us because of her being our mother?'

'Give yourself time. I dare say you'll understand all sorts of things better now.'

Silence wrapped them both. He was a nice chap, but she hoped this didn't make him think she was attracted to him in that way. She'd never met anyone she'd been truly attracted to – or perhaps never been *allowed* to meet anyone suitable.

'Will you write to me and tell me how you're going?' he asked suddenly.

'If you like. Penny and I can send you joint letters.' She could see that he was disappointed in her response, but he was too polite to say so.

As they drew near his sister's house, she said, 'Thanks for being so kind, Harry.'

He gave her one of his warm, puppy-dog smiles. He wasn't good-looking, not with that plump face and pale skin. It was more important to be kind, she felt. She didn't know what she'd have done without his help today.

She would write to him, but she wouldn't encourage him to come courting her.

Penny came to the door to greet them and stopped in surprise. 'Georgie Cotterell! My goodness, is that really you? I was so sorry to hear about your brother.'

Harry put his arm round Georgie's shoulders. 'We need your help, old girl. There's been a bit of a kerfuffle after Philip's funeral and Georgie's now homeless. Let's go inside and we'll tell you all about it.'

When they'd finished their tale, Penny said firmly, 'About time you struck out for your independence, Georgie. I'm so glad you're not going to marry that horrible man.'

'I didn't realise when I got engaged how much people dislike him, or how vicious he can be. My mother made it all seem a very happy thing and it put her in a good mood, so I went along with it. She can be charming when things work out as she wants. Only usually she doesn't do things to make other people happier, just to suit herself.'

Harry sighed. 'Sit down, stop nattering and get to the

point. Can Georgie stay here? If she can't, we'll have to go and find a hotel and—'

'Of course she can stay here, you fool!' Penny told her brother then turned to Georgie. 'Actually, I'll be glad of the company. Edward goes away for months at a time and it can be very lonely out here in the middle of nowhere. I do wish he hadn't joined the navy. But then he's probably safer on a ship than in the trenches, though sometimes I wonder. So many seem to have been sunk lately.'

Georgie asked, 'Are you *sure* it's OK for me to stay? I'm afraid I've been forced on you. And I don't even have any clothes. I'll have to buy a few bits and pieces.'

Penny gave her a hug. 'Yes, very sure. And I can lend you a few things.'

'I can't tell you how grateful I am.'

And then she was weeping again, it was all too much.

'The poor girl's emotionally exhausted,' Penny said and swept her off to bed calling, 'Go and put the kettle on, Harry.'

Chapter Four

In June, a month after the memorial service, Bella received a letter from Mr Marley's law firm. It was from another lawyer who said he was dealing with the estate of Philip Cotterell in Mr Marley's absence. She had been left something in his will. Mr Shadwell apologised for the delay but said he'd had trouble finding her. Could she please come to see him in the company's rooms in London?

She reread that paragraph in puzzlement because the Cotterells and Mr Marley knew perfectly well where she was. She hesitated to contact this new lawyer, didn't want to stir up the pot of Cotterell family hostility again. After all, she didn't need anything. At least, she hoped she didn't.

But after thinking it over, she decided that if Philip had wanted to leave her something, she should abide by his wishes. And if these lawyers or any family member treated her scornfully, well, it was only words and *she* knew she'd done nothing to be ashamed of.

Fortunately the lawyer's rooms were in London, so she could get there quite easily by train. Once again, however, she had to go and ask for time off.

* * *

'I'm sorry to be such a nuisance, Matron, but I do think I ought to find out what Philip's left me.'

'Of course you ought. Anyway, there are other drivers available at the moment, with that new intake of VADs, so it will only mean you cancelling one day's duties. Why don't you go tomorrow?'

'Thank you.' Bella stood up to leave.

'Please sit down for a moment. I've been meaning to speak to you about something else.'

She waited, hoping she wasn't going to be transferred.

'You've not been looking well since the memorial service, Jones. Are you still upset about how you were treated by the Cotterell family?'

'Angry, more like.'

'Hmm. I'm told you're not eating properly and you look to me as if you've lost weight. Do you have any other symptoms?'

Bella hesitated. 'Well . . .' She explained about the unreasonable tiredness she'd been feeling for a few weeks and the evening nausea.

Matron gave her one of the penetrating looks for which she was famous. 'Could you be expecting?'

Bella could feel herself flushing and chose her words carefully. 'I thought people were sick in the *mornings* when they were, um, having a baby.'

'Were you on familiar terms with Mr Cotterell? Is a baby a possibility?'

Bella could feel her cheeks grow even hotter. 'Well, yes.'

'And have you missed your monthlies?'

'I might have. I've never been very regular, so it's hard to tell.'

'Well, if there is a baby on the way, it won't show for a while yet so if you're able to keep on working, I shall say nothing about it and you'd do well to save your money.' She gave Bella a wry smile. 'In the old days you'd have been dismissed on the spot for even a suspicion of immorality, but war changes things, at least it does in my book. The men need comforting, not by casual encounters but by warm relationships with women who love them. And you *were* engaged to be married. This was not just a chance encounter.'

'Thank you. I only ever went with Philip, I promise.'

'I believe you. So we'll wait a week or two and see if you have any further symptoms. In the meantime, go and see what your young man has left you, and let's hope it's money, because you might need it.'

Bella had half an hour before she needed to return to duty so went and sat in the small chapel they'd created in what had previously been a sitting room in the country mansion.

Was it possible? Was it really possible?

Suddenly she hoped fiercely that she was carrying Philip's child. It would be wonderful to have such a legacy from him, absolutely wonderful. And she'd find a way to manage. She'd always been careful and had some money saved already.

For the moment she would put the thought of a child firmly to one side. The important thing now was to find out what Philip had left her and see if there were any last wishes to carry out for him.

* * *

The following morning Bella took an early train to London. She decided to wear her uniform again, because people like the Cotterells would be scornful even about her best clothes. She couldn't imagine any of the family would be there for this meeting, though, thank goodness. They'd not be interested in minor details like her legacy.

The offices were in what had once been an elegant house in a Georgian terrace a few streets away from the station. Although she arrived just before the time given, she was kept waiting for half an hour.

When a young clerk at last came to fetch her, he took her to yet another waiting area, which he said was outside Mr Shadwell's office. He mustn't have realised that she could see down into the foyer if she got up and paced about, which she did because she was angry that no one had even apologised for keeping her waiting.

What she saw down in the foyer made her suck in air in a sudden whoosh, because Spencer Cotterell was there, shaking hands with a plump, youngish man who was very smartly dressed. Spencer looked pleased with himself as he strolled out of the building, triumphant even.

She didn't trust Philip's brother, and especially not with that expression on his face. What was he doing here at the same time as her? She doubted it could be a coincidence.

Her fears were confirmed when the youngish man proved to be Mr Shadwell. He walked right past her into his office without acknowledging her presence by more than a disgusted glance. Five minutes later an office boy showed her in.

The lawyer didn't rise to greet her, only gesturing with a cursory wave of the hand to a hard chair on one side of the desk. He proceeded to speak to her in a patronising tone, as if she were a particularly dim-witted child. 'Please tell me if you don't understand anything, Miss, um, Jones.'

'I speak reasonable English.' With an effort she kept her tone mild.

He blinked, looking surprised, then shook his head a little as if dismissing the very idea of her words being sarcastic and carried on in the same patronising tone. 'I believe you regard Philip Cotterell as your fiancé, even though the family has not recognised the relationship.'

'I *was* his fiancé.' She held out her hand with the diamond engagement ring on it. 'Which is why he gave me his grandmother's ring and introduced me to his friends as his fiancée. I can get several officers to swear to that on oath, if you don't believe me.'

Another blink then. 'Oh. Well, anyway, whatever the rights or wrongs of that, he has left you the entirety of his estate, which consists of a small annuity, a cottage in Wiltshire, in a small market town called Malmesbury, and his motor car. Naturally his family are not pleased about this.'

She didn't even try to speak, had to cover her mouth with one hand to hold back tears. Dear Philip. How had he found time to write a will? He'd had such short leaves and they'd only known one another for a few months. But he was taking care of her even now, and that gave her the courage to face this nasty little man.

Mr Shadwell answered that question before she could ask it. 'The will was apparently drawn up by a fellow officer who had been a lawyer in civilian life, and it was witnessed by two other officers, men of impeccable standing. After that a copy was sent by the army to our legal firm by a major at the local headquarters in France. We have been the Cotterells' family lawyers for several generations, you see.'

After a pause, he added in a disapproving tone. 'There is no doubt that the will was properly drawn up and executed.'

All she could manage was, 'I didn't even know about it.'

'Surely Captain Cotterell told you what he'd done?'

'No, he didn't. Philip's will was the last thing I was thinking about when I was with him. I loved him with all my heart, Mr Shadwell, and what I wanted was for him to survive the war.'

Her words seemed to echo in the room and she could hear Philip's voice from a great distance saying, 'Attagirl!'

The lawyer shifted uneasily, pushing his thick, round spectacles higher up his nose and looking more than ever like a vicious owl about to pounce on a helpless mouse.

'I'd like a copy of the will,' she said quietly.

'Well, um, all right. I shall ensure you get a copy of it, Miss Jones, so that you can read it at your leisure and get help understanding it, if necessary.' He clearly thought it would be necessary.

'Thank you. But as I said before, I do speak reasonably good English, and read it too. Perhaps you'd go over the main points in a little more detail now?'

'The annuity will bring you four hundred pounds a year for the next twenty years.'

She gasped. So much! A whole family could live well on that. She would think herself rich.

'You need not be concerned about the details of the cottage. Mrs Cotterell wishes to purchase it back from you to keep it in the family. She offers you a hundred pounds. I'll draw up the deed of transfer before you leave today if you'll wait a little, then you can sign it.'

'I don't even know what the cottage is like, but I definitely don't wish to sell it. If it's at all possible, I'd like to live there. It'd make me feel closer to Philip.'

'I wouldn't advise that. His mother would not be at all pleased and she has important connections. You'd be wiser to do as she wishes.'

'It's my intention to do as *Philip* wished. If he left the cottage to me, he must have wanted me to live there, so as long as it has a roof and four walls, I shall do exactly that.'

There was a heavy silence, during which he breathed deeply as if holding back annoyance.

She waited him out, though she longed to get away from this stifling office and this arrogant, disapproving little man.

'There is also the question of the motor car, which will be of no use to a woman of your class. Spencer Cotterell is prepared to offer you twenty-five pounds for it and—'

'Does he think I'm a fool? It's worth far more than that.'

'It might be. I wouldn't know. *I* am not a huckster. But a woman like you will not know how to drive it, nor will you have anywhere to keep it, so he is saving you the trouble of disposing of it.'

'If you know nothing about the value of motor cars, I shan't argue with you, Mr Shadwell. I shall simply refuse that offer as well. Now, what must I do to finalise everything?'

'One moment.' He beckoned to her and took her across to the window, pointing below at the back of the building. 'The car is down there. You would need to take it away today.'

He definitely didn't recognise the VAD uniform or what her version of it meant.

'I can easily do that.'

'Really? Where will you find a driver, Miss Jones?'

She indicated her uniform. 'You don't seem to know much about uniforms, Mr Shadwell. I'm an ambulance driver in the VAD, and have been for over a year. And that means driving vehicles of all sorts, most of them converted from large private vehicles.'

She waited but he was staring at her open-mouthed. 'But Mr Spencer Cotterell said you were a hospital cleaner and—'

'I don't care what he said. I've only seen the man a couple of times before today. He didn't speak to me on that occasion, and I doubt he knows anything about me. Now, what do I need to do about the money?'

'You will need to open a bank account and let us know the details, after which we can transfer the money into it. That will take about a week.'

She leant back in the hard chair and stared him right in

the eyes. 'I already have a bank account with money in it. I can give you the details now.'

'Oh. Well, our chief clerk will take down that information, Miss Jones and . . .' He paused as if searching for words, but though his tone was slightly less patronising, what he had to say was not. 'Look, I have to remind you that the Cotterells are a powerful family. Mr Cotterell is in a senior position at the War Office. You would be wise not to upset them.'

'As I've already told you, I shall do as Philip wished. I don't feel the need to see or talk to his family again, so I don't care what they think of me. Now, let's get the practicalities organised, then I'll drive myself back to the hospital. I've driven Philip's car before, so I know how to handle it. A Model T Ford is a lot easier to drive than a big ambulance, believe me.'

He spread his hands wide in a helpless gesture and escorted her out.

In the office area they encountered Mr Marley, whom she'd met at the funeral. At least he wouldn't be condescending towards her.

'Ah, Miss Jones. I hope everything has been sorted out to your satisfaction today.'

For a moment she debated keeping quiet about what Mr Shadwell had said, but the idea of that didn't sit well with her. After all, he must have been instructed what to do by Mr Marley. She would definitely have to find herself another lawyer.

'No, it has not been sorted out to my satisfaction and Mr Shadwell hasn't tried to help me at all. In fact, he was colluding with Mr Spencer Cotterell, who was with him when I arrived and who had been telling lies about me in an attempt to cheat me out of the value of what Philip left me. I take that very seriously indeed and shall now consult another lawyer to check out that Philip's wishes really have been carried out by Marley and Polbrook.'

He looked at her open-mouthed.

Mr Shadwell said hastily, 'Mr Spencer Cotterell came to see me unexpectedly. He, um, informed me of certain things in connection with this woman. It was just a misunderstanding on his part, I'm sure, Mr Marley.'

'Lawyers shouldn't accept things people tell them without checking,' she said sharply before the older man could reply. 'They should be above reproach and impartial. Now, I wish to sort out the details of my inheritance as quickly as possible, then I'll take Philip's car away today, as you've instructed me to, and drive it back to the hospital.'

Mr Marley gave his junior colleague an angry look and beckoned to the head clerk. 'Please see that Miss Jones's business is sorted out quickly, Thomas. And give her all the help necessary.'

He turned back to Bella. 'I apologise for how you've been treated. It was not what I instructed anyone to do. I have a client due any moment, but I'd be grateful if you could please come and see me before you leave. It's rather important. Will you do that?'

Once again she found him likeable and was inclined to give him a second chance, so she nodded and followed the chief clerk.

* * *

Nigel Shadwell went back to his office, furious that he'd been made to look a fool in front of Mr Marley, just when he was hoping to be made a full partner in the firm.

He picked up the phone and asked for an outside line. 'Cotterell? I'm glad you're still at your hotel. She's taking the car, driving it away herself, so you've no need to make arrangements for it. What? Oh no, she's not *selling* it; she's driving it back to the hospital herself. She's a damned ambulance driver, would you believe?'

He sighed as he was treated to a few angry remarks. 'Yes, she's turned down your mother's offer for the cottage as well. She's not nearly as stupid as you thought.'

He listened for a few seconds longer then interrupted. 'No, I can't do anything else to prevent her from doing this. The will was perfectly legal.'

The phone was slammed down at the other end.

Half an hour later Bella was shown in to see Mr Marley. She was hoping this wouldn't take long, so that she could get home while it was still light.

'Miss Jones, please take a seat. First, I wish to apologise to you unreservedly for my young colleague's, um, carelessness in handling your affairs. From what he told me, you were not being offered anything like fair prices by the Cotterells.'

She inclined her head.

'If I can obtain a fairer price, would you consider selling them the cottage? Just to keep the peace? It has been in the family for a good many years.'

'No, Mr Marley. Philip wanted me to have it and I shall

do as he wished. Anyway, I'm going to need somewhere to live.'

'Could you please take a day or two and think carefully about it. I'm not threatening you but I am worried that you're getting into deeper waters than you realise. I'll tell you frankly, Spencer Cotterell and his mother can be difficult. There's no hiding the fact that his spiteful nature is well known and he's become even more bitter since he failed the army medical. As for his mother, she's a cunning woman who likes to get her own way.'

'I've been unhappy myself since Philip died,' she said quietly, 'but I don't take it out on other people or try to cheat them. I shall do nothing to provoke his family but I don't need to think about selling the cottage and car to them. I shan't change my mind.' She wasn't telling him anything about her possible complication, not if she didn't have to. But if what she was beginning to suspect was true, she would definitely need somewhere to live. 'Is that all?'

'An old lady who was living at a village called Honeyfield died a couple of months ago. This Miss Thorburn was a close friend of Miss Gordon – the lady who left Philip the house in Malmesbury – and left everything she owned to her. I didn't trouble Philip at the time, because he was involved at Verdun and had enough on his mind, and Miss Gordon seemed in excellent health. But her unexpected death meant that Philip inherited everything that Miss Gordon owned, which now, unknown to him included her own recent legacy from Miss Thorburn.'

'Good heavens!'

'The second cottage is much smaller than the house you've been left in Malmesbury, so Miss Gordon didn't wish to move there. She was happy where she was. She was going to put a tenant into the cottage but she had a sudden seizure and she didn't even have time to clear out her friend's personal effects. I hadn't spoken of her inheritance to anyone, because she believed it prudent to keep quiet about what she owned. She didn't want people, even distant cousins like the Cotterells, to think she was worth robbing. I think Miss Thorburn was her only real friend and the two were very close.'

He paused and added quietly, 'As Miss Gordon left everything to Philip, and he left everything to you, this means that you've also inherited a second house and its contents, as well as just over a hundred pounds in the bank.'

Bella stared at him in astonishment. 'I can't believe it. I've always had to work hard for my living and to have an income and *two* houses, well, it's beyond riches to me.'

He had been watching her carefully and was pleased by her reaction. She was definitely not a 'grasping harpy', as Mrs Cotterell had told him. 'I'm pleased for you, Miss Jones. Look, I'd be honoured if you'd trust me to handle your affairs from now on. Philip asked me to do that if anything happened to him, you see, and I'd like to keep my promise to him. I can show you his letter, if you wish for proof of that. I can assure you I shall not discuss your business with anyone else in this firm, and I shall make sure no one else has the opportunity to look at my clients' paperwork without my permission in future.'

She looked at him sharply. 'As Mr Shadwell did?'

'Yes. Please keep this to yourself, but I shall not be continuing to employ him. Not only did he deal badly with you, but there have been one or two other rather careless incidents that didn't reflect well on our firm.'

She hadn't expected to like him but she did. He had a grandfatherly air to him, did not talk down to her and he looked honest. Besides, Philip had trusted him. 'I'd be happy for you to continue managing my legal affairs, Mr Marley.'

'I'm pleased.' He held out his hand to her and they shook solemnly, then he gave her his business card. 'If there's any trouble or you need help, don't hesitate to get in touch. I'll tell my senior clerk to give your affairs priority till we've sorted everything out.'

'Thank you.'

'Now, as for the practicalities, I'd like to arrange for you to go and see the two properties you've inherited. If I'm unable to take you myself, I'll ask Nathan Perry to do it. He's an accountant and lives in Malmesbury. He inherited his father's business a few months ago, so he now handles the letting and sale of various properties for us. He's a very shrewd young man in whom I place complete trust.'

Feeling surprised at the turn things had taken, she glanced outside to see clouds scudding across the sky. 'Oh dear. It looks like rain. I'd better get going.'

'Do you need help with starting the car?'

She smiled. 'No, thank you. I drive cars as my

contribution to the war effort. I've had a lot of practice at starting them as well as driving them.'

'I greatly admire young women like yourself. I don't know what our country would do without you.'

Chapter Five

It was going to be a long, tiring drive back to Wiltshire, Bella thought as she unlocked the car door and tossed her satchel inside. When she saw something poking out of a corner of the back seat, she pulled it out and found herself holding Philip's favourite scarf. She paused for a moment, blinking away tears. Then she touched it gently to her cheek, feeling as if it was a sign that he was still with her.

Silly, but there you were. She was surely entitled to some fanciful thoughts on this day of surprises.

She used the dipstick to check that there was enough petrol to get her on her way and found to her relief that the tank was nearly full. The square petrol can was full as well, in case she ran out.

She could probably get home on what was in the tank, but if not, she was quite used to filling petrol tanks and there was a funnel in the car. She was also used to finding hardware shops and wayside bicycle or car dealers which sold cans of petrol. Those who had trained her when she started in the VAD had been very thorough.

She started the car without needing anyone's help with the crank handle, pleased about that. She hoped that

Shadwell creature was watching her out of the window.

Philip had always said she was a sturdy wench who had a sure touch with motor vehicles and hang what people said about women drivers needing a man to help them. With a satisfied nod, she put the car into gear and drove away.

It was a relief to leave the busy city streets behind. Unfortunately half an hour after she started it began raining quite heavily. Thank goodness this wasn't an open tourer. But she had to slow down because water was streaming down the windscreen, making it difficult to see where she was going.

Twice she had to stop to clear the accumulated layers of mud thrown up from the country roads from the bottom of the windscreen to which it had slid. After the second stop she wondered whether to try to buy something to eat, but she wasn't really hungry and it was the time of day when she felt vaguely nauseous so she decided to press on.

An hour later the rain had stopped completely and that made her feel better. She began humming as she drove along a pretty country road patterned now by the longer evening shadows. She kept an eye on the other vehicles because another car had been behind her for a while, presumably waiting to overtake her. It looked like a largish Daimler, but she couldn't be sure and its number plate was completely covered in mud so she couldn't tell where it was from.

Thank goodness Philip had had an Argus dash mirror installed so that she could see what was happening on the road behind her without turning her head round.

When the other car sped up on a long, straight stretch, she pulled closer to the side of the road, waiting for it to move out and pass. Instead it kept accelerating straight towards her. If she hadn't been watching carefully, as she'd been taught, it'd have smashed right into her. It was bigger and heavier than her Model T Ford and could have done a lot of damage. As it was she saw what was happening in time to accelerate herself, so it didn't hit her very hard.

The driver had done that on purpose! she thought indignantly. Why had he done that? She pulled away as fast as she could, keeping watch in the rear-view mirror. She was sure the paintwork on the boot would be badly scratched and it was probably dented too, but she'd saved herself from a serious bang, at least.

She squeezed the bulb of her horn and yelled, 'Stop that!' though of course the other driver couldn't hear her.

When he gave every sign of preparing to ram her again, she became so alert that everything seemed to be happening more slowly than usual. She braked suddenly then accelerated quickly, which confused him and prevented him from bumping her vehicle a second time.

He stayed away from her as they went round a tight bend and then began to accelerate again, another attack coming, she was sure. He must be a madman.

There didn't seem to be any houses nearby or other drivers around so she didn't dare stop. But for how long would she be able to avoid him? The next time he tried she swerved out into the middle of the road as well as accelerating, which made it harder to keep control of her car but at least he missed again and he was having trouble controlling his own vehicle too.

She groaned in relief as she saw another car waiting at a narrow side road for them to pass so that it could pull out on to the main road. Its driver must have seen her attacker's attempt to drive her off the road, surely?

When the newcomer turned onto the road behind her pursuer, he began sounding his horn again and again. She didn't dare take her hands off the steering wheel to sound her own horn in reply.

The attacking driver realised he'd been seen and veered suddenly round her. As he passed, he tried to bump into the side of her car. But she'd braked hard as soon as he was out from behind her. Thank goodness her training in driving ambulances had included how to drive in muddy and slippery conditions where other cars could lose control!

She had a fleeting glimpse of a figure with a cap pulled down and a scarf across his mouth. She couldn't make out what he looked like, but he seemed to be a tall man judging by the position of his face above the steering wheel. To her relief he began moving away down the road at a dangerously fast speed.

She let her car slow down, wondering if she dared stop, but she was shaking so hard now that the crisis had passed that she simply had to pull over. When the car was still, she leant her head on her arms on the steering wheel and groaned aloud, waiting for the shaking to pass.

Someone tapped on the driver's window and with a huge effort she looked sideways.

'Oh, thank goodness!' The man was a minister of

religion, with the white collar showing clearly. He had silver hair and the sort of kind expression that made you trust him instinctively, so she felt safe to open the car door.

'I saw what happened. I'm John Charters, minister of the parish church in Little Gibden just down the road. That lunatic was trying to ram your car! Are you all right, miss?'

'I think so. I'm just a bit . . . well, upset.'

'Anyone would be. Do you know who that man in the other car was?'

'No. He came up behind me suddenly a short time ago and started trying to force me off the road. I can't think why. If you hadn't appeared, I think he'd have succeeded, too, because his Daimler was much heavier than my Ford. He bumped into the rear of my car once but not hard enough to shove me off the road. After I realised what he was doing, I mostly managed to avoid him.'

'You must be a good driver.' He studied her uniform. 'Well, you would be in your job. Look, if you follow me, we'll take the next left turn and go into the village where I live. We must report this to the police at once.'

'I just want to get back to the hospital where I'm stationed.'

'Due back on duty, are you?'

'Tomorrow morning.' It felt good not to have to explain her uniform and duties to him.

'I do think you need to report it, my dear young lady. Anyway, that fellow may be waiting for you further down the road. He must be stark, staring mad and he may attack you again or someone else if he's not caught. It's a good thing I was coming home from a visit to a parishioner and waiting to pull out on to the main road just then. I saw some of what happened and can bear witness to that.'

'I might be lying dead in a ditch by now if you hadn't been there, Mr Charters.' She shuddered.

'Look, I don't think you'll be fit to drive very far tonight, my dear. You're as white as a sheet.'

'I'll be all right once I get a cup of tea and something to eat.'

'If you follow my car, I'll lead you to the police station. We'll go slowly.'

'Thank you.'

'My wife and I live nearby so you can come home with me afterwards and she'll make you something to eat. You can stay the night with us, if you like. We can always find a bed for someone serving our country. And we have a telephone so you can let your commander – or is it a Matron? – know what's happened.'

What Mr Charters was suggesting made sense and she was so weary she gave in.

The police sergeant was just as kind and fatherly, utterly horrified by what had happened to her. After taking the details of the strange car from her and the minister, he phoned through to headquarters straight away to report a dangerous lunatic on the loose. The person he spoke to said Miss Jones was to stay the night at the minister's house, as he'd invited, and someone would come to accompany her back to the hospital the next morning. Bella was still too shaky to do anything but agree.

So then she had to phone Matron to let her know she'd be

late, which led to more shocked questions and explanations when all she wanted was to lie down and sleep.

The kindly couple made her very welcome at their home, but it seemed a long time till she was able to go to bed and change into the plain flannel nightdress she'd been offered by Mrs Charters.

'From the poor box, I'm afraid, Miss Jones, because my clothes wouldn't fit you, I'm so short and scrawny. But the nightdress has been thoroughly washed, I promise you.'

'I'm grateful for it.'

Although it wasn't a cold day, her hostess also supplied her with an earthenware hot-water bottle wrapped in a neat quilted cover. The gentle warmth it radiated was exactly the sort of comfort Bella needed.

She still had trouble falling asleep, though, because images kept going round and round in her mind, and she couldn't stop worrying. Had this attack been arranged by the Cotterells? And if so, by Spencer Cotterell or his mother? Or by both of them working together? If so, the man must have known she'd be travelling home in Philip's car.

Had Mr Shadwell rung them to tell them what had happened to her?

The Cotterells would make formidable enemies, she was sure. Their utter confidence that they could make the world do as they wanted was a weapon she didn't own.

She'd gone along with the idea of a raving lunatic trying to murder someone put forward by the policeman, because you couldn't accuse people like the Cotterells of such an action without proof. But who else could it have been except them? Someone they'd hired or Spencer Cotterell himself.

Were they trying to kill her or frighten her into doing as they wanted? Surely not *kill*? They were people of standing in the community, not criminals. But she could have been killed in a car accident, as hundreds of people were each year.

Should she have accepted the offer to buy the cottage and car for the sake of peace, as even Mr Marley had suggested? After all, she'd still have had the annuity, a more than enough amount of money for her to live on. She still hadn't got used to the idea that she need never work again.

But no, it went against all that was in her to give in to bullying. She just couldn't do it.

She placed one hand on her stomach. It was still flat, but she was beginning to feel that Matron might have guessed correctly. Her monthlies had always been irregular, but she had never before been so late. She should have realised sooner what that meant, but she'd been lost in a fog of grief.

If she told the Cotterells she was expecting Philip's child, would that stop them attacking her? Or would it make things worse? They might try to take her child away from her, even if they didn't want it themselves.

No, better to find some way to hide her condition, and then bring the child up herself, pretending to be a widow.

Matron had advised on the phone to get some sleep and leave thinking about what had happened until the morning, when she would be more alert. But would a solution become any more obvious then? Bella doubted it.

It wasn't till she pulled the hot-water bottle higher and cuddled it to her chest that she managed to fall asleep. She dreamt of the few, the very few times she and Philip had been able to spend the night together. She'd fallen asleep in his arms.

She wept when she woke, because he wasn't there, never would be again, and didn't even know that she might be having his child.

She had breakfast with the minister and his wife, afterwards waiting impatiently for a policeman to arrive. She was pleasantly surprised when a young man turned up just before nine o'clock on a motorcycle. He wasn't in any kind of uniform.

'Sergeant's compliments, Miss Jones, but he thinks it'll be better if I follow you back. Are you going back to the hospital or to your lodgings?'

'To the hospital.'

'Right. Sarge doesn't like the thought of that lunatic lying in wait for you again, but just let him try to attack you and I'll arrest him before you can say Bob's your uncle. Oh, and I'll start back as soon as I see you into the hospital grounds, if you don't mind. We are rather busy.'

'Please thank the sergeant for sending you. I must admit I was worrying about whether whoever it was would try again, but I feel guilty taking up valuable manpower when there's a war on.'

'You're valuable too, Miss Jones. We'd hate to lose one of our ambulance drivers. A lot of men will have benefitted from your driving skills, and it can't be easy with some of the strange, converted vehicles they're using as ambulances on the home front. No, we're not letting anyone hurt you.'

She loved his youthful enthusiasm and his cheerfulness. It made the world seem a better place.

The roads were quiet, with more horse traffic than motor vehicles. Her young protector followed her back to the hospital, sometimes in view, other times out of sight. But there was no sign of the Daimler and no other vehicle followed her car for more than an incidental mile or two, thank goodness.

Bella waved goodbye to her escort as she turned into the gateway and drove round to the rear of the hospital. She felt she ought to see Matron and discuss what had happened before she went back to her lodgings. The older woman could be sharp-tongued at times and kept iron discipline among the VADs, but no one who was in trouble hesitated to confide in her. She could not only be kind but was very wise.

After parking her car, Bella made her way to Matron's office and was shown in immediately by the clerk outside the door.

Matron studied her for a moment or two before speaking. 'How are you, Jones? You look exhausted.'

'I didn't sleep very well.'

'I was shocked at what happened to you. Are you still sure you have no idea who was trying to harm you?'

'I can't be certain so I didn't want to say it on the phone, because you never know whether the operator is listening in. I'd guess it's a member of Philip's family, probably his brother. The police talked about a lunatic, but I don't think that's who was to blame.'

'I agree. There aren't that many lunatics running loose with a car at their disposal. Tell me more about your legacy. Was it something that would upset Philip's family?'

'It's definitely upset them.' Bella went over it all again, including the offers to buy at ridiculously low prices, which had the older woman huffing in indignation.

When she'd finished, Matron sat for a few moments looking thoughtful, then said, 'Well, the legacy solves one of my problems.'

'I don't understand.'

'You can stop work immediately and take refuge in your cottage.'

'The Cotterells know about the place in Malmesbury, so it wouldn't be safe to go there, and Mr Marley wasn't sure what condition the other would be in. It's smaller and it's been standing empty for two or three months.'

'You could sell the Malmesbury house back to the Cotterells at a fair price and not tell them about the other.'

Bella nodded. She'd been wondering about doing just that. But would they leave her alone if she did it? Spencer Cotterell might not be an outright lunatic, but he certainly wasn't completely sane, or he'd not have tried to hurt her.

Matron cleared her throat to get Bella's attention. 'I hope you don't mind, but Philip's lawyer tried to phone you here just before you arrived and I had a little chat with him. Mr Marley seems a sensible fellow and was horrified at what had happened to you. Like me he doesn't feel it was a chance attack *or* a lunatic.'

'I liked him.'

'He's coming to visit you at the weekend, if that's all right, and wants to drive you over to Malmesbury to show you the houses you've inherited. I suggested that at the same time we work out a plan for keeping you safe. I didn't tell him about the baby, but I think you should.'

'I might not be expecting. I'd much rather not say anything till I'm sure.'

Matron gave her a knowing smile. 'I didn't say so when we talked about that before, because you were still getting used to the idea, but I have a gift for spotting a woman carrying a child and mark my words, you have that glow to you, even as tired and worried as you are at the moment. It's quite unmistakable, a softness in the eyes and skin, and a tendency to be more emotional.'

'Oh. Well, I hope you're right.'

'I'm sure of it. And I'm really glad you want the baby. It upsets me to see children brought into this world and raised unloved. You can always tell from their poor little faces whether anyone cares about them or not. The ones in need of love have a sharp, pinched look.'

'Well, this one will be greatly loved.'

'I know, dear. You're a caring young woman.'

For the first time in public, Bella allowed her hand to rest on her stomach, though she'd done it a couple of times in bed. If there really was a child in there, she would love it with all her heart. And she would not only have something of Philip but she wouldn't be alone in the world any longer.

That was a wonderful thought. Her mother was always so

busy and was far too sharp in dealing with the world. They had never been close. She'd felt very alone since her father died.

The next couple of days passed slowly. The other drivers were envious of Bella inheriting a car of her own and were itching for her to take them for a spin in the long summer evenings. But she didn't do that, pretending the engine needed tuning properly and she didn't want to do any driving around until that had been sorted out.

By the time Saturday came she was impatient for the conference with the lawyer and the visit to her cottages, impatient to be *doing* something.

She would have to work out what was best to do with her life from now on. She didn't feel certain about anything.

But she was beginning to feel that Matron was right and she was expecting Philip's child. And oh, it was such a comfort to have no financial worries! She still couldn't believe she'd inherited so much. She'd had to be careful with money all her life. She didn't think she could be extravagant even now, but she wouldn't have to skimp.

Georgie Cotterell was finding it hard to pass the time as a guest, even though Penny had made her feel very welcome. She tried to think what to do next and even wondered whether she should try to join the VADs. But she couldn't stand the sight of blood and didn't know how to drive, so all that remained as far as she could tell was becoming a hospital cleaner, which wouldn't be very pleasant, she was sure.

She visited the village library and borrowed books.

She tried to join other women in sewing comforts for the soldiers, but was told that her sewing simply wasn't neat enough. Penny found her efforts at sewing hilarious and set her to knitting squares instead, which could be sewn together to make blankets.

And all the time, she missed Philip. She might not have spent a lot of time with her twin since he'd enlisted but he'd always been there, sending her carelessly scrawled letters, telling her how much he enjoyed reading her letters. There. He'd been part of her life for ever, closer than ordinary brothers.

The first letter from Harry was a godsend. It was long and chatty and when Penny said she hated writing letters, Georgie volunteered to keep in touch with Harry for her. She decided to write to him once a week, but he wrote more often than that, and it seemed rude not to reply, so they were soon exchanging letters every two or three days.

Then he sent word he was coming home to run a training course for troops being posted to Ireland, where there was a lot of unrest since the Easter uprising in April in Dublin.

It was bad enough to be fighting the Germans but Ireland seemed like a close cousin to her and she didn't really understand what 'the troubles' were about.

Harry tried to explain and said he felt sorry for both sides and there was no easy way out.

What a mess the world was in!

One afternoon when Georgie went into the nearest town to buy some art supplies, because her mother hadn't sent hers when Mr Marley brought her clothes, she saw Spencer across the street. He was staring in her direction with a triumphant look on his face. But he made no attempt to come near her, just stared, in that horrible threatening way he had when he was plotting mischief.

What could he be planning to do to her now?

She began to worry. Surely he wouldn't try to grab her and take her back by force? And how had he found her anyway?

'Is something wrong, Miss Cotterell?' the butcher asked.

She hesitated then nodded. 'My elder brother is down the street. I'm frightened of him. I ran away from home and I don't know how he found me but I'm afraid to walk back to Mrs Richards' on my own in case Spencer, um, accosts me. There's no one else living down that lane, as you know.'

The butcher, a family man, came to peer out of the window. 'That thin fellow near the lamp post?'

'Yes.'

'Not in a good mood, is he? And he doesn't mind who sees it. Would you like to go out the back way? You can slip down the alley and cut across the fields to Mrs Richards' house.'

'Would you mind?'

'Of course not.'

But she worried all the way there that Spencer might pursue her and ended up running flat out. He must know where she was living.

What was she going to do?

* * *

The next day Harry turned up unexpectedly and found Georgie at home on her own, as Penny had gone into the village to sew for the troops.

Georgie felt suddenly shy. She and Harry had been writing long letters and now she felt she knew him better, so she should have been more at ease. But though he was tall and strong, with a healthy air to him, she wasn't attracted to him, and she didn't know why.

'Come in,' she said, feeling awkward. 'Penny will be back in an hour or so.'

After a few minutes of stilted conversation, he reached across the table to take her hand. 'Don't we know each other well enough now for you to relax a little with me, Georgie?' he asked with one of his sweet smiles.

'Yes. I don't know what's got into me. I'm a bit on edge because I saw Spencer in the village yesterday.'

'I don't like the sound of that. He must be following you. Why else would he come to such a small place? Perhaps it's time for you to look for somewhere else to live.'

'I agree. I don't want Penny getting hurt because I'm here. But where shall I go? Spencer's very clever, and I think he could trace me anywhere. He's very persistent when he wants something and he's as bad as my mother for wanting me to marry Francis. I can't work out why they were both so eager that I do it.'

'I think you'd better stay in the house for a few days. I've got a couple of important meetings coming up in London, but after that I've got a few days' leave before they send me somewhere else. I could help you find somewhere to live, if you liked.'

She nodded, but after he'd left she began to worry and in the end, she packed some things together in case she had to get away at a moment's notice. She'd go to Bella's landlady first and beg her help.

In fact, she'd leave in a day or two at most. Thank goodness she had some money. She could afford to hide in a hotel for days without poking her head outside it.

The trouble was she'd go mad with boredom. She was already fretting at having so little to do, because Penny had a very capable woman who came and 'did for her' so there was nothing for Georgie to do in the house.

Why did life have to be so complicated?

Chapter Six

Bella went to wait in Matron's office for the lawyer, surprised how on edge the older woman seemed. She kept looking out of the window and when a car arrived, she exclaimed, 'There's Mr Marley at last! I think that's his son-in-law driving him. He was apparently invalided out and now walks with a limp, poor chap.'

She went to the door, turning to say to Bella, 'You'd better stay out of sight in my office. We've agreed that I'll pretend Mr Marley is a relative of mine in case anyone is watching.'

A few moments later, her voice came clearly from outside, 'There you are, Cousin Gilbert!'

It seemed to Bella that the older woman was rather enjoying the excitement.

She heard a brief murmured conversation, then Matron came back alone, saying tersely, 'Go back to your lodgings, Jones, and tell anyone who asks that you're going out for a nice long walk. Head towards the village and wait for us under that big oak tree near the pond. Mr Marley suggests we all drive over to visit the cottage in Malmesbury first, to see what condition it's in. I hope you don't mind me coming too.'

She didn't wait for an answer but rushed on, 'Oh, and wear your ordinary clothes, not your uniform, with a hat you can pull down to conceal your face. Well, what are you waiting for? Hurry up!'

Bella rushed across the grounds to her lodgings, which were only a few hundred yards away. She trusted her landlady so told her the truth, that she had to go out with Matron and to tell anyone else that she'd gone for a walk.

All this cloak-and-dagger business made her feel more not less anxious, she thought as she flung on her everyday clothes. If people as sensible and down to earth as Matron and Mr Marley thought it necessary, then she too had to take the danger very seriously indeed. The thought of what else the Cotterells might be planning sent a shiver down her spine.

It only took her a few minutes to walk to the tree from her lodgings and she waited in the shade, standing well back from the road.

It wasn't long before a car pulled up and Mr Marley got out to open the rear door for her. She was more used to opening doors for herself and could perfectly well have got in without help, but that would probably have made him feel uncomfortable.

'This is Walter Fowler, my son-in-law.' He glanced round, as if to make sure no one was watching. 'We were just saying it might be a good idea for you to slide down in the back seat and stay out of sight till we've left the village, if you don't mind.' He didn't wait for her agreement but closed the door and went back to his own seat.

His son-in-law muttered what could have been a greeting, then set off again.

Bella felt silly as well as uncomfortable as she crouched on the floor, her face close to Matron's sturdy calves, once hidden under longer skirts but now revealed in the new shorter skirts that were in vogue.

She was glad when Mr Marley said, 'It should be safe to get up now, Miss Jones.'

It was only an hour or so's drive to Malmesbury, which was near the border between Wiltshire and Gloucestershire, but it seemed longer to Bella.

Matron and Mr Marley enjoyed a lively discussion about the progress of the war, starting off with the sinking of HMS *Hampshire* at the beginning of June. It had hit a mine off the Orkneys and sunk. Sadly, Lord Kitchener had been on the vessel, which most people considered a tragedy. Why his death was more tragic than those of the mainly younger crew members, Bella didn't know, but people kept on saying that. On the recruitment posters for the armed forces, Kitchener looked distinctly grumpy to her.

Walter concentrated on his driving and spoke only in monosyllables.

Bella didn't attempt to join in the conversation, either, and was glad when they left her in peace. It was as if Matron understood that she was finding it hard to think straight at the moment. She wasn't used to big dramas in her life.

The 'cottage' in Malmesbury turned out to be a semi-detached three-storey villa, much larger than Bella had expected and situated in a row of similar, well-kept dwellings. It had a neat little garden in front and a bigger one behind.

Mr Marley unlocked the front door and paused on the threshold looking puzzled, then called back, 'Someone has been here since I last visited the cottage. I distinctly remember leaving those papers in a pile on the hall table and now they're scattered all over the floor. Walter, will you please stand near the front door while I inspect the place, in case someone's still inside? And I think it'd be prudent if you ladies stayed in the car.'

'What next?' Matron muttered.

Bella was beyond words.

Mr Marley came out a few minutes later and walked across to the car. 'The whole house has been ransacked. Nothing seems to have been damaged, but I can't tell if anything has been taken because I've only visited it once. I asked Mr Perry to remove any valuables, and I can only hope he's done that. Perhaps Walter should go for the police and we can wait in the garden.'

Bella felt suddenly impatient. 'Well, since no one's there at the moment, I don't see why we shouldn't go inside, as long as we touch nothing.'

Matron looked up at the sky, which was overcast. 'It looks like rain. It can't hurt to take shelter inside, surely, Mr Marley?'

'Cousin Gilbert,' he corrected. 'I think we should keep up the pretence. And perhaps you're right.' He waved one hand. 'Go ahead and explore your house, Miss Jones. We'll wait for you in the hall.'

Bella had gone all over the house by the time the police

arrived. It was bigger than anywhere she'd ever lived before. Her mother would be over the moon to live here, but to Bella, the place had an unhappy feel to it. She didn't know why, but something about it made her shiver. She stood in the doorway of each room in turn, taking in the old-fashioned décor, with heavy velvet or brocade curtains, flowery wallpaper and carpet squares covered in writhing flower patterns and surrounded by dark parquet flooring, dusty now after the months of neglect.

Furniture and ornaments were crammed in everywhere. Her eyes felt tired just looking at them all.

When she'd finished she joined the others in the hall, where Mr Marley and Matron were chatting like two old friends as they waited for the police.

'I'll ask Walter to call at Mr Perry's place of business next because he knows more about the house and its contents than I do. He's been keeping an eye on it since Miss Gordon died. Philip was wondering whether to live here himself after the war but he didn't like the house, I don't know why.'

Philip hadn't mentioned that plan to her, not even when he asked her to marry him. It had all happened so quickly. In four short months they'd met, fallen in love and then she'd lost him. The inheritance from Miss Gordon mustn't have mattered to him or he'd have spoken of it. He'd gone to university and had studied engineering, but hadn't finished his degree because of the war. He wanted to do something connected with motor cars after the war ended because he was sure they were the coming thing.

Mr Marley turned as his son-in-law returned.

'The police are coming shortly,' Walter said.

'Good. Mr Perry's office is nearby, just at the end of the next street. Perhaps you could go there and ask him to join us? Explain what's happened here.' He glanced at Bella and added belatedly, 'Is that all right with you, Miss Jones?'

'Yes, of course. Do whatever you think best, Mr Marley.' She waited till Walter had driven off to say, 'I agree with Philip. I'd not like to live here.'

Her two companions looked at her in surprise. 'It's a very commodious house in a good street,' Matron protested.

They'd think her foolish if she told them the house felt unhappy, so she merely said, 'Yes, but much too big for me.'

'That's your choice, my dear Miss Jones.' Mr Marley began to pace up and down the room. 'I wonder how the burglars got in. There's no sign of broken windows or doors being forced.'

He fell silent as they all considered the most obvious reason there might be for that.

'What can they have been looking for?' Matron wondered aloud.

'The lady's valuables, I should think. But I'm sure Mr Perry has those in safekeeping. Perhaps we should have the locks changed immediately, though. Someone must have a key to the place.'

And that could only be the Cotterells, Bella thought.

Walter came back to report that Mr Perry had immediately agreed to come to the house and also offered to go with them later to show them the house in Honeyfield, because he knew the village well. If they didn't mind waiting for him to speak to the police, that was.

'I think that's an excellent idea,' Mr Marley said at once. 'Dear me, this is all turning out to be very complicated, isn't it?'

A policeman arrived at long last on foot and Mr Perry came shortly afterwards in his car. He confirmed that the house hadn't been in this state two days ago.

Mr Perry seemed a pleasant man of about thirty, Bella guessed, with a kind expression on a face that managed to be attractive in spite of a rather large nose.

'They must have been after Miss Gordon's valuables,' Mr Marley said. 'But as I told Miss Jones, there was nothing of value here to be taken since you were looking after all the silver and Miss Gordon's jewellery.'

He turned to Bella. 'You will be entitled to keep those, even if you sell the house, my dear young lady.'

Bella knew she would rather sell them but it seemed rude to say so. She couldn't imagine wearing jewellery valuable enough to be locked away for safety, or using silver items in everyday life. She'd be forever polishing them.

This whole situation continued to feel unreal, like a confusing nightmare.

The policeman said he couldn't see much chance of catching the intruders and they didn't seem to have taken anything, so it wasn't an urgent matter. But of course, he would report the facts to the sergeant when he got back and they would keep their eyes on the house in case something happened.

He left it to them to arrange how to set the place to rights, strolling off down the street as if he had all the time in the world.

'Not very helpful, was he?' Mr Marley said. 'Can you find someone to tidy up the house, Mr Perry?'

'Yes, of course. Do you still want me to come to Honeyfield with you?'

'If you can spare the time, I'd be much obliged.'

'I'm happy to help in any way I can. I don't have appointments with any other clients today. I shan't even be going home to lunch because my wife and son are out at a friend's.'

'How is your little son?'

Mr Perry's face lit up. 'Stephen is thriving and his half-brother and -sister adore him. We hope to give him a sister soon, though of course you can't choose which sort of child you'll get and whichever it is will be loved.'

'Congratulations. Please give your wife my regards.'

'I will. Now, I'll lead the way in my car, shall I? I'll probably go on to visit Honeyfield House before I come back. I'm one of the trustees there.'

'Honeyfield House?' Mr Marley queried. 'Is that someone's country mansion?'

'It was once. Now it's a convalescent home for women who have no one else to help them. It's one of the charities run by the Greyladies Trust, set up by distant relatives of mine to help women in trouble. My wife and I keep an eye on the place. She used to be the supervisor there when it was first set up.'

Bella liked the loving way he spoke of his family and

also the idea of a place for women in need. It seemed to her that Honeyfield would be a more attractive place to live in than this cluttered house in Malmesbury. She was looking forward to seeing it.

It was a small village, more of a hamlet, really, Bella thought. And pretty. She stared round as they drove slowly through it, trying to take everything in at once. The most important thing was to find somewhere safe to live, more important than anything else to her after that attack on her car.

Was the cottage here safe? How could you tell?

She liked the looks of the village, she had to admit. Most of the houses were built of a beautiful, grey-gold Cotswold stone. They were cosy-looking, a mixture of large and small, with neat gardens and windows sparkling in the sunshine.

There was a small church and a few shops opposite an open space, which Mr Marley called the village green, though it wasn't very big, just a long narrow strip of grass. The village school was at the end of the green and children were shrieking and running round in a small playground. It'd be good to have a school so close later on.

A woman came out of a cottage and stood staring at them, as if wondering what they were doing here.

Mr Perry, who was in the leading car, raised one hand to greet her and she narrowed her eyes for a moment to squint at the car, then smiled as if she'd suddenly recognised him and returned his wave.

He turned into a short street beyond the school at the northern edge of the hamlet, away from the main road that had brought them here. There was the same mixture of houses in the street, with the one next to the end looking unoccupied and ready to fall down in the next big storm. Mr Perry stopped his car outside the house next to it, which was set across the end of the street.

As they pulled to a halt behind him, she saw curtains twitch at a couple of nearby windows. People were usually nosey about what was going on in their street, but they'd become more suspicious of strangers since the war began. Bella hoped this might work in her favour and help keep her safe.

Good neighbours always kept an eye on one another. If she lived here, they might include her too, even though she would be a stranger to them at first. She didn't want to live anywhere without neighbours to talk to and was already wondering how she'd fill her days after she left the VADs. She'd been busy all her life.

Mr Perry unlocked the front door and pushed it open. 'Why don't you go in first?' he suggested to Bella. 'Get a feel for the place.'

'Thank you. I'd like that.'

'Good idea!' said Matron. 'First impressions are so important.'

The front door led into a hall about two yards wide. To the right was a decent-sized living room, and though the furniture was dusty and the room quite dim with the curtains drawn, when she pulled one back, afternoon sunlight streamed in. She felt a sense of peace and welcome. It was very different from the Malmesbury house.

When Matron and Mr Marley came into the house behind her, she asked, 'Whose is the furniture?'

'Yours, now. All this has come to you by a rather twisted route, has it not? The lady who owned the cottage was a very close friend of Philip's aunt and the two saw each other regularly, staying overnight when they visited. Miss Thorburn lived here all her life, was born here, even.'

'I can't imagine only ever living in one house,' Bella said.

'Do the Cotterells know about this house?' Matron asked.

'Not as far as I'm aware. I didn't tell his parents anything about it because he'd intimated to me that he wanted his affairs kept strictly private from them. His mother can be a bit . . .' He paused, searching for a word and came up with, 'Officious.'

One point was particularly important to Bella. 'So Mrs Cotterell doesn't know about this place in Honeyfield?'

'As I said, I don't think so. And I don't intend to tell her, or anyone in my firm. My partner deals with legal matters for her and her husband, and Mr Shadwell was assisting him. I attended Philip's funeral alone because my partner wasn't well.'

Matron was still standing by the door. When the lawyer had finished speaking she waited a moment then made a shooing gesture towards Bella. 'Go and explore the rest of the house now, Jones, while I chat to Mr Marley, then you can show us round.'

Bella set off to explore the house which might become her new home. It was a double-fronted house, with a dining room on one side and a sitting room at the other. The kitchen and a bedroom that was presumably for a maid lay at the rear.

She spent a lot of time studying the kitchen, which was a generous size, with a large scullery to one side and a big pantry on the rear wall. There was a large table for preparing food and a small table by the window, just big enough for two people to eat at.

There was a door at one side and beyond it she found another large room, light and airy with windows on two sides. It had obviously been used as a studio and several pretty watercolours were displayed on the walls, wildflower studies and rural scenes. She was sad to see one painting standing on an easel, unfinished. They were very pretty and well executed.

She returned to the kitchen, unlocked the back door and went into the garden. It needed weeding and tidying up, but it was big enough to support a few fruit trees and bushes, as well as a kitchen garden. The grass needed mowing and there were washing lines with pegs still on them strung across between two posts. To one side, placed to be seen from the studio, was a flower bed overflowing with blooms, with a few weeds poking out among them.

There was a pretty wooden summer house at the rear and she couldn't resist walking across to peep into it. It'd be lovely to sit out in the garden in summer. There was a door at the rear of the summer house, which led to a gate in the garden wall. She'd never have guessed there was a gate here. Where did it lead? She'd have opened it to peep out but there was no key and it was locked.

She went inside the house again. She'd be able to see what lay behind the wall from the rear bedrooms.

The stairs ran up from the hall. She could see Matron and Mr Marley standing out at the front in the sunshine chatting to Mr Perry, so she continued her exploration alone.

There were four bedrooms, two large and two slightly smaller, plus – oh, joy! A bathroom! It had a huge bath and an old-fashioned washbasin and lavatory with a flower pattern on them. The water seemed to be heated by a gas burner. This would be such a welcome luxury, especially with a baby.

Everything was neatly furnished, which would be a godsend, but there was too much furniture for her taste. Still, she had more than enough money and time to make a comfortable home for herself and her child and change things round to suit her.

She went across to a rear bedroom window and found herself looking across what seemed to be a large commercial orchard, beyond which she could see a rambling farmhouse and outbuildings. To one side of it, further along she could see the corner of what looked like a large house. Why had they wanted a gate through into an orchard? She smiled. To steal apples and pears? Hardly.

She jumped in shock as she heard Matron call, 'Are you all right up there, Jones?'

'Yes. Sorry to keep you waiting. I'll just be another couple of minutes.'

She couldn't resist trying a door in the bedroom,

thinking to find a cupboard and surprised to see narrow stairs leading up to an attic. Of course she went up and found a few small pieces of furniture and several boxes stored there haphazardly on the wooden floor.

Everything in the cottage was dusty but as she went slowly downstairs again, she felt as if she'd come home. She could be happy here, she was sure. It was strange how quickly you made your mind up about a house. She hadn't liked the one in Malmesbury even before she'd seen the upstairs, but she did like this one. Very much.

Fate had taken her beloved fiancé away from her and then given her all these worldly goods. She knew which she'd have preferred. Even after a few weeks of knowing one another, she and Philip had been so comfortable and happy together.

'Oh, you fool! Stop thinking like that,' she whispered to herself and wiped the tears away with her handkerchief. She leant over the bannister and called, 'Do come up if you'd like. I'm sure you're dying to see the rest of the house.'

When the others had explored the upstairs, they all gathered in the front room, which was furnished with a sofa, two upholstered rocking chairs and an upright piano with brass candleholders on it. She pressed a couple of notes down, wishing she could play.

Matron came across and played a short melody, grimacing. 'Needs tuning.'

'I didn't know you could play the piano,' Bella said in surprise.

'There's a lot you don't know about me.'

They all fell silent and Mr Perry smiled at Bella. 'No need to ask if you like this house, Miss Jones. I can see it in your face.'

'Do you like it?'

'Yes. Very much.'

'I'd like to move here quite quickly.'

'It'll take a couple of days to find people to get it ready for you to live in, but it won't be a problem.'

But Matron was still frowning.

'Is something wrong?' he asked.

'I think you know about the attack on Miss Jones. I'm wondering how to make it safer for her to live here, perhaps by changing her name so that they can't easily find her. She shouldn't do anything till we've worked that out. She'll have no one in the village to turn to for help till she gets to know people.'

Some of the glow faded from the day at this reminder, but Bella tried not to let that show. If she lived here quietly, didn't upset the Cotterells, surely they'd leave her in peace? What would they have to gain by annoying her?

As Matron spoke, Nathan's vision blurred for a moment and he got the strange feeling that meant his special ability to find both objects and solutions to problems was starting to work. He let ideas drift into his mind and settle, not questioning the rightness of what he was going to suggest, just *knowing* it would be the best thing to do. After all, that strange sense had never let him down or led him astray.

The gift came from the Latimer side of her family,

his mother had told him. Some family members were apparently fey, or whatever you wanted to call it. He wished he'd talked to her more about her side of his family before she grew forgetful and distant, but his father had been a bully and had forbidden her to mention them and in particular the 'weakness', which he called 'jumping to conclusions' to their son.

She'd been so meek and quiet, so *browbeaten* by his father that you sometimes forgot she was even in the room. She'd died as quietly as she'd lived, poor woman.

His own wife was a much more lively woman and thank goodness for Kathleen's strength of mind and loving warmth. He loved his stepchildren too; they were as lively as their mother. No fear of them being bullied at school, or putting up with someone else bullying a weaker child when they were around.

He took a deep breath and shared his thoughts: 'You could tell people that Bella is a distant relative of Miss Thorburn, who's inherited the cottage.'

Mr Marley frowned. 'What if Miss Thorburn told her neighbours she was leaving the cottage to her friend?'

'You could tell them her friend died, so her great-niece inherited instead.'

Matron was nodding approvingly and Mr Marley was looking thoughtful now.

Bella didn't say anything, looking towards Matron.

'Even so, she'd be a woman on her own, even if we pretended she was a widow,' the older woman said. 'What if they go looking for her? They've only to ask in the towns and villages nearby to hear about all the newcomers. There's always someone willing to gossip.'

'Perhaps you could invent a husband for Miss Jones and give her another surname?'

Silence as they all considered Nathan's second suggestion.

'But if he never appears, people will get suspicious,' Bella protested, not liking the idea at all.

It was Mr Marley who snapped his fingers as the solution came to him. 'I think we could ask Captain Tesworth to visit from time to time. I know he's concerned about his friend's widow because he asked me to let him know if you needed any help. I'm sure he wouldn't mind pretending to be your husband, Miss Jones.'

She didn't know what to say to that. She liked Tez, of course she did, but she wasn't sure she could pretend to be married to him. And it didn't seem fair, either. It'd stop him courting another woman.

'He's a very decent fellow and you'd be quite safe with him, even if he stayed the night,' Mr Marley said.

She couldn't hide her shock. '*Stayed the night!* I don't think it would be necessary to go so far.'

Something told Nathan it would be necessary and he said so.

Mr Marley looked from one to the other. 'I would not normally advocate doing something like this, but as I've said before, I'm aware that Mr Cotterell – the son, not the father – can behave in a very, um, underhand way when he wants something or feels himself slighted. I would like you to be as well protected as possible, Miss Jones.'

'Yes, but . . .' She was lost for words.

'And there's another side to the matter: it will give that nice young man something to do. Mr Tesworth tries not to show it, but he's upset about losing those fingers and being invalided out, and can't yet see a new path to follow in life.'

'Perhaps he already has a young woman he likes.'

'I've not heard of any. I know his family slightly and they'd have said something if he'd been courting. He's the youngest of three sons, so he won't inherit the family business and therefore must make his way in the world now he's back in civilian life. He joined the army before he could settle to a profession but I believe they were thinking about banking for him, or was it medicine? No, I'm sure I heard that he'd been working in a bank.'

Bella looked round and saw how much the other two liked the idea of her inventing a husband. She tried desperately to think of a good reason for not doing such an embarrassing thing. 'Not only is it an imposition on Mr Tesworth, but he'll only be able to come here now and then, so how will that protect me?'

'It's the belief that you have a husband that will protect you,' Mr Marley said. 'If the Cotterells search for you, they won't suspect a woman who is living quietly here and has been seen to have a husband, whereas if you said you were a widow, they might well become suspicious.'

'Surely they wouldn't go to such lengths?' It was like a melodrama, the sort she'd seen at the cinema, with the pianist playing soft, sinister music in the background and a black-hearted villain creeping after the heroine, hands outstretched to grab her.

The lawyer shook his head. 'I regret to say that Spencer might pursue matters if he feels slighted. He isn't involved in the fighting and his mother won't let him run the family estate. He can't ask his father to override her because Mr Cotterell doesn't get involved in family life.'

'But people will see that Tez isn't involved in the fighting now, can't be because of his hand. How would we explain the fact that he doesn't live here all the time?'

'We can say your husband has been given a job at the War Office in London. We don't need to explain exactly what in these troubled times, just say "war work" and tell people you're not allowed to reveal the details. His hand will bear witness to the reason why he's no longer actually fighting.'

She couldn't think of any other arguments. 'Well, if he doesn't think it an imposition, I suppose we could think about it. I'm not as sure as you are that he'll agree, though, Mr Marley.'

'I feel quite certain he will and I'll be happy to ask him for you.'

'Yes, please.' There was no way she was asking him, that was certain.

But what about the child? she wondered and looked at Matron, who nodded and turned back to Mr Marley.

'There is also a possibility that Bella is expecting Philip's child.'

'Good heavens!' Then he smiled. 'But isn't that wonderful?'

'I think so,' Bella said. 'But I don't want to tell his family. They're so hostile.'

He sighed. 'I think that's wise.'

Bella was now feeling utterly boneless with exhaustion. She seemed to tire so easily these days. It was a relief when they decided to set off back.

Chapter Seven

Mr Marley's nephew drove them to the hospital and Matron invited both gentlemen in for afternoon tea, since they'd missed their midday meal.

When the two men accepted, Bella stifled a sigh because all she wanted to do now was lie down. 'I think I'll go and rest, if you don't mind. I didn't sleep well last night.'

'You'd better join us for a while, at least, Jones, because we still have the details to sort out, and I have a further suggestion to make.'

When Matron spoke in that firm tone no one argued with her. Bella sat down and found to her surprise that she was hungry after all. She waited for the afternoon nausea to strike at the mere thought of food, but it didn't. Perhaps it'd fade gradually after the first three months as morning sickness was supposed to do. Well, people said that was what happened and she was hoping they were right. She hadn't had much experience of other women's pregnancies because she came from such a small family.

Which reminded her: she'd have to tell her mother about the inheritance and the child. Or would she? Her mother was an inveterate gossip and wouldn't be able to keep to herself the news that her daughter had inherited money. Worst of all, her mother would want to come and live with her if she thought her daughter now owned a large, comfortable house, something Bella definitely didn't want.

And naturally her mother would insist on meeting the so-called husband and be very angry not to have been invited to the wedding. Her mother had never visited her here because she didn't like travelling, so Bella had gone home for a quick visit whenever her mother's letters got too full of hints about feeling neglected. But once there she had to face her mother saying how much she looked forward to the end of the war and being able to have her only child there to brighten her lonely widowhood and care for her in her old age.

Perhaps letters would keep her mother at bay for a while so that Bella could keep her move secret. She'd ask her kind landlady to forward them and her replies. If she told Mrs Sibley that Philip's family was causing trouble, it'd ensure that no one else was given her new address, not even her mother and—

She realised Matron was giving her an are-you-listening look and tried to pay closer attention to what the others were saying.

'I'll have a quick check that my deputy is coping, then we'll work out how best to keep you safe, Jones.'

While Matron was away, Mr Marley asked, 'Are you all right, Miss Jones? You look a little pale. No need to force conversation with me. I'm happy to sit quietly till Matron returns.'

'Thank you.' No need to ask his nephew to keep quiet, either. Walter had hardly said a word the whole time he'd been driving them around. She wondered what had happened to him during the war to leave such a quiet shadow of a man. Driving an ambulance had shown her some of the sad effects of war on those injured fighting for their country, but some of them were invisible effects on the mind that other civilians might not fully understand.

Five minutes later Matron and the tea both arrived at the same time. When the maid had left and cups had been poured for everyone, Matron ignored hers and said abruptly, 'As I said before, you could sell the Malmesbury house to the Cotterells – at a decent price, of course. You didn't like it, after all, and that should make them feel they've frightened you into doing as they want. With a bit of luck, they'll leave you alone after that. I'm sure Mr Marley will be happy to negotiate a better price?'

He nodded vigorously. 'Indeed I will. I think that's an excellent idea.'

'Mr Cotterell wanted to buy the car as well,' Bella pointed out.

'Do you want to sell it?'

'No. I'd much rather keep it. A car will come in very useful and it's small and not expensive to run. Just what I need.'

'Then he can't have it. I could tell them you've put it at the service of the government. Some people have done that with their cars as a patriotic gesture. Do you need time to think about the house?'

'No. I think it's a good idea to offer it to them. Will you

do that for me, please, Mr Marley? It'll be interesting to see what they offer this time.'

'Oh, very little more at first than their original offer, I expect, my dear. But don't worry! I shall push them up. I rather enjoy bargaining.'

Later, as she walked back through the hospital grounds to her lodgings, Bella felt as if a load had been taken off her shoulders. Matron had excused her from any further duties at the hospital and would tell people she'd been transferred. They'd decided she should move to Honeyfield in a couple of days.

She trusted Mr Marley to handle the sale of the other house. She trusted Matron to stop tongues wagging at the hospital.

But she didn't trust the Cotterells at all, except for Georgie of course. They'd written to each other a couple of times and she hoped to keep in touch with Philip's sister. He'd have liked that.

When Mr Marley phoned Nathan to ask him if he could get the house in Honeyfield cleaned as quickly as possible, ready for Miss Jones to move in, Nathan consulted his wife about who best to hire to do the job.

Kathleen, who was aware of Bella's plight, thought for a moment. 'Actually I can't think of anyone better than our Sal to do it. We've only got a couple of women staying at Honeyfield House at the moment and the matron there says there's not enough work to keep Sal occupied. Or we can easily find someone else in the village to help her, if necessary.'

He gave his wife a quick hug. 'Well, we can be sure it'll be well done. Sal is the most ferocious dirt hunter I've ever met, seems to love washing and polishing a floor.'

'She's a good-hearted woman. It's not only the extra money but she'll be happy to help a stranger in a predicament, as people helped her when she was destitute. I'll explain a little about Miss Jones's background and afterwards Sal will tell her friends in the village how nice the stranger is – you did say you liked Miss Jones, so I'm sure Sal will take to her too.'

She paused and added slowly, 'I wonder . . . are there clothes to dispose of from the previous owner? Sal is very short of clothes. She's saving every penny she can so that she can help her little daughter to get a better life than her, so she'll only spend on herself when her clothes get totally worn out.'

'I suppose there will be. And I doubt they'd fit Miss Jones, who has a very trim figure.'

They exchanged smiles. Miss Thorburn had been a distinctly stout old lady and so was Sal.

'Have you heard what married name Bella will be using, Nathan?'

'No. I'll no doubt find out next time I speak to Mr Marley.' He put his arm round his wife's shoulders. 'Now, enough about other people, much more important to me is how you're feeling today.'

Her whole expression softened and her face seemed luminous with love. 'Stop worrying. I feel wonderful. I always do when I'm carrying a child, especially yours, my darling.'

He held her close, deeply moved as always by her love. He had never thought to be so lucky as to find and win a wonderful woman like his Kathleen. He even got on with her father these days because Fergus had mellowed greatly since his second marriage, though his other children seemed to resent their sister marrying a man so much better off than any of them.

Money was all relative. Nathan was still careful with his because he'd had to pull the family business back from the edge of bankruptcy after his father died leaving their business in a mess. Nathan's house-selling venture was doing particularly well, thank goodness, and the little investigative jobs he undertook on the side.

He hadn't yet achieved his ambition of becoming a full-time detective like Mr Sherlock Holmes and only Kathleen knew about that dream. But people had started coming to Nathan for help in finding lost family members or to discuss solutions to their problems. He called his talent 'finding things'.

He was lucky in so many ways these days, so he tried to help others as a way of paying fate back.

Mr Marley was very busy the following day. He telephoned Mr Tesworth first to broach the delicate subject of him pretending to be Bella's husband. He didn't intend to mention the baby. Matron had suggested leaving that job to Bella.

There was dead silence at the other end of the line after he'd explained the situation.

'Not if you don't want to,' Mr Marley added hastily.

'No, no. It's not that. I'm happy to do it. You surprised me, that's all. Philip was my best friend and I'm sure he'd want me to help Bella. He was head over heels in love with her, you know.' He sighed. 'How I envied him.'

'You're young yet. There's plenty of time to find a wife.'

'I don't feel young.'

A lot of men who'd been in the thick of the fighting said that, Mr Marley thought sadly. War was a terrible thing. 'How is your hand?'

'Less painful, thank goodness, but I'm having trouble using my right hand in its place. I was always very strongly left-handed. My handwriting is like that of a five-year-old child nowadays.'

'Practice will make it better.'

'So they tell me. And I'll be able to use my left hand once it's healed. Thank goodness it was only the last two fingers I lost. They tell me there are gadgets to help me hold a pen more comfortably in it later. But that's beside the point. It's Bella's safety that matters at the moment. If you're quite sure she feels all right about such a pretence and that it really will protect her, I'll happily pose as her husband. When is she intending to move to Honeyfield?'

'Tomorrow.'

'Then I'll get someone to drive me into Berkshire tomorrow and Bella can drive me to Honeyfield in her car.'

'She's no longer working at the hospital. Matron had the same idea and said if you could manage it, you were to pick Bella up from her lodgings.' He gave the address.

'All right. Philip always said she was an excellent driver, as good as any man, so I shall look forward to our journey.'

'I've never wanted to learn to drive a motor car myself but you young people seem to enjoy it, and we rely greatly on the young women who've taken men's places during the war, as Miss Jones has done. You won't stop these women driving around after the war ends, though, not now they've tasted such freedom. The days of a quiet home life are, I fear, sadly numbered.'

'A lot of things will be changed for ever by the war, I'm sure.' Tez glanced at his hand and grimaced. He still hadn't heard whether there had been serious nerve damage, but at least the swelling was going down.

'I'm glad you're going to Honeyfield with her the first time, Mr Tesworth. Your being there should set the scene properly for the neighbours.'

'Good. I hope Bella won't be too tired by her drive to take me to the nearest station afterwards.'

'Well, um . . . about that. There are several bedrooms, so Matron and I felt it might be better if you spent the night there occasionally, and especially the first time. It would look strange for a husband to leave before his wife is settled in.' The older man held his breath, hoping this suggestion wouldn't frighten Mr Tesworth away.

Another of those heavy silences, then, 'You're sure Bella won't mind me doing that?'

'No, of course not. Though she's still grieving and you may find her a trifle absent-minded as a hostess.'

'I'm not very talkative myself at the moment.'

When he put the phone down, Mr Marley nodded in satisfaction. It was a bit early, and rather sneaky of him and Matron, but they both thought Mr Tesworth and Bella had a lot in common and might take to one another if they were thrown together.

He phoned Mrs Cotterell next but that conversation wasn't very promising. The woman was still refusing to pay a proper price for the Malmesbury house, still trying to cheat Bella. If the family continued to be so obstinate, he would tell them there was another gentleman who wanted to buy it. That ought to bring them to heel. And if it didn't, Nathan said he could easily find a buyer for a house in such a good location in a pretty little market town.

While he was waiting for the Cotterells to come to their senses, Gilbert decided to have the Malmesbury house cleared of all remaining papers and letters, and go through them carefully. Perhaps they'd give him a clue as to why the house had been ransacked.

And he'd be hanged if he'd include the old lady's silver and jewellery in the sale, even though Mrs Cotterell had told him she'd expect the contents of the house to be untouched. Bella didn't seem interested in the jewellery, so he would offer to sell it for her and she could add the money to her nest egg.

He picked up the phone to tell Matron what he had arranged and reminded her to ask Bella to call herself Mrs Tesworth from now on.

'She can't do that till she's left the area, Mr Marley. We don't want anyone here making connections to her new life.'

'Well, she can arrive in Honeyfield as Mrs Tesworth. And if we are to keep visiting them, we'd better keep up our own little pretence and you can call me Cousin Gilbert.'

'Yes, you're right. And I'm Cousin Evelyn.'

They were both smiling as they broke contact.

Bella kept an eye on the street below her bedroom as she finished packing, watching out for a car. She felt nervous about taking Tez with her to Honeyfield and having him spend the night there occasionally, but Matron had given her a good talking-to about not putting her life and that of her baby at risk.

What would Philip have thought of all this? Matron had demanded. Wouldn't he have trusted his friend to behave in a gentlemanly manner towards her?

Bella knew the answer to that as clearly as if he'd spoken it. Philip would have wanted her to do whatever was necessary to keep her and his child safe, and he'd have trusted his best friend who'd been more of a brother to him than Spencer ever had. She blinked hard as tears welled in her eyes. She'd never been so emotional in her whole life.

To her relief a car stopped outside just then and the inclination to cry vanished as she watched Tez get out of it. He was wearing civilian clothing today, with his arm in a neat black sling. His driver was in khaki. She'd never seen Tez out of uniform before, but the neat felt Homburg hat suited him, as did the grey lounge suit which had a faint stripe that was very fashionable. In fact, his whole appearance was neat and trim, unlike Philip, who had always looked as if he'd thrown his clothes on anyhow.

Tez was carrying a small suitcase and the way he stopped to take a deep breath before knocking on the door made her wonder if he was feeling as nervous as she was.

Well, no wonder! They were strangers who hardly knew one another, with only Philip to bring them together. So it was particularly kind of Tez to help her.

Mrs Sibley let him in, so Bella checked her appearance in the mirror, tried once again to subdue her unruly curls and went down to greet her visitor. 'Thank you for coming with me today, Captain Tesworth,' she said formally for her landlady's benefit.

'It's not "captain" any longer, Miss Jones. I'm officially out of the army, thanks to this.' He glanced down at his hand.

'You've served your country for two years, so you've more than done your bit.' She hoped she was saying the right thing. When he shrugged and continued to look sad, she changed the subject. 'I'll just bring my last case down and put it in the car, then we can be off.'

'I'll help you with that. There's nothing wrong with my right hand.'

His help wasn't necessary because the final bag wasn't heavy and she'd already managed to bring down the heavier one and the box of oddments, like her books and writing materials. But it was obviously important to Tez to do this for her, so she took him up to her bedroom to get the case.

He stopped in the doorway to ask in a low voice, 'Are you sure you're all right with this . . . this charade, Bella?'

She didn't pretend to misunderstand him. 'Yes, of course. And Philip would have approved, I'm sure.'

His expression softened. 'Yes, I'm sure of that too. If I thought he'd object in any way, I'd not be doing it.'

'I'm still not sure all this cloak-and-dagger stuff is necessary, mind you. At least, not to the extent of troubling you.'

'Someone has tried to hurt you already by driving you off the road. Of course it's necessary.'

She shuddered at the memory of how frightening it had been. 'Yes. That's why I agreed to do it. It's left scratches and a dent on the back of the car.'

'We'll find someone to sort that out later. Look, I don't know how much Philip told you about his family, but to be frank, he always said they were a spiteful bunch, except for his sister and to a lesser extent his father, who has always lived apart from his wife and children, and has his own home in London.'

'How sad that must have been for them as children, not to see their father!'

'Yes. And there was bad blood between Philip and Georgie and their brother from an early age – he would never say why. I'm not sure he even knew. He told me more than once that I was never to trust Spencer, whatever he said or did. To make matters worse, their mother always took Spencer's side, whatever the rights and wrongs.'

'I thought her very arrogant when I met her.'

'Yes. She seems to believe herself superior to most other people, though she's actually a rather stupid woman.'

'Do you really think they were the ones behind the attack on my car?'

'Yes, I do. Now, tell me about your family. I should know something about them, shouldn't I?'

'That's easy. I don't have any close relatives except my

mother because my father died a few years ago. I'm not at all close to her. Oh, she wouldn't *hurt* me, I'm certain of that, but she's never cared what *I* want, has only tried to make me do what *she* wanted. That doesn't stop her expecting me to play the devoted daughter and care for her in her old age once the war is over.'

'Were you intending to do that?'

'Definitely not. If I had to emigrate to Canada to avoid it, I would. I could never live with her again. Oh, and I'd better warn you that she can't keep a secret to save her life, so if she ever meets you, please don't let her know we're not really married.'

'I won't tell anyone that.'

As they loaded the suitcase and his small overnight bag into the car, he murmured as if speaking to himself, 'At least doing this makes me feel I'm still useful for something.'

Her heart went out to him but she knew he'd hate any expression of pity, so she said briskly, 'I'm truly glad to have you with me today, Tez, and not to be moving to Honeyfield on my own. Thank you for your help. Now, please get in while I say a final goodbye to Mrs Sibley, then we'll be off.'

They didn't talk much during the drive. To her surprise Bella found it comfortable that Tez didn't try to fill the silence with meaningless conversation. The country roads were quiet, which made driving a pleasure, and the sun was shining. She checked the rear-view mirror regularly, however, and kept her eyes open but she saw no signs of pursuit. Well, there were hardly any other cars on the roads once you got out of the towns.

As they drove, she stole the occasional glance at Tez and was pleased to see him looking more relaxed than when he'd arrived at her lodgings. It was a beautiful June day, with flowers nodding at them from the hedgerows and meadows. Several times they passed groups of people haymaking and, for once, the war seemed very far away.

'You seem to know the way. Have you been there often?' Tez asked after a while.

'Just the once. I'm good at remembering the way once I've been somewhere.'

'I'm the same.'

As they turned into Honeyfield, he exclaimed, 'What a pretty village!'

It was even prettier than she'd remembered. Two small children and a puppy were romping on the green and some women were standing nearby chatting. 'Wait till you see the street where my house is. Pear Tree Lane is like an illustration from a picture book of beautiful villages.'

When she stopped, they got out and stood for a moment or two, looking back from their end at the half a dozen houses on each side of the street. All the gardens were well tended and bursting with flowers except for that of her house and the deserted cottage next to it.

She went to open the gate, *her* gate now. 'Welcome to Pear Tree Cottage, Tez. I'll open up a few windows and show you round before we unload, shall I?'

'All right, darling,' he said loudly, winking at her.

It hadn't occurred to her to use a term of endearment and she could feel her cheeks growing warm.

He chuckled and said more quietly. 'Tell me if you object to my calling you dear or darling, but it adds to the illusion nicely, don't you think?'

'Um, yes. I suppose so – Tez, dear.' She felt such a fool because for a moment, just one very brief moment, she'd wished his endearment was genuine, that she did have someone to love her.

As Bella drove past the hospital grounds, a car pulled slowly out into the road and began to follow her, keeping well back and only moving forward now and then to check that she was still there ahead.

Then, as it rounded a corner, the driver of the second vehicle cursed and had to brake hard because a hay wagon had come to grief due to a broken wheel. It had shed its load of heavy bales all over the narrow lane and one man was lying by the side of the road clutching his arm, with another bending over him.

The wagon driver looked round and yelled, 'I'll be an hour or two clearing this lot up, sir, I'm afraid. The wheel hit a stone and broke, throwing my mate off the wagon. I think he's broken his arm. I have to get him some help before I can deal with this, unless you can take him to the doctor at the cottage hospital for me?'

'Sorry, but I'm in a bit of a hurry.'

The man looked surprised at this answer. 'I see. You'd be best to turn round and go on your way then, sir. Sorry to have troubled you. If you reverse about fifty yards, you'll be able to turn round in the gateway.'

The driver cursed under his breath as he did that, but

though it didn't take him long to find another way to the main road, he failed to catch up with Bella's car again. It could have gone in any of several directions at the various crossroads and there was no telling which.

He stopped to ask a couple of old men working on a ditch if they'd seen a car with a lady driver, but they shook their heads.

'Don't bother with them smelly things,' one of them said.

'Nor they shouldn't let women drive them, neither,' the other added.

So the man got back into his car, slamming the door shut. He drove far too fast for safety on the way home, furious at the way things had turned out.

Inside the cottage everything was gleaming and smelt of furniture polish. There were even white roses sitting in a vase in the hall, giving off a faint, sweet perfume.

Bella showed Tez the downstairs rooms and they ended up in the kitchen. She went across to investigate the cooking and scullery facilities. 'Thank goodness I remembered correctly and it is a gas cooker. Let's put the kettle on before we look at the rest of the house. I'm not the world's best cook, I'm afraid, but I make a good cup of tea. I'm thirsty, even if you aren't.'

'I'd love a cup of tea – two cups, even.'

She turned to light the gas with a match from the box some kind person had left handy to the cooker and he went to stare out of the window at the back garden, then wandered into the studio and examined the paintings.

When Bella joined him there, he said, 'Miss Thorburn

was quite talented. What a pity she didn't finish the final painting. I might have a go at it once my hand has recovered. It'd be a pity to throw it away.' He stared down at his bandaged hand and murmured, 'You don't need five fingers to hold a paintbrush.'

'I didn't know you were artistic.'

He gave her a wry smile. 'It's not something a young man boasts of, especially after he's joined the army. But I did enjoy it. I like to paint landscapes, but flowers too.'

'While the kettle boils, we should bring the luggage in, if you don't mind, Tez. I bought a few provisions yesterday and Mrs Sibley made me a casserole to tide us over till I could do some shopping. I don't want that sitting out in the sun when there's a nice, cool pantry here.'

She opened and shut cupboards, noting a few tins but little by the way of flour or dry goods. She'd have to restock. But there was a tin of sugar, at least, and the same kind person had left her a jug of milk.

'Let me get the luggage in,' he said abruptly.

'How about I fetch the boxes and the food, and you bring in the cases? Leave them in the hall till we've had our cuppa, then we'll take them upstairs.'

It didn't take him long to do that and come back into the kitchen. 'There isn't much luggage, considering you're moving here permanently, Bella. Are you going to be all right?'

'Oh, yes. I'm looking forward to doing some shopping, though. I didn't take a lot with me from home when I joined the VADs, because we were in uniform most of the time. But I can't ask Mother to send the rest of my books and things or she'd know where I live. I'll see if I can find a library nearby, as well. I enjoy reading, not heavy stuff but stories with happy endings and books that teach you things.'

'I can send you some novels to read, if you like. We have a lot of them lying around in the attic because my mother isn't a reader and she'll only allow the leather-bound ones into her sitting room, so that the bookcase looks nice. What sort of novels do you like reading? Ours may be a bit old-fashioned.'

'Anything I can lay my hands on. I'm not fussy. Marie Corelli gives an exciting read, though I can never believe such things could happen in real life. I don't want to trouble you, though.'

His voice was suddenly harsher. 'It's good to be troubled and have something useful to do.'

That was the second time he'd said that. It was her needing to help bring in the luggage that had brought that look to his face. She'd have to be more careful what she said next time he was reminded of his injury. 'I gratefully accept your offer, then, kind sir.'

The kettle was boiling by the time she'd put away the casserole and other bits and pieces of fresh food on the stone shelf in the pantry. She poured the hot water into the teapot and stole a glance in Tez's direction, wondering whether to tell him about the baby. Perhaps she should get it out in the open, in case it put him off pretending to be her husband. But it was hard just to throw news like that at him. She didn't want to upset him again, had to do it tactfully.

He spoke before she had worked out what to say. 'We

ought to have discussed it earlier, but Matron and Mr Marley suggested I spend tonight here. I'll understand if you don't want me to do that, Bella, but if that's the case, I'll have to ask you for a lift to the nearest railway station.'

He still looked stiff and ill at ease, poor man. Mr Marley and Matron shouldn't have put him into such a difficult situation. 'I'd feel better if you stayed, actually, as long as you don't mind. And if my two wise advisers are in favour of it, we'd be foolish to go against their advice, don't you think?'

He nodded and seemed to relax a little.

'Let's go up and choose our bedrooms while the tea brews.'

On the landing she went towards the larger front bedrooms and opened the door of the one on the right. 'I think I'll sleep well here. It has a bolt on the inside of the door in case I feel nervous.'

She stood in the doorway, while he remained like a silent statue at the other end of the landing.

'Will you be nervous on your own here?'

'Probably. Till I'm used to it and the different night noises. And till we're sure the Cotterells are not going to come after me. I'll probably keep a poker handy when I go to bed. Women on their own often do that, you know.'

'I didn't realise.'

'Anyway, if you choose a bedroom, we can go back to our cups of tea.'

He walked round the other rooms quickly then asked,

'Would you mind if I used the other big bedroom? I find small rooms rather oppressive and sleep much better in bigger spaces.'

She wondered if that was as a result of the war, but didn't ask. 'It's fine by me. I only need one bedroom and I'm not likely to have any other guests staying. You may want to change the furniture around, perhaps find a small table to use as a desk. Please feel free to do that. There's too much furniture in the downstairs rooms for my taste, that's for sure. I've never been in such a cluttered house before.'

On the way he stopped at the rear bedroom. 'This would be a charming study.' He walked across to the window. 'It has a pretty view over the back garden.'

'It will be pretty once I've found someone to tidy up the garden.'

'Shall you use the summer house?'

'I think so. It seems sound and there's a surprise inside. I'm not telling you till we go out there.' She still couldn't work out why the gate into the orchard next door was concealed. Perhaps someone in the village would know.

As they sat in the kitchen a few moments later sipping their tea and eating some of the biscuits she'd bought, he said abruptly, 'If you like, I could come here every weekend. You might sleep more easily if you weren't on your own. I can't get a job yet and I don't know what sort of job I'd want. Not in a bank or office or anything like that.'

'I don't want to impose.'

'Well, though I'm staying with my mother she's out a lot, busy with war work. She's a magnificent organiser, knows everyone who's anyone. And the chaps I know from the army aren't often in town since most of them are stationed in France. But perhaps it'd be too much trouble for you to have a regular guest.'

She'd been wondering how safe she'd feel here, because the whole back wall of the garden fronted on to the orchard, so a burglar could easily climb over. 'Not at all. I think that would be a good thing. I'd enjoy the company if you're truly sure you can spare the time.'

'Oh, good! I've always preferred the country to the town and London looks so grey, even in summer. People are worried about bombs and spies and shortages of food, always in a hurry to get somewhere else.'

He reached out for another biscuit. 'I'll bring some food with me next time or pay for my share.'

'How shall you get here? By train to Marlborough?'

He looked down at his hand. 'In a week or two, I may be able to drive myself, so I'll get my car out of storage. If this had been my right hand it'd have been a lot easier to get back to driving.' Only he couldn't change gears yet with this *thing* that used to be a hand. 'I'll have to see if I can find someone to drive me down till I'm able to use my own car again. I'll find a way. There are always chaps on leave and if I leave word that I'll lend them my car for a day or two in return, they'll be happy to help.'

'If you came by train, I could meet you at the railway station.'

'Perhaps you could take me back that way, as long as

you drive off immediately and keep a hat pulled down to hide your face. But you shouldn't wait around in Marlborough for a train which may be late. You know how the war has affected the railway timetables. Someone might see you and recognise you. You won't be all that far away from the Cotterells there – though I don't think they go up to London all that often, from what Philip said, so they might not go near the station.'

'Could you please give me your mother's telephone number? I'm going to get a telephone put in here, at Mr Marley's suggestion, and I'll let you have the number as soon as it's installed. He said he could help me get priority for one. He seems to know a lot of useful people, doesn't he? Like your mother. Until there is a phone you'll have to drop me a letter when you're coming.'

'Or we could arrange it when I leave. So I'd only write if I wasn't coming.' He studied her face. 'You're looking tired again. Are you sure you're all right?'

'Yes, of course I am. Just a bit weary from the driving. I'll go and unpack, then put my feet up for half an hour.' She'd find a better time than this to tell him about the baby. He was looking restless and she was feeling blurry with tiredness.

'I'll go for a stroll round the village, then. I'd like to stretch my legs a bit.'

When he'd gone, she let out her breath in a long half-groan. She hoped the conversations between them wouldn't always be so full of shoals. Light conversation was easy, talking about themselves and their problems much harder. She could see that Tez was still coming to terms with the injury to his hand while she . . . Shaking her head she told herself that she wasn't going to spend her days weeping. That wouldn't bring Philip back.

She went up to unpack and was relieved to find that someone had cleared out the drawers and wardrobe. Thank goodness! Clearing out clothes, especially underwear, would have been a horrible job for a stranger to do.

When she'd unpacked her two suitcases, she lay down on the bed for a few minutes and woke up some time later wondering where she was and how late it was. There was a clock on the mantelpiece, a pretty little enamelled thing, but it wasn't working. She'd have to find the correct time and wind it up.

And she'd buy herself a little fob watch. She'd been issued with one by the VAD ambulance organiser to make sure she kept good time but had had to hand it back when she left. She had come to rely on it and missed it already.

Yawning and stretching, she went into the bathroom, smiling at how convenient it was to have the facilities inside.

How lucky she was to have this house!

At Honeyfield House Sal Hatton was gloating over the clothes she'd cleared out of Pear Tree Cottage. She'd been offered first choice of them by Matron, on Mr Perry's say-so no less, as her reward for doing the job, *as well as* being paid. Well, the clothes would be of no use to the new owner who was a slender young woman, they said.

'Looks like these will fit me just fine, for once.' She

beamed as she held a pair of bloomers up to her waist and studied her reflection in the spotted mirror that graced one wall of the room she and her daughter shared.

Size was always a consideration when you were bigger than most other women. She'd seen Miss Thorburn in the village and she had a fine, buxom figure. I bet she never went hungry for a single day of her whole life, Sal thought. And she hadn't gone hungry for the past few years either, not since Harriet Latimer found her about to give birth, having broken into Honeyfield House with no more than the clothes on her back.

Eh, to think that baby was now nearly five and would soon be starting at the village school.

She'd blessed Mrs Latimer every day since then, because she'd been given a home and a job here as housemaid, and if there was one thing she enjoyed it was cleaning nice houses like this one, making everything sparkle and banishing dust and dirt from every crevice.

There was a new Mrs Latimer at Greyladies now, though, Mrs Olivia Latimer, and she ran the trust which paid for the upkeep of Honeyfield House. Sal didn't quite understand what a trust was, only that it paid for the expenses of this big house and for the help given to women in trouble.

Mrs Olivia was just as kind as her relative had been. And though Mrs Harriet might have moved away now, she came back every now and then to visit them.

Sal put away the underwear and tried on the clothes one after the other, twisting from side to side in front of the mirror. As she took off a lovely blue dress that she liked best of all, she decided she'd definitely have that one. She'd keep it for Sundays and going to church. And wouldn't she look fine then?

While she was going through the clothes, her little daughter played on the floor with her rag dolls. Sal looked down at her fondly. Children grew quickly when they were well fed and Barbara would also need some new clothes soon as well. Sal had decided recently not to let anyone shorten the child's name to a mere Babs because it sounded too common. She wanted her daughter to grow up to have a better life than herself, and that meant having a better name to match it.

Perhaps the present matron of Honeyfield House would let her cut up some of the more worn clothes and the smocks covered in paint stains that had also come from Miss Thorburn's house. There was enough good material in them to make dresses for her daughter. Not that she was very good at sewing, but Miss Pendleby had promised to help and even to teach Sal how to make up or alter simple clothes herself. They had a sewing machine here at Honeyfield House, but Sal was afraid of using it because that needle ran so fast when your foot slipped on the treadle that it could make a mess of things. But she was determined to practise till she could do it slowly and steadily.

She looked down at her big red hands and smiled ruefully. It'd be easier if she had smaller, softer hands, but no matter how much goose grease she rubbed into hers they always showed the effects of scrubbing floors. Well, scrubbing was a good, honest task and Miss

Pendleby complimented her regularly on her work.

'Come here and give me a kiss, my little lovey,' she said fondly and scooped up her daughter for a cuddle.

'I'm playing with my dolls!' Barbara protested and wriggled out of her hands. She made up all sorts of games with those little rag dolls, wonderful it was, to hear her. You'd think they were real people.

There was a knock on the door and Miss Pendleby peeped in. 'How are you going, Sal? Can I help?'

'The clothes fit perfectly. I don't know which to choose.'

'Let me help you.'

By teatime a bemused Sal had a wardrobe near as fine as a lady's, finer than *she* had ever owned before, that was sure. And there were other garments set aside to be cut up for Barbara, ready for the child starting at the village school in September.

And that still left clothes for the women who sought refuge here, if they needed them. Some weren't able to bring anything with them when they ran away.

As she cleared up the tea things, Sal spared a quick thought for the lady who'd inherited Miss Thorburn's house, some sort of distant cousin, Mr Perry had said. She hoped Mrs Tesworth and her husband would settle in quickly.

He'd been wounded in the war, poor chap, and lost two fingers, Mr Perry said. But at least he was still alive. A lot of them hadn't survived. Two lads that she knew by sight from church had been killed even from this small village.

Miss Pendleby was going to call on Mrs Tesworth to

welcome her, but Sal wouldn't presume to do that. She was looking forward to seeing her in church, though. She liked to know everyone who lived in her village.

As she'd told her friend, the Tesworths sounded to be a lovely couple.

Chapter Eight

In the morning after breakfast, Bella gathered her courage together and said, 'There's something else you need to know about the . . . the situation, Tez. Before you commit yourself finally to regular visits.'

He looked at her, waiting. He seemed more cheerful this morning and said he'd slept better here in the peace of the country.

There was no easy way to tell him so she blurted out, 'I need to tell you – I'm expecting Philip's baby.'

For a moment or two he froze, mouth half-open in shock, then slowly his face came to life again and he smiled at her. 'That's wonderful, absolutely wonderful. It means Philip will live on.'

She couldn't stop the tears of relief at how well he'd accepted the news. 'I wish he could have known.'

'Perhaps he does. He'd have been very happy about it, I'm sure.'

She sobbed even harder at that.

When Tez put an arm round her shoulders, she gave in to temptation and leant against him for a few moments, because she'd been feeling so alone with her secret and because he hadn't turned away from her.

He smoothed back her hair, then fished a handkerchief out of his pocket. It was still neatly folded, while hers were always crumpled before she'd had them in her pocket for an hour. 'Here. Use this. I'll squeeze another cup of tea out of the pot.'

As they sat opposite one another, holding cups half-full of tepid tea, he said, 'Philip and I were such good friends, I'm going to insist on being a godfather to the child.'

'Yes, please.' She mopped her eyes again. 'I was afraid of what you'd say, with me and Philip not being married.'

'Some people would condemn you for that, but I wouldn't. It obviously gave him great joy to have found you in such dark times. I'd not seen him that happy for ages.'

For a moment, painful memories of his friend made his heart twist with sadness, then he took her hand across the table. 'I'm very glad I've agreed to play the part of your husband, Bella. There won't be any nasty gossip about you or the child if I do that.'

'But what if you meet someone, a woman you can love? I know: if you do, I'll tell my neighbours here that you've been killed and call myself a widow. You must never feel you can't have a life of your own.'

'That's very generous. But I doubt I shall do that.'

His eyes flickered down to the injured hand and she said impulsively, 'Any woman who would mind about that small injury wouldn't be worth having.'

'It doesn't worry you, though, does it?'

'No. Not at all. I learnt first aid for my ambulance driving and I had to help people who were much more badly injured. One of them died in my arms. You may not think so now, but you've got off very lightly, Tez.'

'I realise that with my head but my heart is still upset about it.'

'Time will cure that.' And her own grief, she hoped. She didn't want to feel this raw and unhappy for the rest of her life, especially not with a child to raise.

They sat quietly for a few minutes and he didn't seem to realise that he was still holding her hand. She found his touch comforting and didn't pull hers away.

When he broke their clasp he stood up, looking restless again. 'What do you intend to do this morning?'

'I thought I'd go and introduce myself at the village shops.'

'Good idea. I'll come with you, if I may. It'll look better if we're together and I don't like to be penned indoors on fine days. I nearly went mad stuck in a bed in the hospital.'

'It'll be nice to have you with me.'

They walked down to the green and went into the nearest shop, which was the baker's. There was a wonderful smell of freshly baked bread. Bella introduced herself and Tez to the proprietor, explaining that her husband would be coming and going from his new job in London, so she couldn't place a regular order for bread.

'That's all right,' the woman behind the counter said cheerfully. 'We always have a spare loaf or two, especially for someone whose husband is engaged in war work.' She bobbed her head cheerfully to Tez. 'I'm Mrs Saunders. It's my husband who does the baking.'

'What other shops are there?' Bella asked after she'd paid for two fresh, crusty loaves. 'I saw the grocer's and we're going there next. Are there any other shops?'

'Farmer Corsley kills a beast on Fridays and his son sells the meat in the butcher's shop just round the corner from the grocer's. Mrs Corsley supplies eggs and table chickens if you put in an order. You can go up to the farm for them or pick them up at the butcher's shop.'

She ticked them off on her fingers. 'Malcolm Leatherby down at the far end of the green repairs cars and tractors and such, and sells petrol too. He's getting on a bit, says he'll sell his business to some chap back from the war once we've trounced them Huns. He has a smallholding as well and grows vegetables. His son was killed at Ypres, poor soul. Left two children, the son did, but they're girls and their mother took them to live in Birmingham with her family, so poor old Malcolm is on his own now.'

'Is there a dressmaker?' Bella was going to need some new clothes soon. Already her skirts were a bit tight and so were her blouses.

'Dear me, yes. Mavis Calwell and her daughter do that. They're so good at it, ladies come to them from all over the district. Get a lovely fit, they do, and a neat finish. But both of them are married to good wage earners, so they can pick and choose what they take on. They won't make anything they think will be unflattering. They're lucky to be able to do that, aren't they?'

'Good. And what about a haberdasher? I need some more sewing things.'

'You'll have to go into the next village for that, though they've got a few bits and pieces at the grocer's, thread and needles and the like. Or you could go into Malmesbury, if you need something fancy, or else Stroud, which has more shops. Not much to choose between them in distance from here, either. Pity your husband won't be here with the car.'

'I'll be leaving the car for my wife till this hand is better,' Tez said.

'Oh. Do you drive, then, Mrs Tesworth?'

'Um, yes. I'm a bit rusty, but I'll soon get back in practice.'

'I leave that sort of thing to the men,' the shopkeeper said.

She sounded disapproving, Bella thought. Well, she could disapprove to her heart's content. That car was going to be a godsend.

'I'm relieved my wife's able to drive,' Tez said. 'She's been able to take me around because I'm not allowed to drive yet with this hand.'

'There is that,' Mrs Saunders said, but she didn't sound convinced.

An older woman came into the shop just then and was immediately introduced to the newcomers, but Bella could see the shopkeeper was dying to have a gossip with her, probably about them. So she said goodbye and headed for the grocer's. She had a long list for them and was hoping they'd be able to deliver it quickly.

After she'd placed the order, she was told to bring her jug next time if she wanted some milk, but Mrs Foster volunteered to put some milk in a jar for her if she'd bring the jar back the next day.

'My husband will deliver your groceries within the hour,' the shopkeeper said. 'I hope you'll be happy here in Honeyfield, Mr and Mrs Tesworth.'

By the time they went outside again the day had clouded over.

'Good thing I was here, eh? Word about us will spread quickly, I should think,' Tez said as they strolled back. He looked up at the sky. 'We'd better hurry. It's getting darker by the minute, looks as if it's going to rain quite heavily. That'll give us a chance to check the cottage for leaks. That roof doesn't look as if it's been well maintained the last year or two. And the cottage next door is a disgrace. I wonder who that belongs to and why they've let it go to rack and ruin.'

It felt almost as if they really were married, Bella thought wistfully as big drops started to fall and they ran the last few yards, laughing.

All in all, it was a lovely, peaceful start to her stay here and it was a pity Tez had to return to London tomorrow. She'd miss his company.

Well, she'd find things to fill her time. She could start making baby clothes, for one thing, and hemming a set of nappies. She might have to go into the next village to buy the material but she wasn't going anywhere near Malmesbury in case she bumped into the Cotterells. The thought of doing that made her shiver.

It was silly to feel like that, really. Why would they pursue her now she was offering to sell them the house in Malmesbury?

In Penny's cottage Georgie had a bad night, tossing and turning, sleeping only in fits and starts. As the sun was starting to rise she fell asleep and didn't wake till mid morning. She went down feeling guilty and found her hostess frowning over a letter. Another letter had been slit open and lay to one side.

'Is everything all right, Penny?'

'Yes. Well, there isn't a problem exactly, Georgie, not yet, but—' She broke off as if not sure how to say something.

Georgie caught sight of the handwriting on the envelope and her heart began to thud nervously. Why had her mother written to Penny? Spencer must have told her where his sister was, she supposed.

They'd been living very quietly here because there wasn't much to do and they didn't have a car. Even so, she had found it wonderful not to live with scolding and peremptory demands to do this and fetch that. She felt almost as if she was recovering from a period of illness.

'I can see it's my mother's handwriting, Penny, so it won't be good news. What does she want?'

'It's rather a strange letter. She's warning me that I should be careful what I believe because you're rather unstable and don't always tell the truth. She says you need help and I should encourage you to go home where you can be cared for properly.'

Penny tapped the paper but made no attempt to show the actual letter to Georgie, which probably meant her mother was writing much more nastily than that. Her hostess's next words confirmed that.

'It's a strange sort of letter for a mother to write, very melodramatic. She actually suggested I throw you out.'

'She's been waiting for me to go running home and beg her forgiveness, and is beginning to realise that I won't do that. She'll send Spencer after me, eventually, I know she will. After he saw me, he'll have found where I'm living and told her. He might even drag me back home forcibly.'

'He can't kidnap you off the street or even drag you out of my house, because I won't let him in.'

'Can't he? I wouldn't put anything past Spencer. *He* is the unstable one, but my mother thinks he's perfect. And if he did come after me and force his way in, who would hear? This cottage is very isolated.'

'Oh, dear. And Edward has just written to say he's being transferred to Portsmouth, where there are married quarters available, so he wants me to move there as soon as I can.' She blushed. 'We haven't had much time together, so that'll be wonderful, but I'm not going to move until I've made sure you're all right. Only where are you going to go?'

'I don't know. I think I'd better find somewhere else to live quite quickly and move there secretly.' Georgie forced a smile but couldn't make it last long. 'Now I'm the one sounding melodramatic. I don't think I'm unstable, but my family, especially Spencer, can be downright nasty sometimes. I don't want you caught up in their machinations after you've been so kind to me.'

'Well, grab something to eat and sit down. We have to decide what to do.'

When Georgie was facing her, Penny said, 'I think the best thing to do is for me to phone my brother. Harry will know what to do, I'm sure.'

'I don't want to trouble him. And he might be back in France, probably is by now because he hasn't written for several days.'

Penny laughed. 'He likes being troubled by you.'

'Oh. Well. He's been very kind.'

'Why do you think that is?'

Georgie felt embarrassed and didn't know how to tell Penny that Harry didn't attract her in that way.

But when Penny phoned the regimental office the clerk said Harry was away and wouldn't be back for a day or two.

Did she have time to wait for him? Georgie wondered. Or should she leave here this very afternoon?

But when she suggested it, Penny insisted on waiting for Harry and in the end Georgie gave in because she hadn't a clue where to go and was still nervous about managing on her own in a strange town.

In the middle of the night, Georgie was woken by something. She lay still, wondering what she'd heard. The sound came again, very faint. It sounded as if someone was creeping round the garden.

She slipped out of bed and went to peer out of the

window, gasping when she saw two men dressed in dark clothing moving towards the house.

Dear heaven, it must be Spencer. Who else would come after her?

Who was the other man? She peered out again as she threw on her clothes. The second man moved out of the shadows into the moonlight. Francis! She'd recognise that cruel, hawk-like profile anywhere.

She made sure the bedroom window was locked and went to wake Penny.

'I can't believe this,' her friend whispered. 'Well, they're not taking you away by force. I'm going to phone Farmer Grey. He's the nearest and I know he'll come to help us.'

'He may not be able to reach us in time.'

'Then they'll get more than they bargained for. Edward gave me a gun to protect myself with and showed me how to use it, too. I thought he was being foolish and only learnt to humour him. He insisted you never can tell when you might need to protect yourself, especially these days because some people are taking advantage of the war to burgle houses or worse. Don't tell anyone else I've got the gun, though. I haven't got a licence for it or anything.'

She got out of bed and opened a drawer in her dressing table, taking out a small handgun. 'Come on. The phone's downstairs and we need to make that call in case they try to break in.'

She got through to the farm but it seemed ages before anyone picked up the phone, by which time they'd heard the sound of breaking glass. 'It's Mrs Richards, at the cottage. We've got men trying to break in and they've just broken a window.'

'*What?* I'm on my way,' the gravelly voice replied. 'Five minutes at most.'

'He'll be here in five minutes,' she repeated for Georgie's benefit. 'Now let's lock ourselves in my bedroom and push that big chest of drawers against the door till Mr Grey gets here.'

When they'd done that, the two women could do nothing but wait. The kitchen windows were small and the outer doors were solid, but thumps from below told of force being used.

'If they get in and try to break my bedroom door down, I'm going to threaten them with the gun,' Penny said. 'It's already loaded. Edward said if there was an emergency I wouldn't have time to load it.'

'I don't even know how to fire a gun. I've always refused to hunt or shoot, though Spencer loves killing animals and birds of any sort. He used to dip his fingers in the blood and chase me.' She shuddered at the memory.

They fell silent as something else smashed at the back of the cottage, not glass this time, but wood.

'I think they're breaking down the door,' Penny whispered. 'Oh, no! Listen.'

They heard footsteps inside the house. Doors were flung open and banged back against walls, the intruders making no attempt to hide their presence, then the footsteps came up the stairs.

The knob of their bedroom door turned but the person

was unable to force it open. He shouted, 'They're here! Come and lend a hand.'

'That's Spencer,' Georgie said. 'I'd recognise the harshness of his voice anywhere.'

'You might as well give up, Georgina,' the other man shouted.

'That's Francis. He always calls me Georgina, says Georgie is undignified.' She shuddered and looked at the chest of drawers. They'd wedged the bed crosswise against the wall to hold the drawers in place. 'Will these keep them out for long enough, do you think?'

'I hope so. If not, I'm definitely going to shoot them.'

One of the two men threw himself against the door and it rattled. But it was made of solid oak, hardened with age, and the lock was the old-fashioned sort with a big key, so it held as the thumping continued.

Suddenly one panel of the door cracked with a splintering sound.

Georgie let out an involuntary squeak. 'They must have an axe.'

Penny raised the gun and tried to hold it steady.

After another two blows the panel burst open. They could see part of a man's face.

'I have a gun,' Penny called. 'And I'm prepared to use it.'

'So have I. You'll probably miss but I won't. I can hit you anywhere in the body that I choose. How about the right shoulder?'

She gasped in shock at this threat.

'Stop meddling, you silly bitch. It's not you we want

but Georgina and if you have any sense you'll get out of our way and allow us to take my sister to where she can be cared for properly.'

'If you take her, I'll report you for breaking in and kidnapping, and the police will come after you.'

He laughed. 'There are only old dodderers holding the forts of justice at the moment and people prepared to swear we were with them all night, plus Mother knows a doctor who'll certify Georgina as needing care. You'll get nowhere with a complaint, believe me.'

Before either of the women could reply there was the sound of a vehicle approaching the cottage.

'What the hell—' Spencer exclaimed and his face vanished from the gap in the door.

'Thank goodness.' Penny sagged against Georgie in relief.

'Damnation!' Spencer raised his voice. 'Georgina, this is only postponed. Wherever you go, we'll find you. And the longer you keep Mother waiting, the angrier she'll be when I do take you home. She's talking of having you locked away in a lunatic asylum.'

'I'm never coming back,' she shouted back. 'Never!'

'Oh, but you will.'

'And I've still got the ring and intend to use it as planned,' Francis called, his voice growing fainter as the men clattered down the stairs.

From below came the sound of people yelling and cursing and the two women went to the window again.

Spencer and Francis met the newcomers at the gate and attacked them without warning, causing more shouting.

A gun went off and Mr Grey called out, 'Stand back, Tam. Let them go. It's not worth dying for.'

The sound of the two men running faded and a car engine started down the hill.

As it drove away Mr Grey turned to yell, 'Are you ladies all right?'

'Thanks to you we are,' Penny shouted back. 'I'm not sure we can get the bedroom door open without some help, though. They've smashed the panels and it looks as if something in the lock has been twisted, because I can't turn the key.'

Mr Grey and his son came in and jemmied open the door, finishing the job of ruining it.

'I'll pay for it,' Georgie said.

'Who cares about an old door? It's those villains I'm worried about. What sort of people go around breaking into houses and shooting at people?'

'My brother.'

'Are you sure it was him?'

'Oh, yes.'

'Then he's a madman. You can't stay here any longer, though. It's too isolated. What if they come back?'

'I'm moving to Portsmouth to be with my husband,' Penny said. 'I'll leave first thing in the morning.'

'I think I'd better leave as soon as I can get a taxi to come for me,' Georgie told them. 'Is there someone nearby who runs a taxi service?'

'You've got somewhere safe to go?'

She hesitated. 'No. But I have some money so if I can get to a railway station, I can go to some town far away from here and rent a room. If I live quietly I doubt they'll find me.'

'You can't be sure of that. Word leaks out. I think you'd be better staying with some people my wife knows. They'll look after you, Miss Cotterell. People don't always help a complete stranger, and they won't know who to believe if he's your brother. He's got an educated voice and that always impresses people. No, we have to find somewhere really safe for you.'

He stood frowning for a while, then turned to Tam. 'Can you stay here with Mrs Richards? I'll call in at Lionel's and send him to take you and her back to the farm. I'm going to act quickly and go straight from here to some people who help women in trouble. The young lady will be absolutely safe with them. How quickly can you pack, my dear?'

'Give me ten minutes.'

'Try not to be longer than that. For all we know those villains are keeping an eye on who comes and goes from the village. I want to get you away before dawn and we'll go by farm tracks they won't know about.'

Georgie flung the last few things into her suitcase, the two women hugged and then Mr Grey drove off with Georgie hidden under some sacks in the back of his truck. He used narrow lanes and stopped a couple of times to make sure they weren't being followed.

'Where are we going?' Georgie asked when he suggested it was safe for her to ride beside him.

He simply tapped the side of his nose and continued driving.

They saw no other cars, heard nothing whenever they stopped.

'We'll be there in another hour,' he said after a while.

But she still didn't know where he was taking her. 'How do you know I'll be safe?'

'My wife had a cousin whose husband was ill-treating her. These people helped her. They'll help you.'

Chapter Nine

Bella felt sad as she prepared their breakfasts of scrambled eggs while Tez hooked slices of bread on a long-handled wire fork and toasted them in front of the fire.

'I'm still good at doing this,' he commented as he put the last perfectly golden slice in the little silver toast rack she'd found in a cupboard that seemed to hold everything for serving one- or two-person meals. She couldn't help thinking that she would be living the same lonely life here most of the time.

'Lovely.' She couldn't help thinking how good it was to have someone to talk to, especially someone as easy to get on with as Tez. He reminded her a bit of Philip, because he had the same acceptance of his fellow human beings, whatever their station in life, and showed the same kindness to everyone and their dog.

The prospect of spending most of the next few months on her own was upsetting her more than she'd expected. Tez would probably come here regularly at first, but she wasn't sure that would last. He had his own life to lead, after all. She had to keep reminding herself of that.

He laid his hand over hers on the table. 'What's the matter, Isabella?'

'I like you calling me Isabella. My father used to call me that, but you're the only person to have called me that since he died. He gave me the name, but my mother shortened it to "Bella". She said it was too much of a mouthful, and anyway, Bella was more suited to the likes of us. It was only one of the many things they quarrelled about.'

His voice softened. 'Tell me what's wrong. Maybe I can help you with something else before I leave.'

'You can't. But thanks for offering.'

'And?'

'I've been wondering how I'll occupy my time after you've left. Day after day. I've never actually lived alone before, you see. Never in my whole life.'

'I'll send you some books as soon as I get back.'

'Thank you. I enjoy reading.' But you couldn't read all day, could you?

'Do you draw? I could send you some sketching materials as well.'

That gave her genuine amusement. 'I can't draw anything recognisable. I was so bad the teachers used to hold up my drawings and make everyone laugh at me.'

He frowned. 'That was unkind. Everyone has different talents. I enjoy drawing and painting.' He looked down at his hand as he spoke.

'You'll still be able to do that once your hand has healed, surely?'

'I hope so but they can't tell me yet how well this injured hand will work. Anyway, we weren't talking about me. Look, why don't I come and visit you next weekend? I know that's less than a week, but I'd like to.'

She stared at him in surprise. 'You'd come back so soon? Don't you have things to do in London?'

He set his knife down and fiddled with the piece of toast he'd been buttering, picking it up as if to take a bite, then setting it down untasted. Avoiding her eyes, he said in a low voice, 'I don't know what I'm going to do with myself either, Isabella. So we're both in the same boat there.'

That hadn't occurred to her. 'But you'll still have your family.'

'They're always busy. Both my brothers are still fighting, and my mother is working hard for the war effort. My father is back at the farm growing food for the country.'

'Your father's a farmer?'

'Not exactly: a gentleman farmer would be more exact. His first love is horses. He lost most of his when the government requisitioned them for the army, but he was allowed to keep some to breed from.'

She felt comfortable enough with him to say, 'You're like Philip, you come from people with money.'

'I don't have much. It's my eldest brother who'll inherit the family fortune. All I've decided is that I'm not going back into banking. My father's cousin got me into that before the war and I hated it. Only, there are going to be a lot of other things I won't be able to do because of this.' He waggled the bandaged hand at her. 'Yet I'm the third son, so I need to earn a living.'

He chuckled suddenly. 'One of my aunts suggested I go into the church, but can you imagine me as a minister of religion? I can't. I'm not even sure what I believe in now, not after what I've seen.'

'You'll make new friends in London.'

'Perhaps. But I'll be missing one old friend very much indeed.'

Her voice was a thin scrape of sound. 'So shall I.'

They were silent. She was fighting tears as she still did when she thought about Philip. She glanced across the table and saw Tez staring bleakly into space, looking as sad as she felt.

'If you do want to come here, Tez, I'll be happy to see you any time, not just weekends. If you send me a postcard, I'll come and collect you at the station in Malmesbury.'

'Letter.'

'What?'

'I can't send postcards because the people delivering them will be able to read them. And we all know they do that, so we have to be very careful with our secret. Your life may depend on such details.'

'Oh yes. Of course.' It was like a story from *Home Chat*, and she still found it hard to believe anyone could want her dead, just as she'd found some of the stories in the women's magazine hard to relate to, full of handsome princes who fell in love with kitchen maids. As if a kitchen maid would even meet a prince in real life!

A few minutes later Tez pushed his chair back. 'I'll bring my suitcase down and we can set off now, if you like.'

She dropped Tez at the station and drove away at once, as he'd advised.

She wasn't looking forward to returning to an empty house.

* * *

At the sight of the car and its number plate, a man stopped dead in the middle of crossing the street, nearly causing a delivery van to run into him. As the driver sounded his horn, the man rushed across to the pavement, bumping into an elderly gentleman.

'Watch where you're going, sir.'

'Sorry.' He ran in the direction the car had taken, but it was just turning the corner. He was quite sure it had been Philip's car. He knew that number plate.

Even though he ran along the edge of the pavement, the car was out of sight by the time he got to the corner. He stopped, cursing under his breath.

After a moment or two he turned and went on his way. It had been a woman driving Philip Cotterell's car, he was sure, though he hadn't been able to see her face.

That meant the bitch was still in the area. Where was she living? Why had she risked coming into Malmesbury?

He'd have to keep his eyes open from now on.

He told Spencer what he'd seen and his friend grew angry. 'One day she'll not be able to get away from us.'

'If she's living nearby we'll find her, whatever it takes.'

Bella drove back slowly. What had she to hurry for? She stopped at the baker's because she had a sudden yearning for the simple comfort of crumpets with butter and honey for tea.

'Husband gone back to London?' Mrs Saunders enquired.

'For the time being.'

'Will he be coming home at the weekend?'

'He's planning to, if his duties permit. It's, um, a new posting because of his injury and he isn't sure yet what he'll be doing or how often he'll manage to get away.'

'You'll be able to get to know your neighbours while he's away. Nice folk they are in Pear Tree Lane. And they'll love to have a new baby to coo over.'

Bella gaped at her. 'How did you know? I didn't think I was showing yet.'

'Bless you, dearie, I had eight of my own and I've got nieces falling for babies every time I turn round. Women in your condition get a look to them.'

'That's what M—a friend told me.'

'Well, she was right, wasn't she? Here you are.' She wrapped up two crumpets. 'And you should keep an eye on the garden of the old Hanson house next door. There are fruit bushes and trees there. Why let the fruit fall off and go rotten?'

'Won't the owner mind me taking them?'

'It's just a lawyer chappie as keeps an eye on the place and *he* leaves them rotting on the ground. Your neighbours share out the fruit. The new owner isn't interested in the cottage at all. He tried to sell it but no one offered, because it needs a lot doing to it and materials aren't as easy to come by in wartime. Even the lawyer hasn't been around since that dratted war started.'

'Oh. Well. Thanks for telling me.'

'We all look after one another in Honeyfield.'

When Bella came out of the shop, a man hurried across the street towards her, clearly intent on speaking to her so she stopped to wait.

He tipped his cap and introduced himself. 'I'm Ellis Larner. My orchard is the one behind your wall.'

'Nice to meet you. I'm Mrs Tesworth.'

'Bless you, we all know your name by now. Mrs Saunders made sure of that after she met you and your husband.' He chuckled. 'Can't keep anything private in this village.'

'Oh. Right.' She hoped he was wrong about that.

'I locked that gate in your back wall when Miss Thorburn died and took away the key. Can't be too careful these days, can you? My wife's been wondering if you'd like the key back or whether you'd rather leave the gate locked.'

'I can't work out what the gate was used for, because it only seems to lead into your orchard, but I'd better have the key, I suppose, just in case I need it.'

'The gate's been there as long as anyone can remember because that whole piece of land used to be part of Honeyfield House's grounds till they sold it and built Pear Tree Lane. In my great-grandfather's time, that was. Miss Thorburn used the gate quite often because she got on well with the old matron at Honeyfield House and they used to take tea together. Going through the gate is a shortcut from Pear Tree Cottage to there, you see.'

'I gather Honeyfield House is a convalescent home.'

He chuckled again. 'That's what they say it is but we all know it's more than that, though we don't tell outsiders about it. They take women and children there who're needing somewhere to hide, you see. Some have run away from violent husbands and good luck to those who help them, I say. I can't abide men who ill-treat women and little 'uns. And some of the women have been got into trouble by men who forced them, and I don't hold with that, neither. So I give the folk there some of my apples and pears every autumn to help them along a bit.'

His words were like a gently flowing stream, so she let him talk on at his own speed. After all, she had nothing to rush home for.

'Anyway, Mrs Tesworth, I can bring the key round, if you like. I'll come in the back way, if you don't mind. Much quicker.'

'Yes, fine. Thank you.'

He turned to walk away, then swung back. 'Nearly forgot. My wife wants me to tell you she'll call on you when she has a minute, but we're looking after four grandchildren at the moment while my daughter gets over having a new baby. My Nell's run off her feet but she's loving it, misses having little 'uns around.'

'Thank you for thinking about me and for helping keep the house safe while it was empty.'

'It's a poor lookout if one neighbour can't help another. They say your husband was injured in the war and is now working in London. We're all grateful to them doing the fighting, poor chaps. If you need anything doing while he's away, just nip through the orchard and knock on our door. My son Joss is very handy too, if I'm not around. He and his wife live in the old farmhouse next to ours. He failed his medical because he has a gammy foot and I can't help being glad of that, because he's safe. And the foot don't stop him doing farm work, don't hurt him, neither.'

'Right. Thank you.'

'Eh, look at me, talking your head off like this when you must have a lot to do settling in. I'll let you get on with it all and bring the key round at teatime.'

He tipped his hat again and strolled off down the street. He looked so at home as he stopped to talk to someone else that she envied him.

Then she thought no more about the key as she went back inside and wandered round, because the empty house made her feel sad again.

Oh, don't be so silly! she thought, cross at herself for moping. *Get on with your life, you fool!*

Tomorrow she would go and buy some material for baby clothes and perhaps start an embroidery, too, because she did enjoy embroidering. Pillow cases, maybe. She could buy a set of embroidery transfers to iron on and give her the pattern.

She'd spend the rest of today starting to go through the house one room at a time and making plans for clearing out some of the furniture and ornaments. She'd make lists, do the job properly, because she didn't want to live amid such clutter. You could hardly walk around at the moment without bumping into little tables with ornaments on them or seeing reflections in the doors of glass-fronted display cabinets containing yet more ornaments.

But even though she kept determinedly busy for the rest of the day, when she went to bed, it all overwhelmed her and once again she wept for Philip. Her heart felt raw with loss still.

* * *

Georgie woke with a start as the farmer's truck stopped moving and he switched off the motor. 'Are we there?'

'Yes, Miss Cotterell. This is Greyladies.'

She stared in astonishment at the beautiful old house, with its steep gables and roof tiled with long grey slabs of thin stone. 'Where are we exactly?'

'At the edge of a village called Challerton. The lady who lives here helps women who're in trouble, with nowhere to go. I'll just go and tell her I've brought you.'

While he was knocking on the front door, Georgie got out and stretched in the early morning sunlight. She seemed to be doing nothing but run away lately, first from her mother, now from Penny's little cottage. She shivered as she remembered her brother breaking in and trying to smash the bedroom door down.

Hearing footsteps she turned to see a lady coming down the shallow steps at the front of the house. She was tall, must have been about forty, and had red hair only lightly frosted with grey. Altogether she was a striking-looking woman; the thing Georgie noticed most was the kindness in her face.

'Welcome to Greyladies, Miss Cotterell. Mr Grey has been telling me a little about your disturbed night.'

'Yes. It was . . . frightening.' She shivered at the memory of how terrified she and Penny had been. It'd take her a long time to forget that, she was sure.

'Why don't you come in and we'll let Mr Grey get back to his farm? You can stay here for a while. Alex and I are living in the old part of the house at the rear, because the War Office requisitioned the rest. There are some friendly internees now occupying the front part, but we can still go through this way. No one minds.'

'*Germans?*' Georgie's mother said there was no such thing as a good German and had railed about keeping those living in Britain interned in comfort.

'Not exactly. They may have been born in Germany or Austria but they fled the country to escape the warmongers and most like to consider themselves British now. They're helping our government in certain ventures, because between them they have a lot of information about their former countries.'

As they went through the house, Olivia said, 'I did invite Mr Grey in for a cup of tea but he's anxious to get back home and make sure your friend is safe. Do you mind if I call you Georgie? I'm Olivia Latimer, but call me Olivia.'

'And you help women in trouble, Mr Grey said.'

'When we can. I gather you're in trouble at the moment. You're very welcome here and we'll do our best to help. I'll tell you a little about the house once you've settled in. The old part was built in the sixteenth century by one of my ancestors. But Mr Grey said you hadn't had breakfast, so let's feed you first.' She opened a heavy door and led the way into the rear of the house.

'Oh, what a lovely place!' Georgie exclaimed. 'It feels as if it welcomes you.'

'Does it? I always think so, but not all my visitors sense that.'

Georgie turned to and fro on the spot just inside the doorway, admiring the hall and its huge oak beams. 'What a lovely staircase! Do you always leave a light burning at the top.'

Olivia didn't attempt to hide her surprise. 'You can see that?'

'Yes.'

'I'll take you up there tomorrow and tell you about the light. You look too tired to explore now. Come this way.'

They went through into the kitchen area and she was surprised to see a long refectory table with both maids and ladies sitting chatting at one end. A man with a charming smile stood up and came towards them.

Olivia linked her arm in his for a moment, love shining on both of their faces. Georgie envied them that closeness, but it showed she'd been right to give Francis his ring back. She wanted love like this or nothing.

'This is my husband Alex. We all eat in the kitchen when we don't have visitors. It's so much easier for our maids, who've been here so long they're more like friends anyway.'

One of the maids got up. 'Not too much of a friend to prevent me getting you some breakfast, Mrs Latimer.'

She brought them food and everyone chatted about the previous evening, when there had been a concert in the village hall by the children of the local school. No one tried to get Georgie talking, though they did address stray comments to her or offer her more food. They seemed to sense how weary she was and left her mainly in peace.

She'd thought she wasn't hungry, but once the food was in front of her, she found herself making a good breakfast and feeling better for it.

When the meal was over, everyone picked up their own dishes and took them into the scullery, so she did the same. Then Olivia suggested Georgie join her in the sitting room and tell her what had brought her here.

She'd thought it would be hard to talk to a complete stranger about her personal situation, but she was wrong about that too.

When she'd finished her tale, her hostess said quietly, 'Perhaps you'd like to stay here for a few days, then we'll find a place for you in one of our houses. You'll be safe there until your troubles with your brother are resolved.' She frowned and added, 'There's just one thing I don't quite understand . . . Isn't your father Gerald Cotterell?'

'Yes.'

'I've worked with him once or twice in London. He's a little stiff and formal in his manner, but he doesn't seem like the sort of man to bully his daughter into an unwelcome marriage, or let others do it, either. Does he know what's going on at your home? Can't he help you?'

'Mother told me he approved of my marrying Francis, though he hasn't talked to me about it because he lives in London. He's never shown any interest in me or my twin, and he and my mother have led separate lives for as long as I can remember. My brother was killed in France recently and my father didn't even come to Philip's memorial service.'

'Oh. I see.'

To Georgie's relief, Olivia didn't say anything else about her father, let alone suggest that Georgie should contact him for help, something she had no intention of doing.

She couldn't imagine him intervening in her troubles, not in her wildest dreams. Well, he never had before and she and Philip had written to him a few times when they were younger and their mother was being particularly unfair.

When he hadn't replied to their juvenile pleas, they'd stopped trying to ask for his help and kept out of their mother's sight as best they could. They'd not even eaten their meals with her and Spencer till they were nearly grown up and able – as she'd told them sharply – to hold their tongues unless they were spoken to.

How Philip could have grown up so cheerful and sunny-natured, Georgie had never understood. She had grown quite despondent at times about her life, which was one reason she'd considered marrying Francis. At least it would have got her away from her mother, because her life had been even more unhappy after Philip volunteered for the army.

Olivia showed her to a lovely bedroom and said, 'You look exhausted. Don't worry if you need a nap. We're very informal at Greyladies.'

Georgie was deep-down weary, but she didn't think she'd be able to sleep.

Somehow, however, the peaceful atmosphere of the old house soothed her jangled nerves and when she felt herself growing sleepy, she welcomed the peace she seemed to slide into.

After she'd left her guest, Olivia went for a walk round the gardens with her husband. He was going up to London the following day to visit his antique shop and she might have gone with him if she hadn't had a visitor who was obviously in great need of help.

Alex had a good manager in place at the London shop, but he liked to call in every week or two to see any new stock and check that all was well.

This time there was also a sale of paintings in London that he wanted to see, in aid of some wartime charity or other. There were so many groups, women mostly, trying to do their bit for their country by holding sales of donated items. He'd bought one or two good paintings from such events, things he'd be able to sell at a profit after the war, and in the meantime the money he paid for them would be put to good use.

'If you run into Gerald Cotterell anywhere, you might sound him out about his daughter's predicament.'

'I can call on him if you like.'

'He might not even be in London. Tread carefully if you do talk to him. We don't want him to think his daughter is here.'

As they strolled further, Olivia passed on another piece of information. 'Our guest could see a light at the top of the stairs.'

'She saw the lady? That's unusual.'

'I don't think she saw our family ghost clearly, but occasionally some people outside the family are aware of Anne Latimer's presence, as you were. They might not see a figure, but they see a light where there shouldn't be one and sense a presence.'

'Your new guest looks sad when she doesn't think anyone is watching her. I don't like to see young women that downhearted. She's exactly the sort of person Anne set up the family trust to help, isn't she?'

'Yes. And I'm determined to find a way to cheer her up, either here or somewhere peaceful in the country. We have plenty of room at Honeyfield House, for instance. That might be a good place for her.'

'You'll work out where to send her. She couldn't be in more capable hands, I'm sure. You work miracles with some of the women you rescue, my love.'

'And at the same time you're working miracles with our finances and helping run the Greyladies Trust. The money seems to go further since you took over.'

'Good. I think there will be a lot for the trust to do by the time this war ends, because so many women will have lost the happy married life they'd expected to lead, or they'll find their husbands return distressed by what they've had to see and do.'

'I agree, Alex. Life is going to change greatly and there are always people who have trouble coping with new ways, always people to help.'

Chapter Ten

Spencer Cotterell was tired of dancing attendance on his mother and his anger seemed to burn higher by the day. He had poor health compared to others of his age and no regular income of his own, as his brother and sister did. He had never understood why they had been left annuities and he'd been left nothing.

He'd hated the twins ever since his mother vanished for a few months when he was nine. He'd cried for her night after night, but she hadn't even sent him a message.

'I'll be bringing you back a brother or sister,' she'd said brightly as she left. 'Do as Miss Palmer tells you.'

He didn't want a brother or sister or his governess; he wanted his mother.

When she did return to Westcott from wherever she'd disappeared to, she'd brought back both a brother *and* a sister, together with a wet nurse, a starched and fiercely protective nanny and a nursery maid. One of these women always seemed to be keeping watch over the precious little brats.

He'd never forgotten his outrage at their invasion of his territory. The twins had taken over *his* nursery, *his* old toys and books from when he was small, everything, and he'd been told to keep out. They'd been fussed over and spoilt – and they'd always had each other. Nothing he'd ever tried had set them against one another.

He'd been glad to go away to boarding school, equally glad when *they* went away to another boarding school later on, soon after he finished school.

He pushed the memories aside. What on earth had made him think of those stupid childhood grievances? What did they matter now?

When he joined his mother at the breakfast table, he said casually, 'I think I'll go up to London and see if I can sniff out any sign of where Georgina might be.'

'She won't be stupid enough to go there or to appear in public.'

'No, of course not, but someone might have seen her. She went off with Harry Lewison the first time. I wonder if . . .'

'What do you wonder?' she prompted.

'I don't know. Just thinking aloud.' He refused to tell her that he kept wondering how Georgie had managed to disappear again the other night, when he and Francis had almost caught her. This time, he'd found, Harry had been overseas, so *he* couldn't have been involved.

Spencer paid someone to check on Penny, who had gone to Portsmouth to be with her husband, but there was no sign of Georgina there that his man could find.

Spencer hadn't told his mother that he and Francis had attempted to capture his sister. Pity they'd failed. Francis had been looking forward to getting his hands on her money and was now in a foul mood. As Spencer often spent a night or two with his friend, his mother hadn't seen anything unusual in him being away.

'I'll come with you to London, Spencer,' she said suddenly. 'I'm tired of Westcott and though your father doesn't want me living in London, he doesn't complain if I only spend a day or two there shopping. There's hardly any social life round here these days, anyway.'

That was because his mother had quarrelled with or alienated in some other way half the neighbours. She really was a spiteful old woman and was getting nastier as the years passed, but *he* still got on with her. He had always been her favourite and she showed him her best side.

It'd be good to have somewhere else where he could live independently. But for that you needed money and he'd never found a job that suited him. And his health wouldn't allow him to do anything too strenuous. He was supposed to be managing the Westcott estate at the moment, but it was his mother who did most of that and she was surprisingly good at the money side of things.

'I think you'd better stay here and finish negotiating the purchase of the house in Malmesbury, Mother. You said it was important to you.'

She heaved a loud sigh. 'I suppose so. It *is* important. But I don't want to pay the full price for it. It really is too bad of Mr Marley to take that whore's side in the sale.'

He didn't think Bella Jones's morals were as bad as his mother always claimed, but you had to admit that the woman had been clever enough to capture the affections of his soft-hearted younger brother and had even got him to propose marriage. Then, after Philip was killed, she'd inherited everything he owned: money and family property that ought to have gone back into the estate, or at least to Georgie.

'You'll have to pay her something like the real value of the house in the end, Mother, so why not give in now and stop wasting your time fiddling around with negotiations?'

She tossed back at him, 'Are *you* giving up on finding Philip's car?'

'It's not nearly as important as the house, so it can wait. Why did Father buy Philip the car, anyway? *You* had to buy mine for me.'

'How should I know why he does things? I've never understood your father. And your car is bigger, so I don't know why you even want his.'

Because it was his, because he was here and Philip wasn't, Spencer thought, but didn't say that.

He studied his mother. She had that shifty look on her face, so he knew there was more to this house thing than that and it was to do with his father. The one thing he couldn't get her to talk about was her relationship, or lack of it, with his father. And strangely, she didn't let anger take over when Spencer tried to find out about various puzzling aspects of his parents' arrangements; she simply said firmly that some things were never going to be discussed.

Last time he'd decided to find out, he'd pressed her hard and got a tiny bit more information out of her. For all the good that did! He was still puzzling over what she'd said.

'Do not ask about your father or try to interfere in his affairs if you want to live comfortably here, Spencer.

Believe me, he is not a man to trifle with. You get your determination from him, but you're not nearly as ruthless as he is, or as clever – few people are – and you'd come off worse if you butted heads with him, I can guarantee. Everyone does.'

She'd sounded so bitter it was clear she'd come off worse in her interactions with his father.

In the end she allowed her chauffeur to drive Spencer to the station and he set off for London, glad to be away from her and Westcott, surely the most gloomy house in the county.

Spencer was feeling more cheerful as he got out of the taxi and walked into his hotel. Then yet another woman stepped in front of him and handed him a white feather. It had happened a few times and this one was the final straw, for some reason. He erupted in fury, grabbing her and shaking her hard, yelling at her to mind her own damned business.

A couple of passing officers had the nerve to step in and hold him back so that she could get away. At least he had the satisfaction of seeing her run like a whipped dog.

From the strange looks he was getting, he judged it wisest to try to mend the situation. 'Thank you, gentlemen,' he said once she'd disappeared from sight. 'I shouldn't have got so angry, I admit. But these women don't stop to think that some of us didn't pass the medical and would have much preferred to serve our country in uniform.'

But the two officers were still looking at him askance and moved on with only the curtest of nods.

He really should have controlled his temper better, but that woman had not only confronted him after a highly frustrating few weeks but had handed him the white feather in front of a group of people he was acquainted with.

That evening Spencer went to a party at a distant relative's house. He found out about it from a chap he knew slightly whom he'd bumped into in the hotel bar, so he pretended he'd been invited and they shared a taxi there. He didn't usually attend the Gortons' bland functions and had never been invited, but he'd gatecrashed once before and they hadn't tossed him out.

Tonight he needed company, any company, and he would surely find people to chat to at the soirée. It was going to be a big party, by the sounds of it. The Gortons never seemed short of money to pay for their pleasures, the lucky sods, even in wartime.

When he went into the house, he could tell that his hostess was surprised to see him, but she quickly pasted a welcoming smile on her stupid fat face.

'We don't often see you in town, Cousin Spencer.' She glanced round at the guests in the main room. 'I think you know enough people to chat to.'

With a wave of her hand she sent him inside and turned to greet the next arrivals.

The chap he'd come with soon met a woman, turned out they'd arranged to meet here, and forgot everyone else. It was sickening the way some people displayed their feelings for the opposite sex. Spencer wasn't fond of women in that way. Or of men, either. In fact he had no sexual feelings at all, thank goodness. It must be very inconvenient, he always thought, to be driven by this strange need.

He accepted a glass of wine from a waiter and took a sip as he looked round. He didn't see anyone he knew and was wondering which group to approach when he saw Tesworth over in one corner chatting quietly to another chap. He had his arm in a sling still. Pity the Huns had only blown two fingers off him. They should have aimed higher and blown off his interfering head.

Still, Tesworth had driven that Jones bitch away from Westcott after the memorial service, so it might be worth chatting to him.

When he got near, Tesworth saw him coming and scowled at him. What had that Jones woman been saying?

'How do you do?' Spencer raised his glass. 'Jolly nice wine, eh? Wonder where they got it from.'

'Delightful wine. Excuse me, but I've just seen someone I need to speak to urgently.'

Left high and dry, Spencer stood and sipped his wine again, chagrined to see other people turning away from him. Damnation! Had those two officers been talking about his behaviour earlier today?

'What have you been doing to upset Tesworth?' a deep voice said.

He swung round. 'Father! How unusual to see you at a function like this. You don't usually have much to do with the Gorton branch of the family.'

'Unusual to see you here too. You don't often come up to town.'

'I come up more often than you visit your ancestral home.'

'I prefer to leave the place to your mother – by mutual consent. I believe I asked you a question. Kindly answer it. What have you been doing to upset Tesworth?'

Spencer shrugged. 'Who knows?'

'Well, let's try this for an explanation. From what I've heard, you and your mother behaved rather badly to Philip's fiancée at his memorial service and it was Tesworth who took her there and drove her home again. Could you not be civil about Philip, even after his death?'

'It was Georgina who caused the biggest upset. She gave Filmore his ring back rather publicly.'

'Yes. That surprised me. Your mother always told me she was in love with him.'

Spencer laughed and for once told the truth, instead of the careful lies his mother wanted him to spread about the ill-matched couple. 'No, never in love. What she wanted was to get away from Mother. Who doesn't?'

His father ignored that last remark and frowned. 'Well, she's made the break now. What did Filmore do to make her dislike him that much and do it so publicly?' He broke off as an older man came up to join them, greeting him with a smile, then saying to his son, 'I'll see you tomorrow, then, Spencer, at breakfast and we'll discuss this further. I'm at my club, not the town house. Eight o'clock sharp.'

He turned to the newcomer, not bothering to introduce his son. 'James, old chap. Just the man I was hoping to see here tonight.'

Now what the hell did his father want to talk to him

about? Spencer wondered. He wasn't often honoured with a breakfast invitation. The old man had seemed rather annoyed, unfortunately.

He knew better than to miss that appointment because when it came down to it, his father was the one who held the purse strings in the family. At least, the strings of the purse from which his mother siphoned money into Spencer's pocket.

He wandered round the elegant rooms, stopping now and then to chat, but grew bored and angry because people didn't spend long chatting to him and quickly found excuses to move on. He left early.

He didn't feel like going back to the hotel yet but he was finding it embarrassing here, so had no choice. His mother kept going on about him finding a wife and setting up home in one wing of Westcott, but he didn't want to encumber himself with a woman, let alone try to father children. He was looking forward to inheriting Westcott and living there alone in utter comfort.

His father had never urged him to marry. Why not? Oh, who cared? Not him. He didn't care about anything much these days except his own comfort.

Spencer made sure he was on time for the breakfast meeting and was shown into the dining room at his father's club by the same elderly steward.

His father looked up from some papers. 'Sit down and order whatever you fancy. I'll just finish reading this report.'

Spencer ordered a full cooked breakfast with all the trimmings, which would save him buying lunch. He hated to scrimp and save, but had to watch every penny carefully. That frugality had given him a reserve of more money than his mother realised. As the elder son, the heir to Westcott, he shouldn't have had to do that, though.

He realised his father was shuffling the papers together and putting them in his briefcase, so prepared to pay careful attention. You had to stay on your toes with such a clever man.

'I'm not pleased that you and your mother saw fit to treat Miss Jones so rudely. And to do it publicly was particularly stupid.'

'She's nothing but a gold-digger.'

His father looked down his nose. 'Kindly refrain from using the latest slang expressions when you're with me. You were educated to use the King's English.'

Spencer shut his mouth and waited.

'I wish to make one thing clear today: I shall be obliged if you'll refrain from blackening Miss Jones's reputation in future and tell your mother also to refrain.'

'All right. And I can tell Mother, but I doubt she'll stop at my say-so. You know what she's like when she takes against someone.'

'Only too well.'

Their food arrived just then and both men consumed a few mouthfuls before continuing their conversation.

'Do you know where Georgie is now, Spencer? I intend to make sure she's all right. Your mother can be . . . spiteful.'

'Georgina went off with Harry Lewison, so I assume he's found her somewhere to stay. I believe he's back in France now, though.'

'Hmm. I'd better ask around. If you see her, tell her she can come to me for help. If you see Harry when he comes on leave, ask him to pass that message on. And do not do anything else to upset her.'

Spencer couldn't hide his surprise. 'You don't usually get involved.' But he didn't say anything about Georgie being with Harry's sister.

'I didn't realise until last night that she'd been pushed into getting engaged to Filmore. I don't like the fellow, but I thought if they cared for one another, she'd be looked after all right. I shall make my feelings about that plain to your mother. I don't feel that man is a suitable friend for you, either. He's not a nice person.'

Spencer shrugged. 'Most of the *nice men* are in the forces. I have to make do with the company of those who aren't.'

'Pity you couldn't go into the army. It'd have been the making of you. Who'd have thought that a Cotterell would have a heart weakness? That comes from your mother's side. How are you feeling these days? Do you need to see a doctor regularly for check-ups? If so, I'll pay.'

Spencer was surprised at that. 'They said I should see someone if it got worse, and it hasn't. Doesn't affect me much at all, actually. What they mainly advised was that I shouldn't exert myself too much physically.'

His father studied him. 'You don't look any different from last time I saw you.' He paused to eat another couple of mouthfuls, then said, 'The main reason I wanted to see you today was to tell you that I'm going to pay your allowance directly into your bank account from now on instead of sending it via your mother. I shall double it and pay quarterly in advance, starting this month.'

Spencer hoped he hadn't let his shock show. 'Thank you. I'd appreciate that.'

'I'm satisfied that you manage your money carefully these days or I'd not do it. You were stupidly spendthrift when you were first let loose on the world, but I'm pleased that you've grown out of that.'

He'd had to without money or credit, Spencer thought.

A few mouthfuls later, his father added, 'If you go after Miss Jones or upset her in any way, Spencer, the allowance will stop completely and permanently.'

Was that the purpose of all this? Spencer wondered. Why was he so concerned about the Jones woman?

But his father changed the subject, and for the rest of the meal they discussed the progress of the current war. What else did anyone ever talk about but the damned war? At least his father seemed to think Britain was making progress.

Spencer paid close attention. If the old man wanted to talk about the war he could do so all day, as long as he kept paying the money straight into Spencer's bank account. And actually, his father knew his stuff and turned out to be quite interesting, which surprised Spencer.

As he walked out of the club, he smiled. He was over thirty. It was more than time he had his own income.

He had to stay away from Miss Jones or the money would be stopped. He didn't like to think of her with all Philip's money *and* the car, but was she worth losing his allowance for? Probably not. Pity.

* * *

Tez attended the hospital for his check-up, arriving on time, annoyed when they kept him waiting for ages without an explanation. He couldn't help thinking about the previous evening as he sat there on a hard wooden bench. You didn't often see Spencer Cotterell at society functions, even those of his relatives.

Well, people didn't often invite him. Tez had heard a whisper that his hostess had looked surprised when Spencer turned up. He could well believe that the fellow wouldn't hesitate to gatecrash a relative's party.

Gerald Cotterell, on the other hand, was a welcome guest everywhere. He was interesting to chat to when he made the effort to appear socially, which he didn't often do, and courteous even to the most boring people. He was well respected even though no one was quite sure what he did at the War Office, only that it was to do with information gathering. Sometimes he wasn't seen for a week or two but that happened to quite a few fellows at the War Office, so it wasn't remarkable.

Philip's brother wasn't looking at all well, but then Spencer never did.

'Captain Tesworth?'

He turned round to see a smiling nurse. He didn't correct the title, though he was Mr Tesworth now. Which felt strange.

'Doctor is ready to see you. This way, please.'

The doctor unwrapped Tez's hand and studied it carefully, asking him to do a series of small movements.

He did as he was told, forcing himself to look at the damaged hand as he moved it around. Now that the worst of the swelling had gone down and the line of stitches had neatened the outer edge of his hand, he found it – well, not as repulsive as he'd expected. Or maybe he was just getting used to the sight of it.

'First indications are that you've been lucky, Captain Tesworth.'

'Oh?' It didn't feel lucky to lose two fingers. The lucky part was in not being killed or losing a whole limb.

'Yes. The associated damage to nerves and the various small bones in the hand and fingers could have been far worse. It's my guess that you'll recover a fair amount of use if you're careful not to push the hand too hard. My advice is to give it time to heal before you try to do much with it. If doing something is painful, stop doing it at once.'

Tez couldn't speak because if he had tried to say anything he might have shamed himself by getting over-emotional. They'd warned him of the possible *bad* results of the injury but no one had said anything about the possibility of it becoming a usable hand again. He nodded and swallowed hard.

'Hard to take good news after so much bad, isn't it?' the doctor asked, grasping his shoulder gently. 'It cheers *me* up to give chaps good news for a change, I can tell you, and Nurse here feels the same as well.'

The middle-aged woman nodded vigorously.

'Now, we'll wrap up the wound again and Nurse will give you a list of gentle exercises. I repeat: go *gently*. I can't stress that enough. It could make all the difference to how much function the hand recovers.'

'Thank you. I will be careful.'

The doctor left the nurse to bandage his hand, this time with much less padding.

'There you are, Captain. Be careful not to stress it too much yet.'

'The doctor said that too. I have taken it on board, I promise you.'

She smiled. 'Yes, but I know how impatient you young fellows can get to recover once you see the first signs of real progress. You need to think long term for this first year.' She tied the sling round his neck again then patted his other arm. 'There. Keep the hand in a sling as you go out and about for a few days more, then gradually start doing things without the sling. And the watchword is?' she prompted as he stood up.

'Go gently.' He would definitely take that instruction to heart.

What would Isabella say if she saw his mangled hand? he wondered as he strolled away from the hospital. Would she find it repulsive? Would she not want him to touch her with it? He prayed not.

What would she say if he showed his feelings for her? He smiled at the thought. He wasn't stupid enough to say anything about his love while she was still grieving. He planned to wait until after the baby was born before he started courting her.

In the meantime he'd protect her in any way he could, most especially from Spencer Cotterell. And if that meant spending every weekend in Honeyfield and lying awake in the next bedroom knowing how close she was and aching with the desire to take her in his arms, so be it.

He didn't have much else to do and anyway, couldn't use the hand much yet. However, he had enough money saved not to have to worry about earning more for a year or two, so he was going to spend a lot of time at Honeyfield, if she'd have him.

He might even do what Isabella had suggested and see if he could paint again. It had once been his favourite pastime, after all.

Chapter Eleven

Georgie loved the old house where she was taking refuge. Her own home was about a hundred years old and considered a fine example of Regency architecture. Greyladies was late medieval and yet so warmly welcoming it felt more like a real home than hers had ever done.

On the day after her arrival Olivia offered to show her round the old part and she accepted with alacrity. Her hostess started by taking her up to the gallery to see the portrait of the founder of the house.

'This is Anne Latimer.' She gestured with one hand.

Georgie studied the portrait. 'It must be hundreds of years old but it looks as fresh as the day it was painted. You've found some excellent restorers.'

'No one has ever needed to restore it.'

'Really?' She studied the painting and the lovely grey gown and headdress the lady was wearing. 'She looks a bit like you.'

'Other way round. I look a bit like her.'

'I'd love to have met her. She has such a wise and loving expression.'

'She was wise. When Henry VIII shut down monasteries

and nunneries, she had to stop being an abbess, but she decided to get married and carry on with good works. She and her husband converted this house from the abbey's guest house, and continued to help people.'

'I hope they were happy together.'

'Latimer women are usually happy in their marriages. They seem to have the knack of *knowing* when they've met the right man. I was extremely happy with my first husband, who was killed early in the war and his loss was hard to bear. But I'm also happy with Alex, though in a different way of course, so I consider myself a very fortunate woman.'

'I like to hear such stories. It restores my faith in love. My mother and father aren't happy and don't even pretend to live together. But go on with your story, please.'

'By the time she died, Anne was wealthy enough to found a trust that would carry on helping women in trouble. She set stringent conditions to inheriting the house, as well. It could only be inherited by female Latimers – and if they married, their husbands had to take their surname.'

'Alex changed his name for you?'

'Yes.'

'Didn't he mind? What about his own family?'

'Like yours, it wasn't a happy one so he didn't mind at all. He finds it very satisfying to work for the trust and help people, though he still runs his antique shop in London – as well as one can do during a war.'

'What happens if there isn't a direct female heir?'

'The house doesn't go to the firstborn. The one inheriting it must be able to see Anne Latimer, and that must be witnessed beyond question. No faking is possible. Who knows how to fake a ghost anyway? And the heir can see Anne very clearly.' She laughed gently. 'Don't look so surprised. Yes, we have a resident ghost here – Anne Latimer, of course – and yes, I saw her when I first came here.'

'How fascinating!'

'You saw a light up here when you arrived, Georgie.'

'Yes, but not a ghost.'

'There was no light up there. What you were seeing was a . . . a sort of reflection of Anne Latimer. My husband saw it too when he first came here. She's touched your spirit and I'm sure she'll watch over you from now on.'

Georgie realised she was gaping like an idiot at a fair, as her mother would have said scornfully. What Olivia was saying ought to have sounded impossible, fanciful in the extreme, but somehow she believed it absolutely.

'I'd be grateful for any help I can get because I seem to have got myself into a real mess. I let my mother persuade me to marry the man she chose, and when I gave him back his ring I knew she'd try to force me so I ran away. She can be very cunning, she frightens me sometimes.'

'We won't let them hurt you again. Or rather, we'll help you to stop them yourself. I think you still have a lot to find out about your own strengths and there will be a few surprises to come. Life always brings surprises, whoever you are.'

She didn't wait for an answer but took her guest downstairs again for a walk round the gardens, introducing her to one or two of the internees they met. These seemed amiable gentlemen, mostly quite old.

After that Olivia took her to see the crypt, which was all that remained of the original abbey, then left her sitting in a sheltered spot with a book.

But Georgie couldn't concentrate on anything, let alone read coherently. All she wanted to do was relax and feel the sunshine on her face. She needed a break from being scolded and carped at, as well as from being afraid of Spencer and her mother.

Adeline Cotterell scowled at Mr Marley. 'I didn't think you'd let our family down like this. Your firm has been representing the Cotterells for years, and now you're insisting on me paying an unfair price for what is, after all, a piece of *our* family property.'

'Your husband sold it years ago. Anyway, I was your son's lawyer, Mrs Cotterell, not yours. I'm therefore doing as he wished, that is helping Miss Jones to deal with his legacy. You've, um, been so insistent that she's agreed to sell the house to you and the price I've helped her set for it is a fair one. I really couldn't advise my client to let you have it for any less.'

'You had no need to do that. What does a female like her know about such things? Or need that much money for? She's a cleaner in the VADs, for goodness' sake, scrubs floors for a living. A hundred pounds will seem like a fortune to her.'

'She's an ambulance driver, actually, but even if she were a cleaner, where is the shame in doing what's necessary to look after men injured in the service of our country?'

'No shame in itself, but not a suitable occupation for someone aspiring to marry a Cotterell.'

He was tired of her going over and over the same ground. 'If you cannot meet our price, just say so and I'll put the house into the hands of Mr Perry who will sell it to someone who can afford it. That, madam, is my final word.'

She looked at his calm face, seeing no sign of yielding. It was only her need to get her hands on that house and its secrets that made her give in and say sharply, 'Very well. I shall pay your price, but since your partner is going to retire from ill health, I shall find a new lawyer to represent me from now on. *He* will contact you about the sale.'

'Very well, Mrs Cotterell. That's your prerogative.'

She stood up and rang the bell, tapping her foot impatiently as she waited for the maid to answer it. 'Show Mr Marley out.'

He left, inclining his head slightly as he passed her but saying nothing else.

When he'd gone she vented her anger by throwing the nearest ornament into the fireplace, where it smashed to smithereens. After that she proceeded to find fault with anything and everything her servants did for the rest of the day.

The only person immune to these diatribes was her personal maid, because the last time she'd shouted at her, Gladys had shouted right back, threatening to leave if she was treated with anything but courtesy from then onwards.

Since Adeline's body was growing older and stiffer, so that she couldn't manage her clothes and personal needs without help, and Gladys knew just how to look after her and help her to get going on the bad days, she had managed not to shout at her maid after that. But that need for restraint didn't help her temper and the rest of the household, including her son, suffered.

This time the anger would not go away because it was tied to another deep-seated anger about the way her husband had treated her. One day she would get her revenge. One day soon, if things worked out.

Francis Filmore heard that Spencer had gone up to London and waited impatiently for his friend to come home again.

But even when Spencer did return, he didn't call on Francis or phone him. What was the matter? They hadn't quarrelled. They rarely even disagreed, since they shared a common cynicism about the world and the war.

He drove round to Westcott at a time he would normally catch his friend in, but was told by the maid that Mr Spencer was out shooting pigeons and wouldn't be back till much later.

So he asked for Mrs Cotterell and was shown in. She might know what was going on with her son.

'How are you today, my dear lady?'

She shrugged pettishly, knowing him too well to pretend. 'Angry.'

'Might one ask why?'

'I've had to pay full price for the house Philip left to that horrible woman, which means I'll have to economise for a while. He should never have been associating with a person like that in the first place, let alone leaving family property to her.'

'Couldn't you just have let her keep it?'

'No, I could not. There are things in it that I happen to care about. And anyway, I don't *want* her living in Malmesbury, right on our doorstep.' After a pause she added in a vicious tone, 'And there has been no sign of my stupid daughter, either. When I find Georgina, I will make her regret defying me, believe me. Do not give up hope of marrying her.'

'I'm sure you will deal with her appropriately. And I want to find her just as much as you do because I do still wish to marry her.' Or more accurately, get his hands on her money. He said nothing about his own and Spencer's attempt to kidnap Georgina and force her to marry him. It didn't do to advertise failures. But he too would be watching out for any sign of her. People couldn't just vanish into thin air.

The doorbell sounded again and this time it was one of Mrs Cotterell's few remaining friends come for a gossiping session, so Francis took his leave.

But as he drove home, he couldn't help wondering why she was making such a fuss about the house – or was it the contents? Who could tell with a woman as cunning as her?

When Spencer got home from his day's shooting, his mother was still furiously angry, so he had to listen to her going on at length about the price she'd have to pay.

'You're the one who wants the house,' he pointed out, which started her off again, shouting and yelling at him even more loudly.

He poured her a glass of brandy and made soothing noises till she'd calmed down a little. 'Why do you want the house so urgently anyway, Mother? I can't work that out. You've never lived there because it belonged to Father's side of the family, so it can't have any sentimental value.'

'Well, I happen to like it a great deal. It's so convenient, near the centre of town. And I've fond memories of the first cousin who lived there. We were great friends. Not so much the second cousin. I didn't realise she'd bought it off your father. He never tells me anything.'

Spencer listened to this in surprise. His father never told anyone more than he needed to.

'That woman favoured Philip unduly. Fancy leaving him everything! You're the elder son. It should have gone to you. Or to me. I've always thought I could go and live there when you bring home a wife and start a family. There are a lot of spare women around now, you know, with so many young men being killed. You could have your pick, find yourself a rich wife.'

'I don't want to marry . . . yet. I'm happy living with you.'

As usual that appeased her slightly, because she couldn't bear to be alone for long. She sipped some more brandy and he frowned because something was nudging his memory and it was to do with that house. Yes, it was coming back to him now. There had been huge rows between his mother and father at one stage when the cousin living in the house had died and his father had allowed another relative to take over house and furnishings without consulting his wife.

That must have been a few years after the twins were born, when Spencer was in his late teens and, for once, his father had come down to Westcott to tell his wife about the new occupant and check that everything was in order there.

His mother had claimed she wanted to allow two elderly

cousins of her own to live in it. 'They'd be company for me,' she'd said several times.

His father had noticed him listening and shepherded his wife into another room and closed the door on their continuing quarrel.

Maybe he should go and have another look round the house once the sale went through, or even before. What had he missed last time he searched the place? He hadn't found any valuables or seen any papers that were worth taking. In fact, the only papers he'd found had been old letters from many years back, dating from the mid-nineteenth century. They'd been crammed into a large inlaid wooden box any old how. He'd pulled out a few, but found nothing of interest, so had shoved the box back in the cupboard.

But perhaps he should check the papers out more thoroughly before his mother got her hands on the house? He'd check out the box, too, and the rest of the house if necessary.

There had to be something there still, otherwise why would she continue making such a fuss about the place?

Tez hired a man to drive him down to Honeyfield on the Friday after Isabella moved into Pear Tree Cottage. There wasn't time to send a letter alerting her to his coming, or if he did, he'd have to wait another day to go there. No, he'd told her he'd be down at the weekend so surely she would be expecting him?

He had to fill in some more army paperwork and attend a final meeting on the Friday morning. No one could dream up forms to fill in and procedures to be gone through like the army. But at last that was done and his final steps out of the armed forces had been taken and ratified. He wasn't sad about that because he hadn't been a career soldier; it just felt strange. He'd had to buy some more civilian clothes and that was it.

He was able to set off mid afternoon, only an hour later than he'd planned. The driver was cheerful about the delay, because neither of them expected the journey to take more than three or four hours.

Unfortunately en route they met with a series of problems that delayed them. First they had a flat tyre, and it took ages to get it fixed. Then they had to stop to render assistance to an elderly man who'd had a seizure while driving and run into a tree. He couldn't have been going very fast because he was in more trouble from the seizure than from the accident.

They got the man to a nearby cottage hospital and even brought back a mechanic to drive his car home, since his elderly wife had no idea how to cope.

It was nearly ten o'clock by the time the car turned into Pear Tree Lane and it surprised Tez how much driving into the village felt like coming home. Even with the recently introduced daylight-saving changes the light was fading and curtains were drawn. Most people thought it was a good idea to change the clocks and push the lighter hours further on in the day. What use was daylight at four or even five o'clock in the morning, after all?

Trust the Germans to think of changing the time first. He had a lot of respect for their enemy's intelligence. Daylight saving was such a good idea that the British authorities had been quick to follow suit.

The curtains were drawn at Pear Tree Cottage too, but there was a light showing in the sitting room so Isabella must still be up.

'I'll unload your luggage and bring it in, sir,' the driver said.

Tez went to use the door knocker. There was no answer but he saw the edge of the curtain twitch and called, 'It's me, Isabella. Come and let me in.'

Only then did someone slide the bolts and unlock the door.

'I didn't think you were coming,' she said. 'I'm so glad to see you.'

She'd been crying, he could tell, even in the dim light shining from the sitting room. She stepped back out of sight as the driver brought in Tez's suitcase and then the two boxes of food he'd purchased from Harrod's, putting them down in the hall.

'Thank you.' Tez fished out the payment they'd agreed on, adding a big tip because of all the troubles there had been on the way.

'Thank you very much, sir. If you ever need a driver . . .'

'I'll definitely call on you.' He closed the door and turned back to Isabella, saying bluntly, 'You've been crying. What's wrong?'

'I hoped you wouldn't notice, or if you did, not say anything.'

'I notice everything about you. And I can't know that you've been crying without trying to help. Was it for Philip?'

She looked first startled then shamefaced. 'I'm afraid not. I was crying because I'm alone. Silly and weak of me, isn't it?'

'Not at all silly. We can talk later and maybe work out some way to cheer you up when I'm not here, but for the moment you're not alone. Let's get these boxes unpacked. I brought some food and I'm ravenous, I must admit. We've had a hell of a journey and were unable to stop for a meal. We left London just after midday.'

'Goodness, that was a long drive. I'll get you something to eat straight away.'

He tried to pick up one of the boxes, but as he fumbled she took over the job. 'Leave me to do that, Tez. A box is a two-handed job.'

'I don't like you doing the heavy lifting.'

'It's not all that heavy. Never mind me. Tell me what the doctors said about your hand.'

'They were pleased with my progress but I have to be careful not to strain this hand. They said if I do that, I should get a lot of the function back, which cheered me up a lot. I was afraid the hand would just be there for decoration because it's seemed numb at times.'

'I'm glad for you. We both have ghosts sitting on our shoulders, don't we? And what are we doing standing in the hall talking?'

She carried the boxes through and began to take the tins and cartons of food out of them, exclaiming at his extravagance. 'These must have cost you a fortune.'

'I wasn't skimping. I wanted to pay my share of the expenses here and to be sure I wouldn't be taking your food. I'm a hearty eater, I'm afraid.'

'Let me make you some sandwiches, then. We won't open the tin of ham this evening. I have some very good local cheese and a tomato to slice up with it, plus an apple pie from the baker's.'

'Excellent.'

'I'll make us some cocoa, too.'

After they'd finished eating and drinking, they both yawned at the same time then laughed.

'Let's go to bed,' she said. 'Your bed's made up now. We'll worry about our new ways of life in the morning. I didn't sleep at all well last night, but I'm sure I'll do better tonight.'

As he stood up, he said, 'Don't forget to lock all the doors.'

Her smile faded. 'That's one thing I'm not likely to forget.'

So she *was* nervous, he thought. Well, no wonder.

There was no sound from her bedroom after the light went out. Tez lay listening but heard nothing so hoped she was asleep.

It took him a long time to get to asleep. She needed him now and he had nothing else to do with his life till his hand had fully healed, so he could try to help her.

The fighting mangled your mind, left you with horrific images. Like many men he had nightmares. But he had none that night, thank goodness. He'd have hated to wake her up.

In the morning Isabella looked well rested and they chatted cheerfully over breakfast.

'How does it feel to be out of the army, Tez?'

'Strange. I know it's only just over two years since I

volunteered, but I feel as if I've been a soldier for ever.'

'Are you going to live in your London flat from now on?'

'No, definitely not. It's more like a cupboard than a home. It was all right when I was only there for a day or two on leave but I'd go mad if I had to live in it permanently. I don't really want to stay in London. I'll find somewhere in the country, I think. I'm not sure where yet.'

She stared at the floor then changed the subject.

He hoped she didn't think he'd been hinting to come there full-time. That might give them too many complications. Though it was a tempting idea.

But he did wonder how she was going to manage the heavier jobs around the house as her body grew more unwieldy and after the baby was born. Her mother didn't sound at all loving and Isabella had said she didn't have any other close relatives. Who was going to look after her? Women usually stayed in bed for a few days after a birth.

'Shall we go for a walk or have you something else you need to do?' he asked after she'd cleared the breakfast things away.

'I'd love to go for a walk if you're well enough. I'm going to explore the surrounding area but I've been out a couple of times and found some pretty lanes and footpaths near the village. But walks are always pleasanter with a companion to talk to.'

They didn't chat much as they walked, but it was a comfortable silence. They stopped a couple of times to look at particularly beautiful vistas and once to stare down across a gently sloping field at a large country house with a steep roof and gables.

'That must be Honeyfield House,' she said. 'It's officially a convalescent home but I'm told it's really for women who need to take refuge somewhere.'

'From what?'

'Husbands who beat them, parents or relatives who treat them badly, who knows? My mother isn't very maternal but she's never ill-treated me. That gate in the back wall of my garden is apparently a shortcut to the back of that house. I've got a key to the gate now but I'm going to keep it locked. The farmer says I can pick up windfalls later, when the apples and pears are ripe. He's very friendly. Says to call on him for help if I need anything while you're away.'

'That must make you feel safer.'

She stopped walking to consider this, head on one side. 'Not really. I still worry about whoever tried to knock my car off the road. What if they come back and try again to harm me? But at least there are people within shouting distance here if someone tries to break in, though the neighbours are mostly older than me, so how much practical help they'd be I don't know.'

'It isn't easy for you, is it? No wonder you were upset last night when you thought I wasn't coming.'

'I expect I'm being cowardly, but that attack still haunts me. Philip's family didn't even bother to hide their hostility. And when Mr Marley phoned me – I must give you my phone number, by the way – to say that Mrs Cotterell has agreed to pay our price, he warned me that she's very angry about having to pay the full price. She's a horrible woman.'

'I agree. You can see her spiteful nature in her face.

Most people betray their nature in their face; the rankers certainly did when dealing with officers even though they didn't dare protest about anything.'

He didn't offer to come and live with her full-time because they didn't know one another well enough for that yet. Besides, he didn't want her to feel obligated to house him if that wasn't what she wanted.

As they walked on a bit further in silence, he decided he might offer when he got to know her better, if only because she would need someone to look after her. Pregnant women could be very vulnerable. Then he looked down at his bandaged hand and told himself not to be stupid. A fat lot of good he'd be at protecting anyone these days.

Instead he changed the subject and when they got back to Pear Tree Lane, they stopped at the tumbledown house next door to pick some raspberries from a tangle of canes.

'Pity the house has been allowed to get so run down,' he said. 'It must have been very pretty once.'

Her voice was so low, he wasn't sure whether she realised she was voicing her thoughts. 'I'd feel better if I had a neighbour living there.'

The following day they went for a drive in the car, not stopping anywhere for a cup of tea because she was afraid of being seen but enjoying being outside on another sunny day.

On the Monday it was cloudy, echoing his mood. He felt obliged to go home. If you could call that box of a flat a home. He almost asked to stay another day but didn't like to impose on her hospitality.

As they drove into Malmesbury, they were both quiet. She dropped him at the station, saying, 'I shall miss your company.'

That made him think he should have suggested staying longer, but it was too late now. 'I shall miss you, too, Isabella.'

She gave him a faint smile. 'I like you calling me that.'

'Then I shall always do so. Don't hesitate to phone my mother's house if you need me, or there's anything I can bring down next weekend.'

'Thank you. I will.'

He walked into the station, stopping to stare when he thought he saw Filmore in the distance. But the man turned off to one side and was so far away that he could have been mistaken.

Anyway, Isabella had already driven off by then, so if it was Filmore, he'd not have seen her, which was the important thing, because he'd have told Philip's brother.

The phone call from Francis was put through to Spencer before he could stop the maid doing it.

'How about coming over for a drink tonight, old chap?'

'I'm afraid there's—'

'I've got something to tell you.'

'Tell me now.'

'I'd rather tell you face-to-face.'

There was a long silence, then Spencer gave in to temptation. 'Just for an hour, then. I don't like to leave my mother for long at the moment. She's in a bit of a mood.'

He got there for eight o'clock, driving himself. 'Sorry I'm late. Mother threw a tantrum today. All the fault of my brother for leaving everything to his so-called fiancée. She still can't accept that.'

'Bit unfair of him.'

'Yes. And Mother's missing my sister's company, though she'd never admit it.'

'She should have been kinder to Georgina when she was living here.'

'Mother isn't kind to anyone. You should have realised that by now.'

'I have, but by her age most people have learnt that you can catch flies more easily with honey than with vinegar. Anyway, I should think you need a glass of brandy after a day like that.'

'Wouldn't say no.'

When they were settled in front of the fireplace with its summer 'dressing' of an embroidered screen, Francis said abruptly, 'I saw Tesworth in Malmesbury today.'

'What was he doing?'

'Getting on a train to London. I checked later where the train was going and it was an express. He's still got his arm in a sling.'

'No sign of anyone else with him.'

'No. But why would he come down here except to see *her*. His family aren't from these parts.'

'Was he still in uniform?'

'No. I heard he was going to be invalided out. Wonder what he'll do with himself now.'

Spencer studied his glass, swirling the brandy round and round, making it last. 'It could be interesting to find out what he was doing here.'

'No sign of that Jones female anywhere?'

'No. Mother has bought the house at *her* price.'

'She must be keen to get it. Did you find out why yet?'

'No.' Spencer changed the subject, talking about the horrifying losses in the Battle of the Somme, nearly sixty thousand British Empire casualties in one day alone. 'We're well out of that, eh?'

'It's one consolation for the scornful treatment.'

After finishing his drink, Spencer stood up. 'I'd better get back.'

'Have I done something to offend you?'

'No, of course not.'

'Then why have you been staying away?'

'Other people sometimes pull my strings.'

'What does that mean? Has your mother got some hold over you?'

He shook his head. 'No. And that's all I'm saying. Let me know if you hear anything else and I'll reciprocate if I hear anything about my dear sister.'

'The bitch has vanished off the face of the earth.'

'For the time being only. I don't know where Georgina has gone to earth but I doubt she'll be able to stay there for ever. She'll reappear one day, I'm sure, and we'll be waiting for her.'

'Well, I'd prefer her to reappear sooner rather than later. I really need that money of hers.'

'Don't we all?'

As he drove home Spencer smiled. *He* didn't need a share of his sister's money now, though he had no doubt his mother and Francis were still eager to get hold of it.

He wasn't going to tell Francis about it or he'd be trying to cadge a loan. His mother knew, because his father had reduced her allowance.

Spencer smiled in the darkness of his car and thought about tonight's conversation. Francis must be even shorter than usual of money to be so direct. Well, *he* didn't intend to offend the old man by going against orders to stay away from Francis. And they were orders, however softly spoken.

It was good to know there was money coming in every quarter that wasn't dependent on his mother's whims. Very good.

But now that he could leave Westcott, he found he didn't want to. London wasn't much fun when there was a war on that you couldn't play a part in, and when certain people didn't want to know you.

And there were too many chaps strutting around in uniform. He remembered how alive and heroic Philip had looked when he came home on leave. And how good most men looked in an officer's uniform, even the ugly ones.

It was humiliating when women gave you a white feather. He hoped he didn't show how much it upset him.

Part Two

Chapter Twelve

In early August, Tez was given permission to drive again. He got his car out of storage the very same day and had it checked over and serviced. The next day he drove himself down to Honeyfield for the first time. He took it easy and had a stop en route, but his hand still felt all right and he was looking forward to surprising Isabella and being able to drive her around for a change.

Isabella *not* Bella. It was now established that he call her 'Isabella' not merely 'Bella'. He was the only person apart from her father who had ever done that, she said.

That pleased him greatly because he knew how much she'd loved her father. He felt to be getting closer to her with every visit. There was nothing romantic about it, but friendship was building and that felt good.

When he drove into her street and pulled up in front of her house, Bella ran outside to the car beaming. 'Tez! You didn't tell me they were allowing you to drive again.'

He grinned at her as he got out. 'They said it was up to me now and I felt sure I could do it. So here I am.' Without thinking he pulled her into his arms and gave her a hug.

For a moment she stiffened slightly, then she hugged him back.

'I've been wanting to do that for a while,' he said quietly.

'We've become such good friends,' she said, deliberately skirting round the underlying meaning of his statement.

He didn't say 'More than friends, surely?' but he thought it and she didn't meet his eyes as she pulled away again.

But she had hugged him back! Was he being a fool or was there hope for him?

'I'll carry my case in.' He only brought a small overnight bag now because a few of his clothes were kept permanently at Pear Tree Cottage. 'You can carry the box, because though I think I could manage it now, I reckon I've given my hand enough exercise for the time being.'

'How did you get it into the car?'

'My neighbour carried it down for me.' Tez always brought food because she wouldn't let him pay towards the running costs of the house. He tried to find food that wasn't easily available in Honeyfield, so as not to upset the grocer and to give Isabella a treat or two.

He put the case at the foot of the stairs and studied her. 'I like your new frock.'

She looked embarrassed. 'I've put on so much baby weight that my clothes didn't fit me. I'm very lucky that we have such a good local dressmaker in the village. I don't think I've ever had clothes which suit me so well. She wouldn't even let me choose the materials on my own but insisted on coming with me into Malmesbury.'

'No one saw you there?'

'No. But I had to risk it, because I was desperate to

get some new clothes made. At least I wasn't there on my own.' She looked down at her feet. 'I need some new shoes as well. No one told me that having babies makes your feet get bigger.'

'Perhaps because of the extra weight they now carry.'

She glanced into the mirror and sighed. 'I'm getting very fat round the middle now.'

'Not fat. Plump and ripe as a peach.'

'You say the nicest things, Tez. You always make me feel better. Anyway, I'm going to go into Swindon for a quiet shopping trip after the weekend. I'm sure no one I know will be there on a Monday morning. I'll wear a small felt hat that won't draw attention to my face and pull it down as far as it'll go. And I won't linger.'

'I don't like to think of you driving there and back on your own. You mentioned last weekend that you get tired more easily these days. Why don't I stay on a day or two longer and come with you? We could share the driving.'

She stared at him and it seemed to him as if this moment, this decision, was a turning point in their relationship. 'All right. Will you have enough clothes or shall I need to wash something for you?'

He'd been holding his breath while he waited for her answer and he let it out in a long slow exhalation. 'I'll have enough clothes, thank you. I leave quite a few things here now.'

'Yes. I noticed when I cleaned the spare bedroom. I didn't realise you'd left so many.'

'Can you find me a washerwoman locally? It'll be easier to get my things laundered here and people won't be surprised since I'm supposed to be your husband. You don't mind doing that?'

She shook her head then changed the subject. 'What's in the other box?'

'A new book for you and my painting equipment.'

'I've been hoping you'd try to use some of the art things in the studio. Those watercolours you showed me were lovely. You should use a talent like that. I wouldn't mind if you stayed over an extra day now and then to work there.'

More progress! he thought triumphantly, but said only, 'You're very kind. I'd like that. There's nowhere I can leave my paints out in the flat, it's so small.'

'I'm not being *kind*; I'm telling the simple truth. You really are a good painter. But I think we ought to clear Miss Thorburn's things out of the studio first. We can do it together. I've never quite liked to disturb them.'

Later he helped her go through the studio's contents and they found album after album of the old lady's watercolour paintings of the countryside.

He whistled softly as he carefully turned the big pages. It was like a photograph album only much bigger, with the edges of her paintings inserted into slits at each corner. 'She was a superb painter. I wonder if she ever sold anything.'

'I shouldn't think so. Mrs Dyson at Number Three says she was a lady through and through. Never left the house without a hat, never lost her temper, never did anything but live and behave modestly.'

'That sounds a rather tedious life for the poor old thing. Yet her paintings are full of beauty and the joys of nature.'

'A lot of women seem to live mainly in the shadows.

Philip and I were planning to do all sorts of things after the war: travel, go to the theatre, dance the night away . . .' She indicated her stomach with a wry smile. 'Now my future life has been decided for me. I'll be raising my child for the next twenty years or so, and I too will be living quietly in the shadows, thanks to the Cotterells.'

'Will that be enough to keep you happy?'

'It'll have to be. I don't have much choice but as I want the baby very much, I'll do it gladly.'

He didn't ask what they'd do about his role as her husband after the war. If he had his way, she'd marry him and he'd make sure she didn't have to live her life quietly serving others. For the moment they were taking small steps that would, he hoped, pave the way. They were very good friends now, never short of something to chat about, sharing many of the same interests.

But the day was coming when he would have to speak out. They couldn't go on like this for ever. They had rushed into the pretence that he was her husband without thinking how to end it. And he'd be desolate if they had to separate.

He must hold back from speaking till after the child was born, he always told himself. It wouldn't be right to say anything till she'd had her child. Till Philip's legacy was no longer growing inside her.

Georgie was sorry to leave Greyladies, but found the place they sent her to, Honeyfield House, a friendly place as well. It was a similar style of house, but not nearly as grand. She didn't intend to stay in these sheltering places for ever. She was determined to find somewhere of her own to live, not to mention something worthwhile to do with her life.

A lot of people talked about making new lives for themselves after the war, which seemed to have been limiting their horizons for a long time, even though it was not yet two full years. It felt as if the war would never end. How many more wonderful young men like her brother would be sacrificed to its needs?

She was much better educated than the three other women in residence at Honeyfield, one of whom had brought four children with her, such quiet, subdued children. They'd been afraid of their own shadows at first, Sal said, because their father had often hit them, but were getting more lively now. If that was 'lively' the poor little dears had a long way to go.

As the women got to know one another, differences of background became less and less important. They shared life stories and Georgie began to understand how, in spite of the irritations and limitations her mother had imposed on her life, she'd had a far easier time than the others.

Money made a big difference, whatever anyone said about money not making you happy. She hadn't gone hungry, hadn't had children to protect, hadn't lost babies due to violence.

A few times she chatted privately to Miss Pendleby, the matron at Honeyfield House. They all did. It seemed as if their matron had been chosen in part at least for her ability to listen and prompt the women into working out solutions to their problems.

'Like you, most of them have been told what to do all

their lives by other people,' she said to Georgie one day. 'I try not to order you ladies around too much.'

'I've noticed.'

'Yes. I thought you would. You're not stupid.'

'But I still haven't come up with a plan for what I should do next. I can't seem to think clearly about it.'

'You will. Give it time. Now, I wonder if you would help me – or rather, help Jean? She didn't get a very good education, to put it mildly, and desperately needs to be able to read properly. So does Sal. If you could help the two of them to practise their reading every day, they'd improve quickly and that would make a big difference to their chances of better lives.'

'I'm happy to do that.'

'Mrs Perry used to come and help them sometimes, but she's expecting a child soon and gets too tired to come out in the evenings.' She smiled. 'In fact, Mr Perry is fussing over her like a hen with one chick.'

'He's a lovely man, isn't he?'

'Yes. The pair of them make very good trustees. I can go to them for help about anything.'

'I wonder if Mr Perry would advise me about what to do with my own money?'

'I'm sure he would. He trained as an accountant and still runs his family's accounting business, though he prefers to sell houses these days and I've heard that he does a little work on the side, finding things and people that are lost.'

'Like a detective?'

'Yes. He's a great admirer of the Sherlock Holmes stories, and so am I. They're very exciting. Did you read *The*

Valley of Fear? It was serialised in *The Strand Magazine* at the beginning of the war. I bought every edition and saved them. I can lend them to you if you like.'

'I'd love that.'

'I'm sure I can rely on you to take care of them.'

'Of course.'

As their chat ended, Georgie said in wonderment, 'You make everything seem so much easier. Thank you.'

'I can make daily life relatively easy for people staying here, but I can't make the choices you have before you easy or make your life run smoothly after you leave. That'll be up to you – and fate. Fortunately, we have groups of women working with the trust in several places around the country, so if you need to settle further away to avoid the people who're upsetting you, we can usually find someone to help you settle elsewhere.'

Which gave Georgie a lot to think about. But though she had adequate money to live on, she still wasn't entirely confident about her own ability to manage her life, especially uncertain about how and where to live. And to live on her own! That frightened her, she had to admit.

And she realised, as a lot of young women did, that with so many young men being killed there wouldn't be enough husbands left to go round after the war, so she might remain a spinster all her life.

She knew Harry was fond of her, but though she liked him very much and was grateful to him for helping her, she wasn't fond of him in that way, unfortunately. So even if he survived the war, she didn't see her future bound in his. She wasn't so desperate to marry that she'd do it without love. Not after her experience with Francis.

Sadly, she'd never fallen in love with any man and had only agreed to marry Francis to escape from her mother, which she had grown to understand would have been leaping out of the frying pan into the fire. It had taken his attempt to stop her speaking at her own twin's memorial service to push her into action.

It took longer to finalise the house purchase than Spencer had expected because it took his mother a while to find a new lawyer who suited her, which he knew meant *soft-soaped* her ad nauseam.

He got fed up of waiting, so tried to get into the house to go through the contents, but found to his annoyance that the locks had all been changed. Marley interfering again, no doubt, damn him.

His mother would soon gain possession of the house, so Spencer offered to escort her there and help with the inspection.

'No, thank you. I want to wander down memory lane and that wouldn't be easy with you clumping around there. I need to be on my own.'

He was quite sure she wasn't going to do any wandering down memory lane. She was a very unsentimental woman. But what was she going to do at the house?

Tez drove the two of them into Swindon to purchase some shoes, taking Isabella's car in case he got too tired and she had to drive back. They parked it in a side street and strolled along to Regent Street.

'It feels like a big city after Honeyfield,' she joked. 'Electric lights, tramways and plenty of shops. I wish we had electricity in Honeyfield. It'd make life so much easier. We had it at the hospital and at my landlady's house.'

'Well, I dare say it'll come to Honeyfield one day. Hold on to my arm and watch out for tripping in the tramlines. We'll try the shops on Regent Street first. You ought to be able to find some decent shoes here. If not, I know a couple of other places to try.'

'How do you know the town so well?'

'My army unit was stationed near Swindon for a few weeks.'

They found a good shoe shop and she bought two pairs. As they were about to leave it, he stopped dead in the doorway and said in a low voice, 'Get back.'

She moved quickly away from the door.

When he saw the assistant look at them strangely, he explained, 'I saw someone I know. It's a chap I don't want to bump into, to be frank. And in any case, I was tempted to buy myself a new pair of shoes. It looks as if fate has sent me back to do so.'

Isabella waited while he tried on shoes, then he checked the street again and said it was safe to leave the shop. He had intended to take her out for tea, but now hurried her back to the car.

She let him get her seated then waited for him to start the car, but he got into the driving seat instead and stared down at the steering wheel. 'It was Spencer Cotterell whom I saw, so don't be surprised when I take a roundabout route out of town. We don't want to bump into him.'

'Oh. And did he see you?'

'I don't think so, but I can't be sure. I wonder what he was doing in Swindon. You'd not think it the sort of place he'd visit on a Monday morning, would you?'

She looked at him in dismay. 'It's going to make my life very difficult if I can't even come shopping here without worrying about bumping into the Cotterells or that horrible man who used to be engaged to Philip's sister.'

'It is a problem, isn't it? I'll just start up the car. I'm getting quite good at doing it with my right hand.'

'I could do it for you.'

'No. I'm not that weak now.'

He got out and cranked the car engine into life, then got back in and drove them out of town, going through the backstreets and then along country lanes to Honeyfield, rather than using the main road.

They hardly said a word on the way back, both of them lost in thought, wondering what to do to keep her safe and hide the fact that she was expecting a baby.

Chapter Thirteen

In Swindon, Spencer parked his car and sat smiling for a moment. He intended to enjoy meandering round the shops and buying whatever he wanted, without having to go to his mother for the money. Or listen to a scolding because he'd bought something she considered unnecessary and had 'wasted good money' on it.

He got out and walked along towards the main shopping street, stopping in surprise when he saw Philip's car. Since there was no one around, he walked up to take a good look at it. It had dents in the back, of course. Pity about those. Had she sold it to someone or was the jumped-up little nobody still driving it about herself?

He glanced up and down the street, but there was no one around so he peered into the interior. She had kept it nice, with the leather upholstery polished and the windows clean inside: he'd grant her that much.

Even with the dents, it was a much nicer car than his own, damn her! His might be bigger but he'd had to buy it second-hand and not only was it older, but its first owner hadn't taken proper care of it.

Should he hang about and confront her again about

selling Philip's car to him? Or wait and follow her to find out where she was living? And then do what? He wasn't sure. He was still surprised he'd had the courage to try to edge her off the road into an accident. He'd not managed to hurt her but at least he'd damaged the car a little. He'd been furiously angry at her rejecting his offer to buy it. He probably should have offered her a little more money, he now realised. She might have been tempted then.

He hung about for a few moments at the corner of Regent Street, uncertain whether to go or stay. He began to stroll slowly along the main street. If he stayed nearby he'd see her coming.

He walked along slowly, stopping now and then as if to look at the goods in the windows but really to check the people on the street. At one point he stopped in front of a draper's window to study a rack of ties. Instead his eyes were drawn to the reflection of a man in the doorway of a shoe shop on the other side of the street. Tesworth! What was *he* doing here? He was staring in Spencer's direction then he gesticulated to someone inside to go back and moved quickly into the shop again himself.

Damn! Spencer couldn't see who the other person was. But it was obvious that Tesworth had seen him.

He acted as if he hadn't noticed the other man and continued to stroll slowly along the street until he came to another side street and turned into it. This was as good a spot as any from which to keep watch on the shoe shop because he could see it through the corner of a shop window without anyone who came out of it seeing him.

Had it been *her* inside? Or was Tesworth out shopping with someone else? Spencer intended to make sure, so lingered there and lit a cigarette. But it mostly burnt unheeded because his attention was on the shoe shop.

Eventually, the door opened again and Tesworth appeared, staring up and down the main street, checking who was around. After a few moments he turned and offered his arm to the lady behind him and they set off in the opposite direction to the watcher. It was indeed *her*.

Spencer smiled. This was his lucky day. Tesworth *was* still seeing Bella Jones. Well, they were both going to get a few shocks in the next few weeks.

But it was he who got a shock when the wind blew her frock against her body as she turned to point out something in another shop window and he saw the protruding belly. She was expecting! Hell fire! Was it Philip's child? Or was it Tesworth's?

No, she was too far advanced for it to be Tesworth's. He was one of those goody-goody chaps Spencer despised for their weakness and would hardly have cheated on his friend. Tesworth must be looking after her now, though, or they'd not be out shopping together.

Spencer allowed himself to contemplate the choices. Would it be best to frighten her and drive her away from the district . . . and if so, how? Or would he take a more serious step, as he'd tried before, and get rid of her once and for all? The thought of that tempted him, but he wasn't sure he could go through with it.

It was one thing to ram her car and claim it as an accident, though when he'd thought about it afterwards, he'd wondered if the police would have accepted that explanation if she'd still have been alive to tell them the truth.

It was quite another thing to kill her with his own hands. He doubted he was a good enough shot to hit her fatally from a distance and he didn't think he could strangle anyone.

No. He'd better not go to that extreme. The penalty for failure would be too high – hanging! Besides, if he killed her now, that would kill the child too. Did he want to do that?

He gasped as he suddenly realised that a child would solve his own problem of feeling pressured to marry and produce an heir.

And why was he standing here daydreaming when he should be following them and finding out where they went?

He ran towards his own car, darting behind a postbox when he saw Philip's car coming towards him along the street. Tesworth was driving it, not her.

Spencer raced along to his car, which started first time, for once. He set off after them along the only main road that led out of this part of town. But though he drove fast, he didn't catch up with them.

Where the hell had they gone?

He drove all the way into Malmesbury but there was no sign of them, and when he stopped to ask a lad sitting on the wall if a Model T Ford had gone past, the lad shook his head.

'No cars have come by for the last quarter of an hour, mister, only two farm carts and a woman on a horse.'

'Thanks.' Tossing him a penny, Spencer drove slowly home.

Where could they have gone? He needed a good county map to see what other villages and hamlets there were along the nearby side roads.

And he needed a rest. He seemed to get tired more easily lately and then he didn't think as clearly.

Maybe the best thing to do would be to tell his mother, and then they could consult a lawyer about getting hold of the brat once it was born. Let's hope this new lawyer she'd found had as sharp a brain as she claimed.

They'd have to find out where the woman was living and when the baby was due, then make their plans accordingly.

He grinned as something else occurred to him. His mother could pay for it all, would be eager to do that. She knew his father was paying him his allowance directly, but she didn't know about his father's sudden generosity in doubling the amount. And he knew his father wouldn't tell her, because he never told her anything if he didn't need to. It was one of her biggest complaints about him.

He'd have to be careful not to upset his father.

When they got back to Honeyfield, Isabella carried in the boxes of shoes without any protest from Tez. He was looking tired now, but he seemed to know the side roads well so she hadn't tried to take over the driving.

He let her install him in the sitting room while she produced a cup of tea. He leant back in the chair, admitting to himself that he'd done a bit too much with that hand today.

'That was a close call,' he said when she joined him.

'Yes. I still feel shuddery inside. I peeped out at him through the shop window. Has Spencer always been so thin and, well, yellowish? I thought he was getting over some illness when I went to meet Philip's family but he looked just as bad at the funeral and even worse today. He's like a caricature of Philip, isn't he?'

'Spencer never looks well. Rumour is that he's not going to make old bones, though no one seems to know exactly why. He didn't pass his army medical, that's for sure. He wasn't fit even as a lad, but you're right. He looks terrible.'

'I was surprised when you told me someone had given him a white feather. How could anyone with eyes in their head think him capable of fighting?'

'He can look a lot better sometimes when he's in high spirits, especially if it's at night.'

'Well, let's not think about him any more. I didn't see any sign of him following us, thank goodness. I'm going to put on my new shoes and start wearing them in.' She got them out of the box and stroked the leather with gentle fingertips. 'I've never had such expensive shoes, or ones that fit my feet so well.'

'Put them on, then. That's what they're for, after all. I doubt you'll need to "wear them in", as you put it.'

'That would be marvellous. I've never owned a pair of shoes that I didn't need to break in to get them comfortable.'

They sat in the two armchairs in the sitting room, drinking their tea. To his amusement she sat with her legs stretched out and kept sneaking glances at her new shoes.

She was a darling! But not his darling. Not yet.

* * *

When Spencer got back, his mother was in a foul mood, so he didn't tell her what he'd found out.

He listened to her rant and rave about how much she'd had to pay for that house, murmuring soothing phrases here and there.

By the time she calmed down he was exhausted and she suddenly noticed it.

'You need to go and lie down. You've overdone things today.'

'Yes. I am a bit tired.'

She studied him, frowning, and he knew what she was thinking, but she didn't say it, thank goodness.

He went to bed but he couldn't even doze off because what he'd seen today kept going round and round in his mind.

He wanted to discuss it with his mother but not until she was in a good mood and ready to make sensible plans about what to do instead of ranting and raving.

It suited him to live here, with all expenses paid and people nearby knowing he'd been turned down for the army on medical grounds. But sometimes he wondered if the price he paid for it of humouring a bad-tempered old woman was a bit too high.

A few days later, settlement came through on the house and his mother decided to go and have a good look round *her* house. But as she was coming down the stairs, she stumbled and fell a few steps, spraining her ankle badly. She made such a fuss about the pain that the doctor took pity on them all and gave her something to make her sleepy.

Spencer told her maid to go and have a rest. 'You've borne the brunt of it, Gladys. You've more than earned a break.'

She gave a little nod to acknowledge this. She never complained about how she was treated. 'Your mother made me promise not to leave her.'

'She won't know whether you're there or not, and I can stay with her till you get back.' He gestured to the bed, where his mother was more asleep than awake and was making little whiffling noises that made him want to stuff something into her half-open mouth.

'Well, maybe just for half an hour, sir. I could do with something to eat to keep up my strength. Thank you.' She looked at him as if she knew he had an ulterior motive but he didn't care what she thought.

As soon as Gladys had left, he locked the bedroom door from the inside and went through the leather handbag his mother insisted on carrying around with her everywhere, contrary to the fashionable practice of carrying a small, purse-like contraption.

The bag felt surprisingly heavy and no wonder. The keys to the Malmesbury house were inside it, three copies of each one, with the set of four small key rings all hanging from a larger one. He could only suppose she was keeping them all in her handbag to make sure he didn't get his hands on them.

He unhooked one small key ring from the big one, with what he hoped was a complete set of keys on it and put the bunch back into her handbag, then stared down at her. How old she was looking! And how disgusting she looked without her false teeth. One day she'd die and life here would be much more pleasant without her, though the house would still belong to his father, in theory. But he doubted the old man would ever give up his busy life in London, or turn his older son and heir out of the family home.

When Gladys came back, he'd unlocked the bedroom door again and was yawning over the newspaper.

'You're looking more relaxed,' he told the maid. 'I think it's my turn for a rest now.'

He was driving away from Westcott within ten minutes, on his way into Malmesbury. He smiled as the keys he'd tied together with string and flung carelessly on to the other front seat clinked every time he drove along a bumpy bit of road.

Spencer parked further down from the house and waited till there was no one in the street before going in. The key turned easily in the lock and he slipped inside quickly, shutting the door at once – then opening it again because the hall was so dark and he didn't know whether the furniture had been rearranged since his last visit. He didn't want to follow his mother's example and sprain his ankle.

He opened the nearest internal door, but the room had the curtains closed. Since it faced onto the street, if he opened them, the neighbours would notice, he was sure, and perhaps knock on the door to introduce themselves. Then they might prattle to his mother about him being here.

He went into one of the back rooms and flung open

the curtains there, then went to close and lock the front door, shaking his head in astonishment at the cluttered interior. His last visit had been after dark and the jumble of furniture and other ornaments hadn't shown up so clearly. Who would want to live like this? The décor was positively Victorian.

And why on earth was his mother claiming to be fond of this house? It wasn't all that big and he found it oppressively dark, with wood panelling in the hall and stairs and heavy curtains everywhere. It must have belonged to a troglodyte!

He followed the short corridor behind the stairs into the kitchen, which was lighter because it didn't have any curtains, grimacing as a mouse scampered across the floor. He didn't think his mother would have hidden anything here.

Not sure where to start his search, he simply walked round the house from room to room, trying to work out where *he* would hide something.

Unless the panelling had a secret compartment, he'd not hide anything in the hall and stairs. Not in the sitting room either, which turned out to be the only room with modern furniture. Soft, overpadded armchairs were grouped near the fire, and one was sitting on its own in the bay window. But the wallpaper was in a dark flock pattern, which would show any breaks for secret panels, and the only bookcase was crammed full of well-used books and looked quite flimsy and modern. No place in it for secret compartments.

He peered into an embroidery box, but that didn't seem like a place where you'd hide anything because it would be kept where any person passing could open it. The interior was neatly set out with rows of cards, each with a different colour of wool wound round it.

He was about to go up the stairs when someone knocked on the front door. He hesitated, then tiptoed into the nearby room to peep out of the window and find out who it was. Damnation! A policeman. He'd better answer it.

He flung the front door open. 'Can I help you, Officer?'

'Yes, sir. I'm sorry to trouble you but a neighbour saw the front door open and knew the house was unoccupied, so called the police. May I ask who you are?'

He pulled out a card. 'I'm the son of the new owner. My mother has sprained her ankle, so sent me to check that everything is in order here.'

'I see, sir. Yes, she mentioned a Mrs Cotterell. Sorry to trouble you. But better safe than sorry, eh? We're here to look after people's lives and property.' He strolled off down the street.

Spencer shut the door gently, but then tripped over the doormat and kicked the hallstand, setting the umbrellas and walking sticks rattling in it before going upstairs.

He walked round the five bedrooms, finding them just as dreary as the downstairs rooms. One seemed to have been used as a storeroom and was crammed with furniture, while the other bedrooms were more sparsely furnished. Whoever had moved the furniture around had done a good job of packing it in tightly. It was going to be hard to check everything in the storage room.

He didn't think Cousin Audrey would have had the strength to do that, so someone must have helped her.

But he kept coming back to the question of why his mother had cared about this place. It was conveniently situated, certainly, but such a gloomy house. And she hadn't got on with Audrey, so perhaps the things she was interested in dated from the previous occupant, Cousin Gertrude. If so, maybe whatever it was had been consigned to the storage bedroom or the attic. Yes, that sounded right.

He couldn't see this involving a large object and his best guess was documents of some sort. He couldn't imagine what his mother would want with old documents, but you never knew where her tortuous plans would lead. She could be a cunning old fox.

He went back into the storage bedroom, edged along the narrow gap between the door and the window and threw the curtains wide open. Turning, he stared round as the objects here were revealed more clearly.

Two caught his eye instantly, matching tallboys, with two small cupboards at head height above the five drawers. Each piece had carving writhing its way down side columns on either side of the drawers, and round the oval mirrors set into the cupboard doors. It was exactly the style of furniture his mother had in her bedroom at Westcott.

On an impulse he began to go through the contents of the tallboys, pulling out each drawer, tipping its contents onto a bed shrouded in dust sheets so that he could examine the whole drawer and underneath it. Each time he shoved the things back into the drawer anyhow.

There was nothing in or attached to any of the first set of drawers except an old lady's clothes and he nearly didn't tackle the second one after the disgusting exercise of sorting through her bloomers. How could women wear such ugly things?

He scowled at the second tallboy, groaning aloud, but he might as well finish this job properly, so he took a deep breath and started going through it just as thoroughly as the first tallboy.

He was sighing over how he'd wasted his time as he started to check the lowest drawer, but a minute later he yelled in triumph when he found a large envelope stuck on the bottom of it with pushpins. His mother considered them one of the more useful modern inventions for holding papers on cork boards.

The sneaky bitch! he thought admiringly. Not many people would check thoroughly enough to find this.

The sound of his yell seemed to echo down the stairwell and for a moment he thought he heard footsteps coming up. He even went out onto the landing to check, but there was no one to see. Of course there wasn't. He was letting this dreary old house get to him.

He opened the envelope, whose flap wasn't stuck down, and pulled out a set of smaller envelopes. When he saw his father's handwriting on them, he hesitated. It didn't do to upset his father so perhaps he should stay out of this.

But his mother had hidden these and valued them so highly she'd bought a whole house just to get them back. He should at least find out what they were.

Putting the final drawer and its contents back in place, he picked up the envelope and stuffed it inside his jacket.

Downstairs he shivered, once again feeling as if someone was watching him. Oh, he was being stupid! How could they be? The house had been empty and locked up for months.

He closed all the curtains again before leaving. He might not tell his mother what he had found yet, not till he'd examined the documents and thought about their contents. It depended what they were. He wasn't opening anything till he was alone in his bedroom, though.

That made two things he was keeping secret from her.

Outside he saw a woman peering out from the house opposite. He took off his hat and used it to flourish a mocking bow at her and she vanished quickly. Stupid bitch. It was probably she who'd called the police.

It began to rain as he was trying to start his car and wouldn't you know it, the damned thing coughed and spluttered. It took him ages to get the motor going and by that time he was soaked. He shivered all the way home.

But the precious envelope had been safe and dry inside the car, and he couldn't feel miserable after such a successful expedition.

How lucky that his mother had had that fall!

At Westcott he found her awake and querulous now that the light sedation had worn off.

'Where have you been, Spencer? You're absolutely soaked. Go and change your clothes at once. In fact, have a hot bath and warm yourself up properly.'

'I'd rather have a brandy.'

'Have that as well. We don't want you falling ill.'

'Don't start fussing. I've survived this long and I think I can survive a little longer.'

'Long enough to marry? What if you died of pneumonia?

You need to leave an heir to carry on the family name. Why won't you do that for me?'

He sighed. Here she went again. Suddenly he was tired of prevaricating. 'Because I doubt I could father an heir, if you must know.'

She stared at him blankly for a moment or two, then asked, 'What do you mean?'

'I can't do the act that creates a child – and I've tried several times.'

She flushed bright scarlet. 'You just haven't found the right woman.'

'I haven't found any woman that I can do it with.'

To his surprise she took hold of his hand. 'Oh, Spencer, why didn't you tell me about this?'

'I told Father once. He sent me to a doctor, who said it wasn't likely to change. I was born malformed.'

She lowered her voice to whisper, 'Do you like *men*? Is that it?'

'No. I don't like anyone in that way.'

'Oh dear. You poor darling.'

She had been so genuinely sympathetic for once that he took her hand. 'I found something out last week, something that might help us. Wipe your eyes and listen.'

When she had calmed down, he told her that he'd seen Isabella Jones in Swindon and what he suspected. He didn't mention who she was with.

'She's expecting?'

'Oh, yes, definitely.'

'Is it Philip's child, do you think?'

'Bound to be. She's not stupid enough to have played

him false. What if we got hold of the child and raised it to be heir to Westcott?'

But she only burst into tears again and cried even harder. 'I don't *want* Philip's child inheriting. It's not the same.'

'How can you say that?'

But she shook her head and that stubborn look came back. 'I daren't talk about it or your father will kill me. Literally.'

'I hardly think he's capable of murder.'

'Well, he'd do something awful to me, something just as bad as murder, like destroying me socially. He'd go to any lengths if I upset him.'

He didn't think his father would kill her or anyone, but he might indeed do something to make her sorry. Why was she talking about his father destroying her socially? What had happened between them to create this marriage that wasn't really a marriage? Something, Spencer was sure. Two people didn't hate one another without there being a good reason. But he didn't pursue that point. He might come back to it later.

'Then think about the child, Mother. If we can get hold of it, bring it up ourselves, *voilà*. You have your heir and will spend your life raising him.'

'Or her.'

'Heaven forbid. If a female will do, get Georgina back.'

'Your sister has wounded me to the core – me, who has cared for her all her life. I don't think I want the ungrateful creature back.'

'Well, Francis wants her back. He's desperate for her money and our share of it, as we agreed with him, would come in useful for you and me, you must admit. Especially if there's a child to raise.'

'No, Spencer. Definitely not. I don't want that woman's child here.'

Beyond that she refused to speak, so he decided not to tell her about the big envelope until after he'd seen what it contained. He didn't intend to say anything to his father, either, or at least not until he was sure its contents wouldn't upset the old man.

The thought of having his independent money from now on gave him a lot of pleasure.

As his mother was growing bored with being confined to bed, she decided to get up for dinner, so Spencer couldn't deal with the envelope until much later. He was still feeling a bit chilly, so he put on a thick sweater before facing the dining room. It might be summer, but his mother had been right. He should have changed out of his wet clothes and had a hot bath.

Oh, well, the clothes felt dry enough now and a couple of stiff brandies would soon warm him up.

After an interminable evening of conversation, he helped his mother to limp to her bedroom, then made his way up to his own.

He put on his winter dressing gown over his clothes because he still couldn't seem to get fully warm, then locked the bedroom door before tipping out the papers onto the bed.

The envelopes had dates pencilled in the top right corner, so he put them in order and opened the earliest one. They seemed to be copies of payments to someone called Mary Jane Baxter, and they were in his father's handwriting.

The reason for the payments puzzled him until he got to the fifth one. He suddenly realised what was going on and let the paper drop onto the floor as shock stiffened his fingers.

No wonder his mother had been frantic to get them back. If his father found out she had them, he'd go mad at her and make her life very miserable indeed till he got them back. She wasn't really going to try to blackmail him, was she, or coerce him into doing something? If so, she was braver than Spencer.

When his father had made a plan, no one was allowed to interfere with it. She should know that better than anyone. But this plan was . . . well, incredible. Why had this been necessary? Had his mother been unable to bear any more children?

Why should that have mattered? His father already had an heir: Spencer. So why had he been so desperate for other children? Yes, Spencer's health hadn't been good, but he hadn't been at death's door.

He wasn't rushing into anything. He'd need to find out more about the reasons for this first.

He gathered the papers together and stuffed them into a drawer before ringing for the maid.

'Sorry to trouble you, Olga, but I seem to have caught a chill. Could I please have a fire lit in here and yes, I know it's summer but I'm cold. And would you also bring up the brandy decanter, please?'

She looked at him sourly. 'Yes, sir.'

He looked back just as sourly. Except for Gladys, his mother seemed to hire the most unobliging servants in the world. Or perhaps they were all she could find, given how many of the younger women were working in munitions and what were usually men's occupations because of the war. Yes, and earning men's wages too – it was shocking.

He sat on the bed, waiting, and when the fire had been lit, thanked her and locked the door again before pouring himself a stiff brandy, then another. He didn't often drink deeply but then he didn't often come across such amazing information.

There had to be some way he could use this to his own advantage.

Three brandies later, he opened the drawer and got out the small envelopes, stuffing them into the big one again and putting it on top of his wardrobe as a temporary measure. Then he rolled himself in the bedcovers fully dressed and fell asleep.

Chapter Fourteen

A couple of miles away from Westcott, Francis sat thinking good and hard. He hadn't been able to find Georgina, and heaven knows, he'd tried hard to do it without giving away his real intent. He'd driven round the countryside, visiting all sorts of out-of-the-way places to make enquiries. But no young lady of her description had come to live in any of them recently.

The last time he'd seen her had been at the cottage with Penny Richards, when the damned farmer had turned up and chased them away.

He'd found out that Penny was now in Portsmouth with her husband, but Georgina seemed to have completely vanished. She couldn't have got away on her own, so the farmer had to have taken her somewhere. But where? And how to get the information out of him?

He stopped and slowly began to smile. Or perhaps he could get the information from someone who knew the farmer. Yes, that might be it. He wouldn't find that 'someone' by staying at home staring at his shabby furniture or by driving round country lanes.

He continued to smile as a new method of searching formed in his mind.

* * *

Francis decided it was time to go back to the village nearest to the farm. He hadn't made enquiries here because he was worried the farmer might recognise him. But perhaps it was worth the risk because someone here would surely know where the farmer had gone when the two ladies left the farm cottage. Nothing stayed secret for long in a small village and why should this one be any different? It was worth a try.

He stopped in the shadows at the entrance to the pub to check that the farmer wasn't there, then strolled inside. The landlady came to greet him and fuss over him, as she well might when he saw what a low-class clientele the pub had.

He pretended he'd had a flat tyre and would like a drink and perhaps something to eat. If it wasn't too much trouble.

The landlady couldn't do enough for him, offering to show him into a private room at the side, which was more suited to a gentleman like him.

He followed her into it, hoping she'd stay and chat when she brought his meal and drinks.

She came back with the pint of beer he'd ordered and was all too ready to chat, so he mentioned his friend's sister who had come to stay near here, but seemed to have moved away.

'I thought I'd call in on her, but I can't find her. I had a letter from my friend only yesterday from the front, you see, and I felt sure it'd cheer her up to see it. I'm not medically able to fight myself, but I do what I can to help our brave fellows and their families.'

She gave him a pitying look and nodded, which annoyed him. Surely he didn't look *that* bad? He wasn't in poor health like Spencer, just had a bit of a problem with his breathing occasionally.

'The lady's brother was injured slightly, which could be a good thing because it got him away from the battles that are raging near the Somme – shocking, the losses there lately, aren't they? I thought the news that he's survived might be of comfort to her.' He sighed theatrically. 'It's not only our brave soldiers who are suffering but their families. One's heart goes out to them.'

'You're so right, sir. We've lost two lads from our village this year. Their mothers are broken-hearted.'

A man yelled to her to come and help serve and she excused herself. 'I'll be back with your food in a minute or two, sir. You can tell me more then and I'll see if I can help you find your friend's sister so that you can set her mind at rest.'

He sipped his beer, and it was good, then waited impatiently for her to return.

When she did reappear, she was carrying a loaded plate. He complimented her on how good the food looked but carried on the conversation while he could, describing Georgina.

'I saw her in the village several times but oh, dear, you've just missed her. She was staying with Mrs Richards at Hawes Farm Cottage, but *she* had to join her husband in Portsmouth, so your friend's sister must have had to find somewhere else to stay. I wonder . . .'

He waited.

'One of the labourers from Hawes Farm is drinking here tonight. I'll see if he knows anything about where she went.'

'Show him in here. I'll be happy to buy him a drink for his trouble.'

'Oh, I couldn't do that, sir.' She mimed holding her nose. 'The smell would put a gentleman like you off your food, not to mention his dirty great boots damaging my best carpet.'

The look of pride she shot at the garishly patterned carpet warned him not to go against her wishes. 'And very handsome the carpet is, too. Perhaps you can find out for me, then? I'd be very, um, grateful.' He rubbed his finger and thumb together suggestively to indicate a financial reward and saw her face brighten.

'I'll ask the man directly we have a quiet moment at the bar. The evening rush should be over soon. You get on with your meal now, sir. You don't want it to go cold, do you?'

'Indeed I don't. It looks wonderful.' The food was very tasty. His own cook-housekeeper didn't produce anything nearly as good.

When the landlady came in again, she took the plate and accepted his compliments with a smile that tried but failed to be modest. 'I'll bring you some apple pie and cream for dessert, shall I?'

'If it's as good as this was, I'd love some.'

She came back a couple of minutes later with a huge slice of apple pie taking up half a dinner plate, and slathered in thick cream. His heart sank at how big it was. He was going to have trouble eating it all on top of that meal.

'About the young lady you're looking for . . . the man I was telling you about doesn't know for certain but he thinks he heard the farmer saying that she'd gone off to a convalescent home somewhere. He heard the word "Greyladies" but he doesn't know where that is.'

'Oh dear, how can I find out?'

She beamed at him. 'Well, my husband and I can't help overhearing things when we're serving in the public bar, and I'm fairly certain I heard something a while ago about a convalescent home over in Honeyfield run by some people who call themselves the "Greyladies Trust". That's all I know, but if it helps you find the lady and set her mind at rest about her brother, I'm glad of it.'

'Madam, you are a wonder. I'm sure that'll lead me to her. Now, I'll just finish off this delicious food and then get on my way. I can't thank you enough.'

He fumbled in his pocket for his purse and pulled out a half sovereign and a sixpence. 'Would this be enough to pay for my meal and show my gratitude for your help? And a little extra for the man you spoke to.'

'Oh, sir, I couldn't.' But even as she spoke she was reaching out for the gleaming gold coin and tucking it and the sixpenny piece into her apron pocket.

He didn't want to make her suspicious in case he had to come back and ferret around for more information, so he forced down the pudding and left with a cheery wave.

Once outside he groaned and massaged his belly. He

didn't normally eat even half this amount, but it had been well worth it. Going to the pub after the local labourers would have finished their working day had been a master stroke, if he said so himself.

By the time he stopped his car outside his house he had severe indigestion but it was worth it. He had a feeling the landlady's information would be helpful and doubted she'd tell anyone what they'd been discussing, because then she might have to mention the tip he'd given her. In his experience, married women of her class kept any extra money they acquired well away from their husbands.

Honeyfield, eh? He knew where it was but had never visited it. He'd take a little trip out tomorrow and see what he could find. Or perhaps he'd send his manservant. Yes, that would be better. Dibble hadn't enough to occupy him, but Francis didn't want to lose his services so he'd kept him on. He now owed the poor chap quite a few months' wages, but he'd make it plain that these could only be paid after he married Georgina.

Elderly though he might be, there was no one like Dibble for ferreting out information, which was another reason for keeping him on. Francis would even let him take the car because Dibble was a careful driver and loved going for a run in the car.

He nodded in satisfaction. He'd get that bitch back and make her sorry she'd humiliated him at Philip's funeral, then teach her to obey him in future.

But best of all, after he'd married her, he'd get hold of her money. Well, his share of her money. Unfortunately, he needed Mrs Cotterell and Spencer's help to arrange all this, not to mention their presence at the wedding so that everything appeared respectable.

Spencer didn't wake till long after his usual time for breakfast and only then because someone started hammering on his bedroom door.

'Mr Spencer! Mr Spencer! Are you awake, sir?'

Groaning as he moved and caused pain to stab through his head, he rolled out of bed and opened the door. 'What the hell is it, Olga? Is the house burning down?'

She scowled at him. 'The mistress was worried about you staying in bed so long and sent me to check that you were all right.'

'Of course I am. Tell her I had a poor night's sleep and am still making up for it.' He turned to go back into his room.

'Sorry, sir, but madam was most insistent. She wants to see you as soon as possible.'

'Oh, does she?' He rubbed his aching forehead and cursed his own folly for drinking so deeply last night. It never agreed with him, but sometimes he had a fit of what-the-hells and got drunk anyway, numbing the pain of life in the way other men often did. At least the alcohol shut off that little voice in his brain that sneered at everything he did.

It took him a while to wash and dress, and he cut himself shaving because his hands were trembling.

When he joined his mother in the breakfast parlour his head was still thumping and although he managed to say, 'Good morning, Mother,' politely enough, he didn't say anything else till he'd poured himself a cup of tea with plenty of milk to cool it down. He put several spoonfuls of sugar in it and took two or three big mouthfuls.

'I gather you were drinking brandy last night, Spencer. That was stupid of you. You know it doesn't agree with you. You look absolutely dreadful. I shall tell Olga not to bring it to you in future.'

'I *feel* dreadful and my head's thumping, so if you could speak more quietly, I'd be grateful. Tell her what you want. If I want some I'll go and buy my own.'

She scowled at him but thankfully did moderate her tone. 'I want to go to look over my new house and I don't want the chauffeur spying on me, so I've decided you can drive me there.'

He thought for a minute, nodded incautiously and winced. 'Happy to do that.' She looked like a fat old hen, though better with her teeth in again.

'When I saw the Jones woman in Swindon the other day,' he began, 'there was something else.'

'What else was there? Why didn't you tell me everything?'

'I didn't think it relevant but now I do.'

He smiled, let his words hang fire between them for a moment, then tossed the verbal grenade at her. 'Tesworth was with her.'

'Tesworth? I thought he'd have left her to it after the memorial service.' She paused and stared at him. 'The child couldn't be his, could it?'

'No. Philip was his best friend, more like a brother. Take my word for it, a gentleman like him would never betray a friend so close to him. I don't know what his interest is now, though. Philanthropy? Or does *he* fancy her as well? She isn't bad-looking, you have to admit.'

'If you like that blowsy sort. Did you follow them? Where is she living now, do you know?'

'I don't. I was going to follow them but unfortunately my car was parked some distance away from theirs. She's still driving Philip's car, by the way. They passed me as I was going back to get my car but they didn't see me. By the time I got mine started they'd disappeared. I took the main road north, which was the direction they were heading, but there was no sign of them, so they must have turned off down a side road.'

'I suppose we'd better hire a detective and set him to find her.'

'Let me try first. After all, the baby won't arrive for three or four months yet, from the size of her belly. I know a chap who would keep an eye on her quietly.'

'Hmm.'

'And anyway, you wanted me to take you to that house you insisted on buying, didn't you? Why you wanted the place, I still can't figure.'

'I told you: leave that to me and don't poke your nose into it. You do not wish to upset your father.'

Well, that was one thing Spencer could agree with her about, especially now that his father was being more generous. 'I'll take you over there this afternoon, Mother, then I'll go for a drive and make a start of searching the nearby villages for that bitch. I'd notice the car and know its number plate. I'll come back for you after a couple of hours. How's that?'

She nodded and stopped talking at him for a while, looking as if she was thinking hard as she covered every inch of her toast meticulously in jam. Wartime shortages were beginning to be annoying, but they weren't allowed to affect her comforts, whatever the things she wanted cost on the black market.

He went back to the sideboard for another cup of tea but didn't eat much. After that he spent the time till they were leaving in his bedroom, lying on the bed, dozing a little, with his alarm clock set to remind him to go down to lunch.

As the hangover faded, his thoughts turned more and more to that Jones female and how he could turn her condition to his advantage.

And before they went out, he left a message with the garden lad for his uncle to contact him. If anyone could keep an eye on her, it'd be him. He was the most nondescript-looking chap Spencer had ever seen, and yet one of the most cunning, prepared to do anything for money.

The countryside was a mass of green still, but no longer the lighter greens of springtime. Hedgerows were bursting with plants and flowers, damn them! Spencer cursed as his eyes streamed and he kept sneezing while exploring one village after another.

He didn't see any sign of Philip's car and he didn't ask for her by name. He didn't want anyone warning her that someone was looking for her. All he wanted for the moment was to find her and pay someone to keep an eye on her and let him know when she had the baby.

When he gave up and went back to Malmesbury he found his mother sitting waiting for him.

'You took long enough!'

'I told you I'd be a couple of hours and you agreed to it.'

'Well, I finished more quickly than I'd expected. Someone has been in this house and gone through the drawers, stolen the things I'd hidden.'

'What were these things?'

She hesitated, then said, 'Papers. Useful proof of what your father once did in case I ever need to challenge him about it.'

'Oh? Does he know you've got them?'

'He's not sure. I've not said anything and shall deny that I have them unless I need to use them.'

'You intrigue me. Are you really going to keep my father in the dark about what's in these papers?'

'Yes. Believe me, it's safer for you. I'm going to give my lawyer a letter explaining the whole situation. If anything happens to me unexpectedly, he'll give it to you and then you'll have to do what you can. And whatever happens, don't tell your father about the child. Not yet, anyway.'

How she loved to scheme and plot, he thought, hoping his scorn hadn't shown in his face. 'Well, I'd rather nothing happened to you, Mother, if you don't mind. It'd be lonely here without you.'

She blinked hard and looked at him with tears in her eyes. 'My son, my only son. I'll make sure you get your inheritance for as long as you need it, Spencer, whatever your father tries to do. After that, who cares what happens to this place?'

'I'm the eldest son, Philip's dead. Who else could get it?'

'Anyone your father left it to. The estate isn't entailed.' She sighed. 'My life hasn't worked out as I'd expected. And I wish you'd told me sooner that you can't father a child, I really do.'

'It's not something one wishes to broadcast.'

'No. I can see that. But I'm your mother. *I* should have been told. Anyway, we'll let the subject drop for the moment. I'm debating whether to ask the police to look into the burglary here.'

He looked at her in alarm. That would put the cat among the pigeons because he'd been seen in the house. 'Do you really have to?'

'I'm thinking seriously about it.'

'I don't think you should.'

'Why not?'

'You don't want to draw Father's attention to this house, surely?'

That made her think, he could see.

'Oh really, Spencer. I don't know what you're making such a fuss for.'

'Promise you won't do it.'

She looked at him suspiciously. 'You know something. Tell me.'

'I've heard something,' he said carefully. 'Leave it with me for a few days and I'll investigate further. I won't be able to do that if you call in the police.'

If he hadn't spent the day feeling so bad, he'd have had

a couple of brandies that night as well. But he didn't dare. The drinking bout had made him feel worse this time than ever before.

One of the things he'd hated Philip for most had been his good health and abundant energy.

Chapter Fifteen

Dibble didn't bring the car back till late that evening. He came to see Francis straight away, smelling of beer and swaying slightly. He'd better not have scraped the car! 'Well? Did you find her?'

'I've not seen the lady you're searching for, sir, but I have found out about the Greyladies Trust and its house in Honeyfield. I followed your example and went to the local pubs.'

'Yes. I can tell.'

His tone was aggrieved. 'You can't sit in one unless you buy a drink.'

'No. I suppose not. Go on.'

Dibble explained about the house in Honeyfield, which was supposed to be a convalescent home but was actually a place where women in trouble could seek shelter. 'Unfortunately, it's impossible to get near it. It's set in huge gardens surrounded by high walls and there's a heavy gate at the entrance that's locked at night.'

'Draw me a map of the village and show me where this house is situated.'

'I'm not very good at drawing, sir.'

'Do your best.' He studied the resultant mess of scribbles and alterations. It wasn't very clear, but it'd help because he'd have to go there at night. He had pretty good night vision, had always thought he'd make a good spy. He only hoped they didn't have a big dog at this place, though. He didn't like dogs and they didn't like him, for some reason.

Well, he wouldn't go till the following night. He needed to fill up the car with petrol first and sort out a gun – not to kill anyone with but to protect himself or threaten someone with. And he'd think carefully about what else might come in handy.

The following evening Francis drove to Honeyfield, left the car outside the village and made his way to Honeyfield House. The map might have been poorly drawn but the verbal descriptions Dibble had supplied made up for its deficiencies. As he'd learnt the necessary route by heart, Francis found his way there easily enough.

There was indeed a gate and it had a huge padlock on it. But it was of wrought iron and easy to climb over. There was no gatehouse, so in his opinion the gate was a waste of time. No, not quite. It'd keep out vehicles. If he was able to kidnap Georgina, he'd have to drag her nearly half a mile to get her to the car.

He listened carefully for a dog barking but there was no sound of that, so he made his way slowly and carefully along the edge of the drive towards the house.

When he got there, he saw that they had the curtains drawn tightly over all the windows, even in the kitchen, with not a chink to peep through. And a large man seemed to be keeping guard to the rear next to what had once been the stables but didn't seem to be any longer. There were no sounds of horses moving about inside the low building.

He could see the man quite clearly by the light of a lantern outside the kitchen door. He was sitting on a bench opposite the door on the other side of the rear yard. He had his shirt sleeves rolled up and a cudgel propped nearby, and looked more as if he was courting than keeping guard, because he was chatting to a fat woman.

She too had rolled up her sleeves and had surprisingly muscular arms for a woman. She seemed to be making her companion laugh a lot.

Not much chance of getting past them both and he'd bet the woman would pile into the fight if he tried to knock the man unconscious.

What the hell was he going to do? Wait a while and watch what they did, he decided. It was all he *could* do. He changed his position a couple of times, not enjoying this part of the evening. He hated having to keep still.

The woman leant across to the man, not joking now, and whispered in his ear. Probably arranging to sleep with him, Francis thought sourly. He could do with a woman himself. It'd been a while.

The man looked at her in surprise, then gave her a hug and whispered back. Yes, definitely an assignation being planned, Francis decided.

After that the two of them sat together in silence.

About ten minutes later the back door of the house opened and a woman poked her head out. 'Sal! Barbara's crying.'

The fat woman got up at once.

Francis stayed where he was, smiling now. Bingo! Georgina was indeed staying here. Good of her to come out and show herself to him. Saved him a lot of trouble, that did.

He wasn't equipped to snatch her tonight, given the circumstances. He'd need help for that. Maybe Spencer would come with him, and they could hire another couple of men. It would be almost like an army exercise. He'd have been good at strategy, though he'd have hated the mud of the trenches.

He intended to prepare for getting hold of Georgina very carefully. He'd need somewhere to hide her till she could be persuaded to marry him. His present house was too small. The servants would see her.

Where better than her old home? Yes. That'd be perfect. They could tell people Miss Georgina was sick and being cared for by her mother if anyone asked and then keep her locked in a bedroom, or even the attics or the cellars, wherever was furthest away from the servants. Till she could be persuaded to do what they wanted.

He edged away and went back to the gate, climbing over it without being challenged by anyone. Ha! The grounds of this place were easy to enter. He'd bet the house would be just as easy to break into.

The large man heeded Sal's warning that she'd heard something moving in the bushes and it sounded too big to be an animal. She had the best hearing of anyone he knew, so Cole sat and listened with her, nodding to show he'd picked up the faint sounds now. They'd had people try to break in before.

After Georgie had called Sal in to attend to her daughter, the watcher moved backwards and started to make his way towards the gate, so he must have been reconnoitring.

Cole followed the faint sounds of movement along the drive. The man was either a fool or overconfident, or both. He made quite a lot of noise.

Definitely a fool! he quickly decided. Once he was away from the house, the intruder didn't even try to hide.

There was enough moonlight for Cole to see that he was tall and thin, and something about his clothing and bearing said he was a gentleman. You could usually tell. Well, they'd had gentlemen try to break into Honeyfield House before and they hadn't succeeded. Nor would this one if he came back.

Cole stayed near the gate, watching the intruder walk away down the road. He waited, listening hard, until he heard the sound of a motor car engine starting.

'Just you try to get into our house, mister,' he muttered as he walked quietly back to his bench. He'd tell Matron about the intruder tomorrow and they'd put a few other measures into operation.

He leant back and sighed happily. This was the best job he'd ever had. He was treated well, given as much as he wanted to eat and paid regularly.

And on top of that there was Sal, a fine figure of a woman. He was courting her and he thought he was making progress.

She'd told him about the rape but said she'd never

willingly given her body to anyone except her husband otherwise. If he ever caught up with the sods who'd done it, Cole would make them wince where it hurt a man most.

Since Sal was a widow, they were both free to marry, so why not propose to her? He didn't just want her body; he wanted her companionship.

Yes, life was good here and he wasn't going to let anyone upset the apple cart. So Mr Scraggy Gentleman had better watch out.

When Sal had settled her little daughter, she went to join the others in the kitchen. 'A man was prowling round the gardens just now.'

They fell instantly silent.

'Cole went after him but I looked out of the window and Cole's back now so the man must have gone away.'

So Matron called Cole in and asked him what he'd found out about their latest intruder.

'I followed him to the gate. He had a car down the road. I'm pretty sure he's a gentleman. Don't ask me how I know, there's just something about the way some of them move around, as if they own the world.'

'I wonder who he is and where he's from?'

'I don't know, but as soon as he caught sight of you, Georgie love, he left. Made me wonder if you were the one he came for.'

'Oh, no!' She looked at him in dismay.

They gave Cole a cup of cocoa and started to go through the incident all over again.

'I think we should take some extra precautions, Matron,'

Cole finished up. 'If this fellow brings others back with him, well, I'm a good fighter but I'm only one man.'

'What exactly did the man look like?' Georgie asked. 'And what sort of car was he driving?'

'There was enough moonlight to see that he was tall and very thin. Oh, and I noticed he had a sort of sway to his shoulders as he walked. Strange way of walking, I thought. I didn't see the car, just heard it.'

'Oh, heavens!'

They all turned to look at her questioningly.

'That sounds like Francis,' she said with a shiver. 'The man I used to be engaged to. If he's found me, I've got to leave. He can be nasty when he wants something.'

'Don't go away,' Sal said. 'It'll be easier for us to keep you safe here.' She gave Georgie a sudden hug. 'Aw, don't look like that. Them ladies who run this place will pay for extra help. They know what it's like. Saints, them Greyladies are, or just as good as. And so are the others who help them.'

Georgie still didn't look convinced, so Matron patted her hand. 'We've had situations like this before. There are things we can do.'

'What exactly?'

'I'll tell you tomorrow, when it's all organised. There are one or two men from the village who help us from time to time. I'll tell you who it is once I've seen who has the time to help. One thing is fairly sure: they're not likely to come after you in daylight. Too many people knocking about in the village and the fields nearby.'

Cole put his mug down. 'Thanks for that, Sal. I'll go and

take a little walk round, make sure he hasn't come back.'

'I'll come with you,' Sal said. 'I'll hear him before you do if he has.'

'We'll use your hearing tomorrow night too.' He nodded to the group of women and left.

Georgie went to bed soon afterwards, but she didn't sleep well. There was something nasty about Francis and she was quite sure he'd stop at nothing to get her back. But there wasn't anything he could say or do that would make her say the words that bound her to him for life in marriage.

She'd been fooled by him once, thinking him a pleasant enough man, but she wouldn't be fooled again. He was a friend of her brother Spencer. That said something about the type of man he was.

In the morning Georgie got up early, helped clean the house, which the children always seemed able to turn topsy-turvy within minutes, and did the reading lessons with Sal and Jean.

The two women were pathetically grateful, eager to learn to read properly and improving daily, it seemed, because they took the books away and practised together over and over. The sight of them sitting with their heads bent over a book brought tears to her eyes.

When she went outside she was surprised to see a large, fierce-looking black and tan dog lying in the sunshine. She wasn't sure who it belonged to or how friendly it was, so stayed by the door and waited to see what it would do.

A man came out of the stables, a small lean fellow with

a twisted face as if he'd been badly injured at some stage. But the eyes that looked out of that wreck of a face were kind and calm.

'I'm Patrick Doohey, miss. Come and meet my friend Jago.' He snapped his fingers and the dog ambled over to stand beside him, higher than his waist. 'Shake hands with the lady, Jago.'

It obligingly held out one huge paw, so Georgie shook it.

'He'll know you now,' Patrick told her quietly in a lilting Irish accent. 'If I ask him to shake hands, it means the person is a friend. He's never made a mistake about that. Best dog I ever had, my Jago is.'

'And what does he do if someone comes along who isn't a friend?'

'Depends what they're doing. If he's on guard, as he is now, and they try to pass him, he won't let them. And if I give the word he'll knock them down and stand over them.' He patted her arm, as if gentling her. 'Don't you be afraid of him, now. He's here to help with the guarding of you.'

'That's good to know.'

Two of the children came rushing round the corner just then and stopped in terror at the sight of the dog.

Georgie watched as Patrick introduced them and went through the same shaking hands ritual, which they clearly enjoyed.

'Go and tell the others to come and meet Jago,' he told them. 'He can't play with you, though, because he's on guard duty here, keeping everyone safe.'

Matron came out to join them and Georgie asked, 'Is

this one of the precautions you were telling me about?'

'It is. We do our best to look after our visitors, whoever comes after them. And Patrick hires his dog out for guard duties. He's well known in the area. We're lucky he has a few days free and can help us.'

Georgie felt better after that, but still there was a shadow of worry lingering. Her mother could be very cunning. And didn't like to give up when she wanted something.

Oh dear! Georgie did wish she could live a normal life and feel safe again. She let out a soft huff of laughter as she contemplated this. When had she ever lived a normal life? It seemed as if she'd been at her mother's beck and call ever since she was old enough to run an errand.

In another part of the village of Honeyfield, Tez stopped his car in Pear Tree Lane and saw Isabella watching for him from the window. The way she instantly looked more cheerful and waved to him vigorously made him decide to take a risk.

He knew how lonely she felt at times and had wondered about asking if he could stay here permanently and maybe after a while he would be able to . . . No, he mustn't do anything about that yet.

She opened the door with a beaming smile and he stood by the car for a moment, enjoying the sight of her pretty face. There was something about being pregnant that seemed to give a woman an inner glow, if that wasn't too fanciful a thing to say.

As he was about to go inside the happy moment was shattered when another car pulled up in the street. To his horror he saw that Spencer Cotterell was driving it.

Tez hurried down the path, not sure whether she'd noticed who the newcomer was, but of course she had. Her face had gone white and she looked horrified.

It was no use pretending they hadn't seen him, so Tez made sure he was slightly in front of her as they waited to see what he wanted.

Spencer got out of the car, walking purposefully towards the house. He stopped a couple of paces away and stared from one to the other, letting the silence add to the tension.

'What are you doing here?' she asked in the end.

'I've come to see you and find out if what I was told was true. And I see it is.' He stared down at her belly.

'I have no desire to see you or speak to you, so you can just go away again,' she said firmly.

'Oh, I think you do need to speak to me. And you should invite me in to do it, Bella, because what I have to tell you will be better done in private.'

She exchanged glances with Tez, who could only shrug and leave it up to her.

'Come in, then.'

Tez followed her in and made sure he still stayed between her and Cotterell.

When she indicated an armchair, the visitor stood in front of it and waited for her to sit down on the sofa opposite him before sitting down. Tez took the place next to her on the sofa.

'Very cosy here, aren't you?' Spencer sneered. 'Didn't take you long to find another protector, did it, *Miss* Bella Jones? I've been asking around in the village and it seems he comes here every weekend. And you're calling yourself *Mrs* Tesworth. Tut! Tut!'

Tez could see her blushing but there was nothing he could do or say to help the embarrassment of her position. Not yet, anyway.

Cotterell continued speaking, his tone mocking. 'The people in the shop think it's sweet how much in love you two are and how you miss your *husband* when he's gone. Wonder what they'll say when I tell them you're not married but living in sin?'

He looked round the room. 'You set her up nicely here, didn't you, Tesworth? Or did she use the money she got out of my mother for the Malmesbury house?'

Isabella found her voice. 'If you've only come here to sneer at me, you can leave immediately.'

'Oh, I'm going to do more than sneer, don't worry. I'm going to talk about *that*.' He jabbed one forefinger towards her stomach. 'I'm assuming it's Philip's child.'

'None of your business whose it is,' she said.

He turned to Tez. 'I doubt it's yours, because you and she didn't get together till after Philip was killed. And reluctant as I am to admit it, I doubt she cheated on him.'

Isabella laid one hand on Tez's arm. 'Don't discuss anything with him.'

He stared at her and gave a quick nod.

She turned back to her visitor. 'Please get on with what you're here to say, Mr Cotterell. I'm sure you have a purpose in coming here but I find you a most unpleasant visitor and shall be glad to see you go.'

He leant back and grinned at them, suddenly even more

happy that he'd pushed his mother into agreeing to this. 'Oh, you're right. I'm not just here for a social visit; I'm here on some rather important official business.' He pulled an envelope out. 'This is from our lawyer, giving you notice that my mother and I intend to claim that child and bring it up properly, instead of leaving it here in a nest of sin.'

'What on earth makes you think I'll give up my child?'

'You won't have a choice. It's his considered opinion that no court will support a whore like you bringing up a Cotterell when the child could be raised by a decent family of blood relations.'

Tez thought longingly of punching him in the face. 'Shall I throw him out for you?'

She shook her head but didn't speak.

Spencer waited but she still said nothing and he seemed disappointed by that. 'Aren't you even going to comment?'

'Not till I've seen my own lawyer.'

'Won't do any good. You don't have the moral standing to fight back.'

He tossed a large envelope on to the small table between them and stood up. 'Look after yourself for the next few months. We want a healthy child out of this.'

He sauntered out of the house and it was Tez who accompanied him and then came back and locked the front door.

When he went back to Isabella, he was expecting to find her in tears. Instead she was looking both angry and fierce.

'Aren't you going to open the envelope?' he asked gently.

'You do it. I'm trying to keep calm, for the baby's sake,

but my heart is racing and I feel as if I'm going to explode with anger.'

He opened the envelope and read the letter, but it merely said in long, legal phrases what Spencer had summed up for them.

'I'll have to run away,' she said. 'But I'll need to do it carefully so that they can never, ever find me and my child.'

'There is another alternative.'

'Oh? What?'

'You could marry me. I'm sure I'm respectable enough for any court and we can say the baby's mine. We won't be able to claim that we were already married, but we can get a special licence and do the job as quickly as is possible.'

'Oh, Tez. How kind of you! But I won't take advantage of you like that. It wouldn't be fair to you.'

'On the contrary, I fell in love with you almost from the minute I set eyes on you. I couldn't do anything about it so soon after Philip's death, but I dared to hope that you might turn to me. I was waiting for you to have the baby before I proposed. Well, you've needed time to get over your grief.'

'Do you ever stop missing someone?' she asked, almost as if she was speaking to herself.

'I'll never stop missing Philip. But now, well, I'm asking you please to marry me and let me help you keep and raise his child. You will both be loved, believe me.'

She stared at him in shock as it sank in that he really did care deeply for her.

'I know you don't love me, Isabella, but we're good friends and I'm sure we can live happily together. I'd be delighted to act as father to Philip's child. I've already told you I want to be a godfather, after all.'

'But—'

'I hoped you'd grow to love me before I proposed, but thanks to the Cotterells there won't be time for that. Isabella darling, please marry me.'

Chapter Sixteen

Spencer drove home feeling pleased about what he'd done. It had been sheer pleasure to confront her while holding the whip hand. He'd been dying to get back at that bitch.

He went into the sitting room and found his mother staring into space.

She jumped in shock as he spoke to her. 'Sorry. What was that you said?'

'I asked if you were all right, Mother. You appear to be a bit, um, distracted.'

'It's your father. He's coming down tomorrow or the day after. He's not sure which yet. He wants to speak to us both, says it's important.' She couldn't hide a quick shiver.

He sat down, feeling surprised, studying her carefully. She gave the impression today of being even more afraid of his father than he'd realised. Well, the old man could be severe, but he would never actually *hurt* a woman, surely? 'Why are you so upset about that? You probably won't be seeing him again for years afterwards.'

'Because I don't know what he really wants. He doesn't come down here for years and then suddenly I get a phone call, not from him but from his secretary, saying he'll be arriving on Friday or Saturday afternoon, he doesn't yet know which. It's bound to be something bad that brings him here. It always is.'

Spencer waited but she didn't reveal anything else, so he said lightly, 'Well, he'll no doubt tell us what the matter is on Friday.'

'I'd rather be prepared before I face him.'

'You're not making sense. Prepared for what?'

'Well, for one thing, what we're going to do about that woman. How did it go today?'

He leant back, smiling. 'I shocked her rigid, and serve her damned well right. After all, the lawyer told us she won't stand a chance against us in a court.'

'I know. But I've been thinking about what you're planning. I don't want to be responsible for bringing up a child again. I've done that before and it's an utter bore. And anyway, I'll probably be dead before it grows up.'

'A bit late for saying that, don't you think? But if you won't take on the job, I'll do it.' His father surely wouldn't complain about them bringing up Philip's child and making him the heir.

'You're not in good enough health.'

'I'm not on my last legs yet and I can hire a nanny, can't I?'

She looked at him and he saw tears well in her eyes. 'You're getting weaker, Spencer. I can't help noticing.'

'I'll live long enough to bring up a child, believe me. I know I probably won't live as long as you will, but I'm still able to enjoy life.'

'But what if you *don't* live long enough? I can't see

your father taking over the child-rearing. He was never interested in you.'

'Or the twins.'

'That was because I told him to stay away if he wanted me to mother them.'

'I don't understand.'

'You don't need to understand the details and it's better if you don't.' She breathed in deeply. 'Anyway, we can discuss that after we find out what he wants. Go through what happened today in detail: what you told her, how she looked, I want to know every single word she spoke, every expression that crossed her face.'

'She looked to be in blooming health, damn her!' But he went through everything he could remember, hoping this information would calm his mother down.

It didn't. She went on and on about it, worrying that they'd jumped in too quickly with the Jones woman when there must be another three or four months to go before the birth. Then she asked him to repeat the details of their encounter all over again, for heaven's sake.

You'd think from his mother's comments that *he* had done something wrong. And yet, it had been she who'd brought in the lawyer and then insisted on giving the woman warning straight away. She'd said it would reconcile the woman to losing her baby. She'd also hired a local man the lawyer knew of in Honeyfield to keep watch on things in the village from now on.

He mentioned the man he knew of and she said no, she wanted this lawyer's man to do it because he had family in Honeyfield and would fit in well.

'Oh, very well!' He'd give his man a few bob to pacify him, in case he needed to use him later.

His mother hadn't mentioned his sister Georgina for days, so he tried to turn the conversation to her, because she needed dealing with as well. But his mother refused point-blank to talk about her, which was strange. You'd think she'd want her daughter back, but she just waved one hand dismissively and said she had enough problems on her plate and would leave that ungrateful girl for Francis to deal with.

'He's certainly planning to get hold of her and she won't find it pleasant. He's still furious at her.'

'Good. I hope he catches her and that'll serve her right. He won't let her get away again.'

Spencer was rapidly losing the last shreds of his patience with his mother and was relieved to be called away to the phone before he said something he'd regret.

'Spencer? It's me, Francis. Can you come round at once? Something's cropped up, something very important. It's to do with your sister.'

'I don't think—'

'Do you want to get her back or not? *And* her money! And surely you don't want her to continue spreading lies about us all? Once she marries me those rumours will die down, I promise you.'

Spencer sighed. He'd better keep an eye on things. He didn't want Francis going too far with Georgina. 'All right. I'll be round in about an hour. Have to settle my mother down first. She's upset about something.'

'She's always upset about something.'

So was Francis lately. Spencer put the phone down and went to tell his mother that Georgina had been sighted and there was a chance of Francis getting her back.

She stared blankly at him for a moment or two, then said, 'I suppose it's better to have her where we can keep an eye on her. I did wonder if we should just leave her be. I can't make up my mind.'

'Well I can. Francis should be the one to keep an eye on her. He seems very sure he can persuade her to marry him. He'll have a hard time doing that. She's as stubborn as they come.'

'He'll find a way to tame her and serve her right. Now, that's enough about her. I'd better see Cook and discuss what we'll have for dinner when your father comes. And I need to make sure his bedroom is absolutely immaculate. He hates anything in there to be disturbed, even though he hasn't slept in it more than half a dozen times since he left me just after the twins were born.'

Why did she always keep up the fiction that his father had left her? Spencer wondered. He still remembered the rows, even though he'd only been a child then. If anything, they'd parted company by mutual agreement and with mutual sighs of relief. And she'd never cared two hoots about the twins. Though if what he suspected was true, it was no wonder.

You didn't have to go to war to see people fighting one another. He was surrounded by them. No wonder he was a bit tired lately, given all the problems that kept cropping up.

Oh well, he'd better get round to Francis's house and see what the latest news was about Georgina. And he'd make sure Francis didn't go too far.

Isabella stared at Tez for such a long time that he was convinced she was going to refuse to marry him. Then she nodded and said in a low voice, 'Yes. I will marry you, Tez. And not just for the child. I've grown fond of you.' She gave a sad smile. 'I feel as if I know you better than I ever knew poor Philip. Well, no wonder. We've spent more time together than he and I did.'

'I'm glad you've agreed to marry me.' She hadn't said the word love, but what she'd said was more than he'd hoped for.

'We'd better book a wedding as quickly as we can.'

'How quickly can we do it?'

He frowned, then said slowly, 'I don't know much about it because this is the first time I've thought seriously of getting married. But some chaps have gone home for a few days' leave and got married straight away, and I knew they hadn't had banns called or anything like that. It'll have to be in a registry office, of course, not a church. Shall you mind that?'

'Not at all.'

He snapped his fingers as he suddenly realised what to do. 'I think I should phone my mother and ask her advice. She knows everybody and if anyone can help us fix it all up quickly, she can.'

Tez went to the phone and was on it for a long time, then came out looking surprised. 'That mother of mine is a miracle worker. She wants us to go up to London straight away.'

Isabella was startled. 'Today?'

'Yes. You won't believe this, but she's just fixed up a wedding for another chap who's home on leave and says she can slip us in with him. It's something to do with an archbishop she knows or is related to or something. I couldn't make sense of it all. But if she says she can arrange it, believe me she can. She's an amazing woman. How long will it take you to pack? If this haste doesn't put you off, that is.'

'It doesn't put me off. And the sooner we marry the better. It'll take me fifteen minutes at most to pack. But what shall we do about keeping our departure secret? I wouldn't be surprised to find Spencer Cotterell had got someone keeping an eye on us.'

'I don't think it matters. We'll notice if a car is following us and we'll be able to give it the slip. And if it's just someone in the village who's reporting to him, the person probably won't have a car. I haven't seen any new cars around and I'd notice with only half a dozen or so in the area. So you don't need to worry about anyone following us all the way to London.'

'You're right. Sorry. I get a bit nervous after someone tried to push my car off the road.'

'Not surprising. Now, I'm back to driving properly now, so we'll go in my car, eh?'

She nodded, then hesitated before coming across to him and kissing him on the cheek. 'You say your mother is amazing, but so are you, Tez.'

He put his arm round her and dared to return her kiss

gently. 'No. Just one who loves you, Isabella, darling.'

'I feel honoured and I'm truly fond of you, too.' She moved away. 'I must pack. I won't have a fancy wedding dress, I'm afraid.'

'Who cares? I'd marry you if you were dressed in a sack.'

She smiled. 'Oh, I think I can do better than that.'

He watched her run lightly up the stairs, then went out to check his car. As an afterthought, he took a part out and disabled her car – well, he hoped he'd disabled it. He didn't want anyone trying to drive it away. He'd seen how enviously Spencer looked at it as he left.

He'd been surprised by how Cotterell suddenly looked as old as his father, whom Tez had occasionally seen in London. And something about Cotterell seemed strange. He was almost but not quite wild-eyed, almost but not quite feverish in the way he acted. Tez hadn't been the only one to comment on his strangeness and ladies tended to avoid Cotterell.

Oh, what was he worrying about that for? He was going to marry the woman he loved and the rest of the world could go hang, for all he cared.

Isabella came rushing out of the house to join him. As she locked the front door, he put her case in his car with his own, then started up the motor and got in.

He felt truly happy as he drove off. This was what he wanted more than anything in the world.

He was determined to make Isabella happy, absolutely determined. He'd love Philip's child too. How could he not?

And if he hadn't lost his fingers, he'd not be here to rescue her. He never thought he'd be glad of it!

* * *

The old man digging his garden and keeping an eye on Pear Tree Lane straightened up when he saw the car leave. Once it had passed, he cut across the green to the back lane on the other side and ran down it to the stile. Sitting on the top bar, he waited, looking down the hill at the patchwork of fields and roads spreading over the gentle slope.

Ah, there it was! He watched carefully where the car went as it made its way from the village along the narrow road that twisted across to join the main road.

He stayed there till the car was out of sight, then went to use the telephone at the village shop, paying a high price for making a call out of the area.

He didn't care. The man who was paying him to keep watch would want to know what was happening as soon as possible.

Where were those two going?

He'd been shocked to hear they were living in sin, shocked to the core to know that it was someone else's baby, not Mr Tesworth's. He didn't approve of that sort of behaviour and had been surprised to think of a nice lady like the so-called Mrs Tesworth acting immorally.

But he hadn't said anything to anyone else in the village, and he was in a telephone cubicle at the side of the shop, so the nosey bitch behind the counter couldn't hear what he was saying.

Spencer was still out when the call came through, so his mother took it. She quickly realised this must be the man keeping watch on the Jones woman and made him tell her his news.

Frowning, she hung the earpiece up on its stand and paced up and down, chewing at her gums, wondering what to do about this. In the end, she rang up Francis and asked to speak to her son.

'They're running away,' she said as soon as she heard Spencer's voice.

'Who are?'

'Tesworth and *her*. Your watcher just rang to tell you they've gone off in the car and he thinks they're going to London. He watched from the hill to see which direction they took.'

'Oh, hell! It doesn't rain but it pours. Who'd have thought they'd get out so quickly? Well, there's nothing I can do about them at the moment and really, unless they skip the country, which is just about impossible in wartime – and who'd want to risk being torpedoed anyway? – they'll probably come back to the village.'

'What do you think they're going to London for?'

'To see if they can get married, I should think. But it won't affect the custody of the child, because *he* isn't the father and she won't dare claim that he is under oath. And anyway, you can't just get married. There are all sorts of formalities to be gone through first, like calling the banns or buying a special licence. No, the only thing they can do is start the process.'

'You're sure of that?'

'Yes, of course I am. I checked it all out before I went to see them. Now, if that's all?'

'For the moment. Will you be home to dinner?'

'Yes.'

'We'll talk further then.'

* * *

Francis looked up when Spencer rejoined him. 'What was your mother fussing about?'

'The Jones bitch and Tesworth have run off. I reckon they'll be trying to get married, but that takes time. And anyway, they've nowhere else to go, even if they do marry. No, they'll go back to Honeyfield and then we'll all have to wait for the baby to be born.'

'We've a more urgent matter to deal with first. Your sister. I want to snatch her tomorrow night.'

'No can do. My father is coming down for a visit, goodness only knows why. He hardly ever does that, so my mother is panicking.'

'He's coming tomorrow?'

'Either tomorrow or Saturday, arriving in the afternoon, apparently.'

'Well, I need you tomorrow, so you can just tell him you already had an engagement.'

Spencer whistled softly. 'You don't *tell* my father anything of the sort. He usually tells you what to do.'

'Tell him the truth then, that we're going to bring back your sister.'

'No, I don't think so. It's not the sort of thing he'd approve of.'

'I was going to bring her to Westcott to hide her, because your house is so big.'

'What, with my father there? Definitely not.'

'All right, but you'd better help me. I know too much about you.'

There was dead silence, then Spencer gave in. 'He might come tomorrow or Saturday. Let's hope it's not tomorrow.

Everything will be easier if I don't have to make any excuses to him. Go through the details of what you're planning and we'll see if there's any way of making things happen more easily. I don't want to get into a damned battle! You should have joined the army if that's what you're after. Apart from anything else, fighting would attract the attention of the local police and we don't want that.'

'If we have enough men, it'll be over and done before the police can get there. I'm good at planning things. You're right. I'd have been good in the army. Pity I didn't pass the medical.'

Spencer had heard all this before and though he admitted Francis was quite good at planning things, he didn't think his friend was as good as *he* thought he was. And Francis would never have coped with the physical side of things in the army. He wheezed whenever he had to exert himself.

'I'm waiting for a call from the chappie who's keeping watch on this Honeyfield House for me.'

Spencer rolled his eyes but said nothing. How many spies could there be in Honeyfield?

'Norman's prepared to help us get into it. He seems to have some sort of grudge against the chap keeping watch there.'

'Heaven help us, what next?'

Francis grinned. 'Amazing, isn't it, that both of the women who're causing us trouble are living in the same village and don't know it?'

'Well, they're not close friends or anything, are they? They only met a couple of times. Why should they have kept in touch?'

* * *

When Tez and Isabella arrived in London, they drove straight to his mother's house, parking in the mews behind it.

Mrs Tesworth was a tall, elegant woman who looked as intelligent as her son. There was something similar about their eyes, a sort of awareness and understanding of the world, Isabella thought. But his mother seemed pleasant enough, thank goodness.

Tez outlined the situation quickly, but emphasised that he had been wanting to marry Isabella anyway when the time was right.

His mother studied the young woman her son wanted so badly and nodded slowly. 'You don't seem like a gold-digger, Isabella.'

'Mother!' he protested.

'I had wondered a bit about that after I got your call,' she said mildly. 'I didn't know whether Isabella realised how little money you'll have.'

'I have some money of my own, anyway,' Isabella said stiffly. 'More than enough to live on. Philip left me everything.'

'Good. Because we aren't rich and Tez is my third son. Anyway, we're not here to chat. I like the looks of you and my son isn't a fool.'

Isabella was amazed at her frankness but on the other hand, she felt she knew where she stood with Tez's mother, and that wasn't a bad thing when something happened so quickly.

'We have to go and see the archbishop's secretary at once.' Mrs Tesworth studied her visitor openly. 'Who's your dressmaker?'

Isabella was surprised by this non sequitur. 'A woman in the village.'

'She's good. Your clothes will serve for today but not for the wedding. We need to do something about that.' She rang the bell and a woman answered it.

'This is Lacey, my maid. Lacey, this is my son's wife-to-be, Isabella. Can we find her something to get married in tomorrow morning?'

The maid studied the younger woman. 'Yes. I think so, madam. I can adapt one of your old frocks from when you were expecting.'

'Thank you. You are, as always, a miracle worker.' She turned back to her son. 'Well, let's go.'

Tez winked at Isabella and she felt comforted. She clutched his arm as they were swept out of the house by Mrs Tesworth. She felt like a fish out of water here in this quietly luxurious house, but she tried not to let that show. She'd do anything to keep her child safe.

And Tez was a great comfort to her in many ways, large and small. Such a lovely man.

The interview was very brief. The archbishop's secretary asked them a few questions, scribbled down the answers, and said fretfully, 'This is all very irregular, Mrs Tesworth.'

'There's a war on, my dear cousin. We can't always stick to the rules if we're to keep our fighting men happy.'

'Yes. And that's the only reason you're getting away with it. Well, they'll have to get here at seven-thirty in the morning. There's no other time they can be fitted in.'

She gasped. 'Good heavens! For a wedding? I can't

remember the last time I got up so early for any reason.'

He gave her a dirty look and she sighed. 'All right. We'll do it.'

When they stood up to go, she kissed the secretary on the cheek. 'Thank you, coz. Tez deserves to be happy, don't you think, after what he's been through?'

He looked at Tez's injured hand and his expression softened. 'Yes. All our brave lads do. Tomorrow at seven-thirty in the morning. Do not be late, either, Marguerite.'

'We won't.'

On the way home she said feelingly, 'I hope you appreciate what I'm doing for you, Tez darling, the favours I'm calling in.'

Chapter Seventeen

To Spencer's relief, his father didn't turn up at Westcott on Friday afternoon. He waited till six o'clock then went to find his mother, who had been dithering and fussing all day.

'Since Father hasn't turned up today, I'm going over to see Francis this evening.'

She grabbed his arm. 'You can't! What if he turns up after you've gone? And anyway, you're looking terrible today. You need to rest.'

'I'm bored with resting! As to my father, he said *afternoon* and he usually sticks to what he's arranged. But if he does turn up this evening you'll have to give him my apologies and tell him I had a prior arrangement. He won't want you to entertain him; he'll probably want to work on some papers, knowing him. He's always busy with paperwork!'

It had been the excuse most often given to Spencer during his childhood for his father not being able to spend time with him and he had never believed that to be the real reason.

He unclenched her fingers from his arm. 'I really don't think he'll come now, Mother.'

She dropped into the nearest chair. 'I hope you're right. But this means that I've got all the hanging around waiting to do again tomorrow. Do you think there's any chance that one of his staff will ring to cancel the whole visit?'

'Who knows? Anything can happen with *him*.'

Spencer made his escape and drove off quickly to Francis's house. To his surprise there was no dinner waiting for him, only a nervous friend ready to set off for Honeyfield as soon as he arrived.

'Thank goodness you're here. I was starting to think you weren't coming.'

'Well, I am here.'

'We can go straight away. It'll be dark by the time we get there.'

'But I haven't eaten.'

Francis grabbed an apple from the meagre fruit bowl on his sideboard and tossed it to him. 'This'll hold you.'

'So we're actually doing it, then – invading someone's house and grabbing Georgina?'

Francis grinned. 'We are. Quite exciting, what? Our own little war games.'

And Spencer found himself getting excited too. He didn't bother with the apple, wasn't hungry now that something was happening. Was this how men felt before going into battle? He'd never know, but it was good to feel excitement coursing through his veins instead of boredom, good to feel alert, instead of lying around with a headache, feeling listless.

* * *

When he saw Mrs Farquhar stroll along by the village green and call in at her friend's house, Norman took advantage of Mrs Nosey Parker's absence from Pear Tree Lane to go for a stroll of his own.

One man nodded a greeting as he passed and he forced himself to smile back. It was useful having an aunt still living here in Honeyfield. He'd been able to visit her for a few days without anyone being suspicious as they would have been of a stranger. And he'd slipped his aunt a pound for his keep, far more than his food would cost her, saying he'd pay more if he stayed longer. She was always glad of extra money.

He'd seen the new couple from Pear Tree Cottage drive off earlier and had chatted to old Dan, who seemed to have been watching them from the churchyard. Dan was angry at them for some reason, muttering about immorality. Silly old fool! He should stick to cleaning the church and leave other people to manage their own lives.

Dan seemed to think the Tesworths had gone off to the fleshpots of London. Fleshpots! Norman spat at a nearby bush at the mere thought of that. London was just a big city and if you didn't have a lot of money, you didn't get much chance to have fun there, especially in wartime.

It was hard to earn enough to survive on, let alone go out drinking and having fun. He knew that from experience. Even a visit to the cinema cost more in London, though the pianists accompanying the films were no better than those in the provinces.

All he'd got while in London was a white feather from some ugly young woman. That was rich. He'd laughed in her face. As if he bloody well cared about a feather! He'd gone to a lot of trouble to stay out of the army, thank you very much, and wasn't at all ashamed of pretending to have a weakness in the arm that had been badly scarred when he fell into the fire as a child.

Glad not to have Mrs Farquhar peeping out of her front window, Norman still took the precaution of slipping into the garden of the empty house and making his way from there over the low garden wall into the rear garden of Pear Tree Cottage. He had a vague memory of there being a gate in the back wall and if so, it might lead out through the orchards to the back of Honeyfield House. Mr Filmore would surely pay him extra for finding a sure way to get into the big house without alerting anyone by going down the drive.

He walked round the garden but couldn't see a gate. His memory wasn't usually faulty, not about places he'd been to. He decided to have a sit in the summer house for a while and go over it all in his mind. It was too crowded at his aunt's house to think straight and he was having to sleep on the sofa, and ruddy uncomfortable it was, too.

And then he noticed the door at the back of the summer house and the memories clicked into place. He and another friend had crept round the gardens one night and – yes, of course! You got to the gate in the wall *through* the summer house. Silly arrangement, but there you were. You could be as silly as you pleased if you had the money.

He opened the summer house door and smiled broadly, but his smile faded when he tried the gate behind it and found it locked. There was no key in it, either. He'd rather not break it open. Perhaps the owner had hidden a key nearby? People did that sometimes; honest folk were such fools.

He hunted under flowerpots and under the ivy on the wall and was just about to give up when he heard a faint clink as he ran his fingers over the bricks. He pulled more of the ivy back at that spot and found a key. The mortar had been scraped away between two bricks and the key only just fitted into the gap. It was so rusty, he didn't suppose it'd been used for years, but when he tried it in the lock of the gate, it turned with only a small effort. Someone must have been oiling the lock.

Now what should he do? Mr Filmore wouldn't be getting to Honeyfield till about ten o'clock, but it'd be dark by then so not easy to reconnoitre. Norman glanced up at the sky, which was overcast. Coming up to autumn now. He didn't like winter.

What if he nipped out into the orchard and had a quick look over the back wall of Honeyfield House? He'd take care no one saw him. It was always good to be prepared. He didn't want the police brought into this, so if he knew the lie of the land, he might be able to help Mr Filmore snatch the woman with less fuss.

It was daft, kidnapping a woman, and he wouldn't have got involved if he hadn't needed the money. And if he hadn't seen that there might be an opportunity of thumping that bloody Cole senseless as they did it. He'd hated that goody-goody sod since they were lads together, and they'd fought one another a few times.

Decision taken, Norman opened the gate and slipped

through it, pausing for several minutes to listen. But there was no sound of anyone from the farm working nearby, so he walked along by the wall, finding two places where he could stand on something and peer over.

The third time he did that, he managed to haul himself into the branch of a big tree that hung over the wall. He sat there for a few minutes and was rewarded by the sight of a woman who looked just as Mr Filmore had described coming towards him. It had to be Miss Cotterell. Unfortunately she was with another female.

The more he studied her, the more sure he was that she was the one Mr Filmore was after: tall, thin and ladylike with long curly hair. Then her companion called her 'Georgie' and that confirmed who she was.

If he could get rid of the companion, damned if he wouldn't be able to snatch the woman now. He could gag her and tie her up, then hide her in the tumbledown old house till Mr Filmore arrived.

Next minute fate gave him a helping hand and the other woman suddenly exclaimed, 'Oops! I forgot to take that apple pie out of the oven. I'll be back in two minutes. Wait for me here.'

Grinning, Norman edged on to another big branch that drooped down the other side of the wall. He dropped down on to the soft earth beneath it and crept up behind the woman.

At the last minute she seemed to sense his presence, but it was too late by then. He grabbed her and clapped his hand over her mouth.

She fought hard, he admired that, but he was stronger by

far than any woman and in the end he had her on the ground, gagged and trussed up. He'd always found it useful to keep bits of rope and string in his pockets. You never knew when they'd come in useful. And she had a thin, dangly scarf thing round her neck, so he also used that.

Slinging her over his shoulder, he went back up the tree, glad she wasn't any heavier because it took a huge effort to get her up into the branches. She kept wriggling, so he whispered, 'If you don't stay still, I'll have to knock you out.'

That stopped her struggling but she glared at him, her eyes full of hatred. As if he cared about how she felt! He moved carefully, not wanting to damage her because Mr Filmore was apparently going to marry her. It seemed a strange way to get a wife. Who wanted one, anyway? Not him!

Norman had nothing against her. It was just a job. So he was glad he didn't have to knock her out. Still moving quietly he took her back to the gate, locked it after them and edged carefully through the rear gardens of the houses, panting now.

The tumbledown house was perfect for his purpose, so he set her down and fastened her to the old pipes in the laundry wall next to the sink. He made sure she was tied securely then stood back and studied her. No, she'd not get away.

'You're not going to be hurt,' he told her because behind her efforts to get free he could tell she was terrified. 'There's a gentleman as wants you, and he doesn't want you hurt.'

He would wait on the road that led out of the village for Mr Filmore's car to arrive and guide him to the deserted house.

It was, he thought smugly again, his lucky day.

* * *

When the man had gone Georgie tried to get free but soon gave up struggling because she hadn't had any effect on the thin ropes binding her and biting into her wrists and ankles. She couldn't believe she was lying here helpless. It had all happened so quickly.

As time passed she grew more and more uncomfortable. Her only hope was that the people she was living with would come looking for her. And with the dog's help, surely they'd find where she'd been taken.

It was Francis who'd arranged this kidnapping, obviously, from what her kidnapper had said. But if she hadn't insisted on going out for a breath of fresh air, he wouldn't have caught her. She'd been stupid. But you got so fed up of being shut indoors all the time.

Darkness crept slowly over everything and she couldn't hold back tears. They trickled down her cheeks, drying in cold trails on her skin.

Where were her friends?

Why hadn't someone come to rescue her?

And what was Francis going to do with her? Her kidnapper said she wouldn't be hurt, but that wasn't true. Francis would hurt her if he had to. He'd think he could *force* her to marry him.

She wouldn't do it. But she wasn't looking forward to proving that to him.

Gerald Cotterell was just about to finish work early and let his chauffeur drive him down to Honeyfield when his secretary came back from an errand. As she was the best secretary he'd ever had, he always paid attention when she came in to tell him something. She often passed titbits of information that came in useful.

'You'll never guess who I saw just now at the archbishop's palace, Mr Cotterell.'

He waited, one eyebrow raised. She didn't gossip for no reason, so it must have been something unexpected and of possible interest to him. She knew he collected information like a magpie collected glittering stones. To his mind, jewels were overprized, while information could turn keys in many locks, especially during a war, as enough of the military bigwigs understood, thank goodness.

'I saw your son Philip's friend Mr Tesworth with a young lady. What surprised me was that she was the young lady who was engaged to your son. She looks just like the photo you showed me.'

He nodded, frowning. 'A pleasant enough young woman, I gather. I have no objection to her marrying Tesworth now Philip's dead.'

'Well, sir, the reason I thought you ought to know about it is that she's expecting.' She cupped one hand at her stomach suggestively. 'Must be five or six months along.'

It wasn't hard to do the sums in his head. 'Ah. Now that could be interesting. Did you happen to find out what they were doing there?'

'Yes, sir. They were with Mrs Tesworth, arranging to get married.'

'Hmm. Please tell my chauffeur I shall not be going to Gloucestershire till later but I shall need him shortly for another purpose.'

'Yes, sir.'

'Could you find me Mrs Tesworth's address, please?'

'Of course. It'll be in our files.'

She was back with it in a couple of minutes.

'Tell my chauffeur to come round now.'

Gerald sat in the back of the car, his mind working furiously. He had kept out of the way of his children, partly because he wasn't paternal but mainly to keep them safe and respectable in his wife's household.

When Philip had been killed, he'd been more upset than at any time since the only woman he'd ever loved had died.

He doubted he was mistaken in his analysis of the situation: that unborn child must surely be his son's.

His eldest child, Spencer, had been no use to him as a son, born with serious faults to his masculinity that had horrified Gerald and made him loathe the infant. He'd looked into his wife's family background and found out that Spencer wasn't the only one to be afflicted that way in her family. He didn't think she knew nearly as much about that as he did, given the way her family concealed the problem.

He hadn't attempted to get any other children with her after that, however. He didn't want faulty offspring.

'We've arrived, sir.'

'Sorry. I was lost in thought.'

'Shall I go and see if Mrs Tesworth is at home, sir?'

'No, thank you. I'll do this myself. Wait for me here, please.'

When he knocked on the door Gerald felt diffident about what he had to ask as well as what he might find out. Such a feeling was unusual in him. He was not an emotional person, never had been.

But this was something he needed to know, and if it was Philip's child, that needed to be taken into account in his future arrangements.

Mrs Tesworth hesitated when a card was brought in and the butler told her the gentleman had said it was very important indeed that he see her at once. The visitor wasn't a friend of hers, though she knew him socially.

'Something wrong, Mother?'

'Gerald Cotterell has just turned up and wants to see me on a matter of importance.'

'Ah.'

Isabella looked from one to the other. 'Is that Philip's father?'

'Yes. Have you ever met him?'

'No. He wasn't at the engagement party and Philip seemed relieved at that. I was surprised when Mr Cotterell didn't turn up to his own son's memorial service, though.'

The door opened and a man stepped into the room. 'Please excuse me for pushing my way in, Mrs Tesworth, but this is extremely important and I must see you—' He stared round and added, 'All of you.'

She nodded dismissal to her butler. 'Do come in, then, Mr Cotterell.'

'Thank you.' He took the seat she'd indicated, but it was Isabella he was studying. 'Forgive me, but I have to ask if the child you're carrying is my son's, Miss Jones.'

Tez took her hand. 'Isabella is engaged to marry me, so I—'

But she squeezed his hand and said quietly, 'I think we

owe Mr Cotterell the truth. It needn't make any difference to our getting married.' She turned back to the visitor, studying his face with interest. The resemblance to Philip was strong, but the warmth that had characterised his son was lacking completely. She laid one hand on her stomach as she told him, 'Yes, this is Philip's child, but I don't care how many lawyers you and your wife produce, I'm not giving the child up to you.'

He looked at her in astonishment. 'Lawyers? Giving up the child? Who asked you to?'

'Your wife.'

'What the hell has that stupid fool of a woman been doing now?'

Norman made his way back to the green, staying out of sight, heading out of the village now.

There was no way he could carry her away from here without someone seeing him. They'd need to bring the car and take her away in that.

He was pleased when Mr Filmore turned up earlier than he'd expected.

When he lowered the window, Norman bent down to tell the men in the car what he'd done.

It was good to see the shock on their faces.

'I hope you'll see fit to pay me extra for that, sir? I've saved you a lot of trouble tonight.'

'Definitely! Well done. Let's go and get her.'

Norman crammed into the car with them and gave the driver instructions for getting through the village. When they stopped, he suggested the two gentlemen pretend to knock on the door of Pear Tree Cottage. 'There's no one in but it'll give you an excuse for being here if Mrs Nosey Parker across the street looks out, which she usually does.'

While they were doing that, he suggested he and the sturdy-looking man they'd brought with them go and fetch the woman. Pair of weaklings, the two gentlemen were, just playing at being tough.

He led the way quickly through the garden and into the house.

That's when he heard a dog baying from the orchard. 'Oh, hell, someone's come after her. Hurry up.'

They ran out with their burden and he shoved her into the car on the gentlemen's laps, saying, 'I'll ride on the running board. It'll be better if you drop me off at my aunt's so that no one can find anything unusual if they come round knocking on doors. I'd appreciate being paid.'

When they got near his auntie's, he rapped on the roof. As the car slowed down, he jumped off the running board and ran inside, hearing them drive away quickly but not turning round to watch them.

He told his relatives to say he'd been there all evening if anyone asked. 'I'll make it worth your while,' he promised.

'What've you been doing?' one of his cousins asked.

'Never you mind.'

His aunt said sharply, 'You heard our Norman. Do what he says. We don't want any of our family in trouble with the police.'

Once they'd left the village and turned on to the London road, Georgie heard Spencer say, 'Take the gag off her.

She seems distressed. We don't want to harm her.'

'It won't hurt her to suffer a little,' Francis protested. 'It'll make her more amenable later.'

'No. I'm going to take it off.' Spencer did so, then he and she stared at one another in the dimness.

'Fine brother you are!' she exclaimed.

'I've never liked you. You need a strong husband if you're not to disgrace the family.'

'What I need most at the moment is to use the lavatory. I can't hold it much longer. Do you want me to pee all over you?'

He shuddered. 'Give me your word you're not making this up in an attempt to escape.'

'I swear I'm not.' In spite of her determination not to appear weak, a sob escaped her. '*Please*, Spencer. That horrible man wouldn't let me relieve myself. It's been *hours*.'

'All right. Stop the car somewhere so my sister can relieve herself without anyone gaping at her. I'll just untie her.'

When they stopped, he refused to let Francis help her do this. 'Not till you're married to her, old chap.'

'Do you think you can force me to marry him?' she asked in a low voice as Spencer was watching her put her clothes straight and another man was nearby guarding them.

'Yes. Or at least *he* can force you. You might get hurt a little in the process but he's intending to teach you to obey him, not to maim you.'

'And you're going to let him hurt me?'

'Yes. I get some of your money after you're married, you see.' He took her back to the car.

'I hope you rot in hell!' she told him as he stood back to let her get in. This time they let her sit between them.

It seemed a long time till they reached their destination and Georgie felt sick with apprehension when she was dragged out of the car. Francis grabbed her hair and twisted her head back to say, 'If you make one sound as we're going into the house, I'll knock you out.'

That was the second time someone had threatened that, but he looked as if he'd enjoy doing it. She was more afraid of him than she'd expected. He had a mad look in his eyes she'd never seen before.

He frogmarched her into the house, bumping her against a couple of doorposts on the way in on purpose.

It hurt. But it also told her that he'd treat her like that for the rest of her life if she agreed to marry him. She had to stay strong and refuse.

Surely someone would come looking for her? And find her in time to stop him hurting her badly?'

Chapter Eighteen

When they explained to Gerald what his wife was threatening to do, Isabella understood suddenly why every member of his family was afraid of him. He didn't display any signs of temper and she couldn't work out why he suddenly looked so menacing, but she was relieved *she* wasn't the one in his black books. How did he manage that?

'What time is your wedding tomorrow?' he asked.

'Seven-thirty in the morning. It was the only time they could fit us in.'

'Good heavens! Well, I hope I'm invited? Apart from the fact that I'd like to attend, it'll look better if I'm there, don't you think?'

'Yes, of course you're invited,' Mrs Tesworth said at once. 'If you can get up at such an uncivilised hour. I can't remember the last time I left the house by seven o'clock.'

'I'm usually up and working by eight o'clock, so it won't be much different for me.'

'Well, you must come back here afterwards for a glass of champagne to celebrate.'

'Not this time, I'm afraid. Given the urgency of the situation, I think we'd do better to go straight to

Malmesbury and confront my wife and Spencer. After this, I intend to stop the two of them making a laughing stock of our family name, once and for all. She's avoided scandal till now, but this is going too far. Strange that Spencer's involved. I thought I'd removed any reason for him to commit a crime for money. I don't often misjudge people.'

'Perhaps he thought you wouldn't find out,' his hostess said.

'He should know me better.'

They heard the phone ring in the hall just then and the butler came in. 'I'm sorry to interrupt, Mrs Tesworth, but the caller asked me to tell you that it's a Greyladies matter and ask if you could spare her a few minutes?'

'Would you excuse me, please?' But she was walking out of the room even as she spoke and didn't wait for their answers.

'Isn't it the Greyladies Trust that runs Honeyfield House in our village?' Isabella looked uncertainly at Mr Cotterell.

'Yes. I gather Mrs Tesworth is involved, though she keeps that to herself.'

'I admire her for that.'

'Yes. I too appreciate the good work done by the trust and those who're involved,' he said quietly. 'But I don't know the details of any specific houses they run. Honeyfield House, eh?'

'It's supposed to be a convalescent home, but it's actually a place where women in trouble can find a safe refuge. Everyone in the village knows about it, but they don't usually say anything to strangers.'

'Ah. As I said, I admire the work done by the trust. And

I do not approve of physical violence on principle. There are usually more efficient ways of dealing with problems.'

Mrs Tesworth came back looking anxious. 'It's fortuitous that you're here tonight, Mr Cotterell. I'm afraid your daughter Georgie was kidnapped from Honeyfield House late this afternoon. No one is certain who did it or where she was taken. All they've found so far are traces that she'd been kept in an old deserted house for a while, and a car was seen to drive away from the village after dark but no one could give any details about it.'

The frightening look came back on to his face and his voice sounded like ice fracturing. 'Francis Filmore is behind this, I have no doubt. After your wedding, we'll go straight to his house and rescue her. In the meantime, I'll arrange for someone local to go to keep watch on Filmore's house and keep an eye on things to make sure they don't hurt her.'

'You're that certain it's him?' Tez asked in amazement.

'It's my business to know things, and that includes what my family's doing. He's been a friend of my elder son for years, so I've kept an eye on him for years. Both Spencer and Filmore have surprised me today. They'll both regret it.'

He stood up. 'I'm afraid I have to go and make the arrangements. Don't attempt to intervene. Leave the rescue and other details to me.'

When he'd gone, Isabella blew out her breath in a whoosh. 'He's – well, rather intimidating, don't you find?'

'My dear, everyone is afraid of upsetting him,' Mrs Tesworth said. 'I'm just glad he's on our side in the war. He's apparently made a big contribution to our side's struggle.'

'He's terrifying when he gets that look on his face,' Tez agreed. 'I'm glad he's not *my* father. Thank you very much for that, Mother.'

Mrs Tesworth managed a smile. 'I'd not like to have married him. Your father was much easier to manage. But at the moment we do need a terrifying person like Mr Cotterell to help us.'

She looked at Isabella. 'You look exhausted, dear, but do let Lacey give you a fitting for your wedding gown before you go to bed. I'll send a maid to wake you at six o'clock tomorrow morning. Make sure your things are all packed before we leave for the wedding.'

To Georgie's relief, Spencer wouldn't let Francis start to deal with her that night.

The two men went into the next room and she heard them arguing. When Spencer came back, he was on his own. He said grimly, 'You'd better sleep in my room, Georgina. You'll be safe there. I hadn't realised he was quite so, well, vicious. But then, he considers me his best friend so I'd not have seen that side of him as clearly before.'

'Thank you.'

He shrugged. 'Got to draw the line somewhere. I don't approve of rape, especially where my sister is concerned. I wish I hadn't got involved in all this.'

Spencer was looking dreadful, yellowish and haggard, but she didn't comment on that, just did as he told her without arguing because he was her only hope of safety tonight.

They passed Francis in the hall and he glared at her. 'You're too soft, Cotterell. Now would have been the perfect time.'

She held her breath.

'She's my sister. There is a limit to what I'll allow, even tomorrow.'

'Not if you want the money.'

'Even so.'

When they went into the shabby bedroom, Spencer said abruptly, 'Don't get undressed. It'll be safer.'

'I don't have any night clothes with me anyway. Are you all right, Spencer? You don't look well. Is there anything I can get you?'

He shrugged. 'A new body. I overestimated my strength tonight. I'm better if I lead a quiet life but I get bored with it.'

'I'm sorry you're not well.'

He looked at her in surprise. 'I believe you actually are.'

'Well, you are my brother.'

'Our relationship is not quite as simple as you think.'

'What do you mean by that? I don't understand.'

He refused to tell her any more, just said she should go to bed. She accepted the quilt and pillow he took from the bed and tossed at her, nestling down as best she could on a lumpy old chaise longue near the window.

He locked the door and waggled the key at her. 'I'll take this. It'd be no use you trying to get out without Francis hearing, but we don't want to give him any excuse to get hold of you tonight, do we? I'll think what's best to do in the morning, when I'm not as tired.'

He took the key into bed with him and she supposed he'd put it under his pillow. Surely the locked door would keep Francis out? Surely even he wouldn't knock the door down?

She'd expected to lie awake worrying but when the warmth of the quilt made her feel drowsy, she didn't try to stop herself falling asleep. She would need to be very alert in the morning. Anyway, she'd soon wake up if there were any noises in the now-quiet house.

Tez and Isabella's wedding was a perfunctory affair. They were the first couple getting married that day and the Church of England minister officiating yawned several times. He scowled at Mrs Tesworth, whom he seemed to know, but he hardly even glanced at the people he was marrying.

'I now declare you man and wife,' he ended up. 'You'll have to sign the register before you leave.'

'And we'll need a marriage certificate, John,' Mrs Tesworth said sweetly.

'I'll send one round to you when I have time, Marguerite.'

'We're not leaving today till we have it.'

He looked at Isabella's belly then shrugged. 'I suppose you want to flaunt the marriage in people's faces.'

'If we have to.'

He pulled out his watch. 'Oh, very well. At least this farce will be over and done with completely then. I do not approve of these rushed marriages. Now, let's hurry. I have another wedding to conduct at eight o'clock.'

Isabella felt sad that her wedding should be such a rushed

affair, but Tez put his arm round her and whispered, 'When everything's sorted out, we'll have a glass of champagne together and a little celebration of our own. I'm delighted to be married to you, however we've had to do it.'

His words brought comfort to her as they were rushed through the rest of the formalities and then shown outside.

Mr Cotterell, who had shared with Mrs Tesworth the task of witnessing the union, instructed Tez to follow his car to Gloucestershire once they'd dropped his mother at home.

'You get off straight away. I can easily get a taxi back,' Mrs Tesworth said at once. 'I have engagements I must go to this morning, so I'll leave the rescue mission to you. Do let me know what happens, Tez darling, and welcome to the family, Isabella.'

And she was gone, strolling along the street, stopping to stare in a shop window, even though the shops weren't open yet. As they drove past her, they saw her hail a taxi.

'Nothing ever puts my mother in a flap,' Tez said. 'Or Philip's father, it would seem.'

'Did you notice those two men waiting for him in the car? They looked rather grim and fierce, I thought.'

'He needs a bodyguard sometimes, apparently.'

'What does he do exactly?'

'People say he gathers information for the War Office and the government, and analyses it. He apparently has an amazing memory for detail. But no one knows any more than that. He runs a special, secret unit with an office somewhere in the City, I think. Not sure where. I've never had anything much to do with him.'

'Nor had Philip. I wonder why.'

'Who knows?'

They rode in silence for a few minutes, then he said, 'It's nice that we're together for this drive, isn't it, instead of having to make polite conversation in front of someone else? I hope we can talk frankly, now and always.'

'Yes, it is nice and I hope so too. So I'll start by saying how much I like you, Tez.'

He grinned at her. 'That's an excellent start but I'm aiming for more than that before we're through. I can wait to consummate our marriage till after the baby's born, you know. It won't be easy, but for you I'd do anything.'

'I'm not a naive girl and I don't see why you should have to wait.'

'Well, isn't it obvious?'

'Not really.'

'I want to be sure it isn't going to upset you to, er, consummate the marriage.'

'My mother thinks women can't enjoy making love, but I certainly did and so did Philip. He didn't have to coax me to do it. I wanted to.'

Tez's smile grew broader. 'That is going to make things a lot easier, I must admit. Thank you for not pretending.'

She was feeling less and less awkward. There was something about knowing you were married that brought you even closer together. 'Well, how did you think I got pregnant, Tez? We were overenthusiastic.'

He chuckled. 'Some women claim they were only doing it because their men were going off to fight. Come to think of it, I'm more used to women who pretend about how they feel in all sorts of ways and who do need coaxing with presents and little treats.'

'I don't pretend about anything if I can help it.'

When he reached out to squeeze her hand, she grasped his for a moment and it seemed like a promise they were making to one another, one that was much more important than the brief ceremony they had just gone through.

But they could do nothing about their life together till after they'd rescued Philip's sister. That at least they could do for the man they'd both cared deeply about. 'I hope Georgie is all right.'

He spoke grimly now. 'So do I. Heaven help Francis Filmore if she isn't. Her father will make very sure he regrets it.'

When Georgie woke up the next morning, the room was light and it seemed quite late. Unfortunately there was no clock in the room and she didn't want to disturb Spencer by going to look at his pocket watch, which was right next to where his head lay on the pillow.

Someone was stirring in the house but the noises she heard were only faint, as if people were trying to be quiet. Clearly, from the brightness of the sun, it was not a household that rose early.

When she looked across at the bed, Spencer seemed scarcely to have moved since he'd got into it last night, so she lay still for a while. The longer she could wait to get up, the better. The people at Honeyfield House knew about Francis, and so did her friends.

Then she couldn't wait any longer, simply had to use the

chamber pot. She could see it under the bed and thought it'd wake her brother up when she fished it out, but she managed to slide it out quietly and he still didn't stir. Good, she could do this in private. Well, she could if the door was still locked.

She went to try it and the handle wouldn't turn, thank goodness, so no one had unlocked it from the other side. She turned to look at the bedside table but the key was nowhere to be seen. Perhaps Spencer had shoved it under his pillow.

Not knowing what to do with the chamber pot afterwards, she pushed it back under the bed, grimacing in disgust, and tiptoed across to look out of the window. Perhaps she could get it open and climb down a drainpipe or something.

But no! They were at the back of the house, there was no drainpipe within reach and the land sloped downwards so they were higher above it than at the front. What's more, there was a basement below them, with a small yard in front of it.

That made for such a long drop to the ground, she was sure she'd break a leg if she jumped out. She couldn't make a rope of sheets, as you read about heroines in books doing, because the only sheets were wrapped round her brother.

So she went back to staring out of the window. There were large trees at the bottom end of a long, thin garden, and beyond them the backs of some small businesses. Not an elegant neighbourhood, then.

She was ravenously hungry by now, but Spencer was still sleeping. She tried to tidy her clothes, but they were too badly rumpled to do much and her hair was its usual wild morning tangle. She looked round the room, but there was no sign of a brush or comb, no sign of Spencer's overnight bag, either. Surely he'd brought one?

Time passed slowly and she wished she had something to do, something to read. The figure in the bed was so still, she wondered if Spencer had taken a sleeping powder last night. He sometimes did, she knew.

What was going to happen to her? She couldn't help worrying about what Francis was planning to do to persuade her to marry him. She tried not to give in to her fears, but it was hard to keep her spirits up, however much of a talking-to she gave herself.

Eventually the noises in the rest of the house grew louder. They sounded to be coming from below her. Then there were footsteps on the landing outside the bedroom and someone knocked on the door.

'Time to get up now,' Francis called.

She watched the door handle turn.

'Why have you locked yourself in? Come on, Spencer! We'll have breakfast, then do something about your sister.'

And still her brother didn't stir. That was strange.

Francis rattled the door and yelled again, so she crept across to her brother and shook him. He rolled over, his mouth slack, his eyes staring sightlessly at the ceiling.

Surely he couldn't be . . . she felt for a pulse in his neck and jerked back in shock when she couldn't find one. And what's more, his flesh was cool to the touch, too cool for a live human being.

How could he be dead?

She panicked then and stood whimpering, unable to think straight.

'I'll break this door down if I have to!' Francis yelled from outside.

She jerked in shock at the sound of his voice, checked Spencer's pulse again and still found nothing. Indeed, the more she studied him, the more dead he looked.

She went to the door and rapped on it to get Francis's attention, before calling, 'Spencer's dead.'

Silence greeted this, then, 'What have you done to him, you bitch?'

'I've done nothing. I thought he was asleep so I kept quiet, but when you knocked on the door, I tried to wake him. Only he can't wake up because he's dead.'

'Open the door and let me see. He's probably just unconscious.'

'He's not breathing. There's no pulse. His skin is cold.'

'Well, open the bloody door, for heaven's sake.'

'He's got the key. I don't know where it is.'

'If he had it last night, it's in the room with you. And if he really is dead, he's not going to hand it to you, so you'll need to look for it.'

'Yes. I suppose so. Give me a minute.'

She found the key quite quickly, under the pillow as she'd expected, but couldn't bring herself to open the door and let Francis in. As she stood dithering, it occurred to her that it would be safer to stay behind a locked door. And do what she could to delay things.

She looked round for somewhere to hide the key in case he broke the door down and grew angry with her.

In the end put it under the seat pad of a stiff upright chair near the window. She could claim she hadn't had it. Stepping back she looked at the chair seat and the key didn't show.

The door rattled again. 'Hurry up!'

'I can't find it.'

'Of course you can. It has to be in the bed with him.'

She tried to play him along. 'I don't want to touch a dead man.' As quietly as she could she got another of the stiff wooden chairs and wedged it under the door handle, then looked round. Could she move the chest of drawers behind the door as well? She tried to push it but it was much too heavy so she had to leave it.

The door shook and rattled, and when she didn't answer Francis began thumping on it. 'Stop playing the fool. I can break the door down, you know. And I don't *believe* Spencer is dead. You've overcome him and tied him up, so I need to rescue him.' He bellowed for someone called Dibble to come and help him.

She didn't answer. Let him break down the door. While he was doing it, she was going to stick her head out of the window and scream for help. In fact, why wait? She'd delayed Francis for as long as she could.

She slid the bottom of the window up and leant out, yelling for help at the top of her voice.

Then she sat on the window sill, feet hanging out. If Francis got into the room, she'd have to let herself drop to the ground and risk breaking a limb. She wasn't going to stand there tamely and let him manhandle her – or worse.

* * *

The watcher saw her come to the window and as she looked all right, he followed instructions and didn't reveal his presence.

But when she came to the window a short time later and started yelling for help, he decided he'd have to do something. She still looked unhurt, though, and there was no one with her, so again he hesitated.

In the back of the butcher's shop nearby, Mr Tully stopped cutting up a lamb carcase to listen. 'What on earth's that?'

His apprentice stood still and they both listened.

'Someone's yelling for help,' Percy said. 'A woman.'

He was out of the back door in a trice and the butcher after him.

'Your hearing's better than mine. Where exactly is it coming from?' Mr Tully asked.

'That house behind us.' The lad pointed. 'Look! She's sitting on the window sill, still screaming for help.'

'Ah. That's where that nasty sod Filmore lives. I'd as soon have nothing to do with him. You run and fetch the police.'

'But she's still yelling for help, Mr Tully. And she looks ready to jump. We can't just leave her. He may hurt her. I saw him kick a dog the other day. It wasn't doing anything, just sleeping in the sun and he up and kicked it.'

The lad was fair dancing up and down now. 'What if he *kills* her before the police can get there?'

Mr Tully raised his face to the sky and asked, 'Why me?' feeling aggrieved. Why should he be the one to hear the cries? He wasn't cut out to rescue damsels in distress.

You never saw a stout, older man acting as the hero at the cinema, did you? For obvious reasons.

'We can't just leave her.' Percy didn't wait for permission but ran off and yanked open the rear gate of the house. He flung it back so hard one of its hinges broke and it hung half-open. But that didn't stop him. He kicked it fully open and vanished into the tangle of bushes.

'Young fool,' Mr Tully muttered, but she was still screaming so he followed his apprentice across the back garden. Someone had to see if the woman really did need rescuing. And if she did, he could guess what from. That fellow had been seen to take home ladies before – well, not ladies, women of a certain sort.

'What's wrong, missus?' the lad was yelling up to the young woman sitting on the window sill.

'I've been kidnapped and I've locked myself in this bedroom only he's breaking down the door. I'm afraid he's going to kill me.' She looked over her shoulder as she spoke and the two men outside could clearly hear the crash and the splintering of wood. 'He's coming in.' She started to move closer to the edge of the window sill.

'Don't you jump, missus!' Mr Tully called. 'You'll break your neck. We'll come into the house and get you.'

She hesitated. 'Hurry.' She began to scream again.

Then someone dragged her inside and her screams cut off abruptly.

Mr Tully's ire was now roused. He could recognise terror when he saw it. It was he who pushed open the back door of the house, which wasn't locked, thank goodness, and rushed inside.

The housekeeper was standing in the hall just outside the kitchen listening to what was going on upstairs. She turned as the back door opened and screeched in shock at the sight of them.

'Another damned, screaming woman,' Tully muttered to himself. He pushed past her and charged into the hall and up the stairs, followed a short time later by his apprentice, who had paused to pick up the poker and brandish it experimentally.

The housekeeper collapsed into a chair and had hysterics, but by that time she was alone again so it was a waste of effort and her shrieks soon faded away. After a few moments she followed the two men out into the hall to see what was happening, muttering, 'I'm giving my notice. I am. I'm not standing for this. He's gone too far this time.'

By the time Mr Tully reached the broken pieces of bedroom door, Francis had ripped Georgie's blouse open in the struggle and was shaking her good and hard, yelling, 'Shut up! Shut up, damn you!'

She was making a spirited attempt to scratch his eyes out, still yelling at the top of her voice.

When he clouted her hard and knocked her to the floor, Mr Tully saw red. 'Stop that at once!' he roared in a voice that was noted for its power but more often used for starting Sunday School races than for confronting villains.

Francis swung round and saw a bald middle-aged man, with a jutting belly. The man was red in the face and wouldn't normally have frightened anyone, but what stopped Francis in his tracks was the big cleaver his unwanted visitor was waving threateningly.

When a lad came into the room brandishing a poker, Francis retreated to the far side of the bed.

'Go and fetch the police, Percy. Run for your life,' Mr Tully said.

He turned back to Francis and waved the cleaver again. 'If you move, I'll knock you into the middle of next week, and probably slice off your ear while I'm a-doing of it. I just sharpened this.' Swish went the cleaver again.

By that time, however, the watcher lurking in the garden had gone for the police and Percy met the two constables before he'd run fifty yards.

He skidded to a halt. 'He's kidnapped a woman and got her locked in his house. Mr Tully's keeping him away from her.'

'So it was true,' one of the constables said.

They exchanged startled glances and unhooked their truncheons from their belts.

'Show us,' the other said.

Percy looked beyond them to the stranger. 'Who's he?'

'Someone sent to keep an eye on her,' the man said. 'I'm coming in with you.'

At the house, however, they found Mr Tully sitting on the top stair, rubbing his head, with Georgie in attendance.

'Where's Filmore?' Percy asked.

'Gone. He threw the bedside table at Mr Tully and then hit him over the head with an ornament, before running out of the room. I didn't dare chase after him, and anyway, Mr Tully needed help. Didn't you see Filmore?'

'No. We came in the front way, so he must have gone out of the back.'

Percy rushed across to the window and peered out. 'I can't see him at the back.' Without being told, he ran into the nearest front bedroom and yelled, 'He's gone round the front and he's running down the street now.'

The constables ran back down the stairs, but the stranger had already raced off ahead of them and was considerably more nimble than they were, so began gaining on the panting, wheezing fugitive.

The two cars got to Malmesbury just before lunch after driving faster than Tez considered safe, though he didn't like to say so. Well, if poor Georgie had been in Francis's hands since yesterday, who knew what he'd have done to her? So he managed to keep up with Mr Cotterell's car.

If Francis had raped her, Tez would beat him to a pulp. He couldn't bear men doing that to women and he'd had to reprimand some of the men under him in the army when they talked longingly of doing it to German women. That hadn't made him popular with some of the rougher sorts.

This time he'd have to leave retribution to Georgie's father, who would be best placed to do whatever it took to sort this situation out. Mr Cotterell would be more capable of meting out salutary justice than anyone else, Tez was sure.

The car purred along but as it approached the house where Filmore lived, the passengers saw a man rush out from the side and another man erupt from the front door to chase after him.

Cotterell's car accelerated and caught up with the running men, just as Filmore turned down an alley at the far end that had bollards across it. The two guards were out of the car in a flash and chasing after him.

Mr Cotterell got out and stood watching them, arms folded, so Tez and Isabella joined him.

Tez cheered loudly as the leading pursuer did a flying rugby tackle that brought Filmore down and the man behind him helped drag Filmore to his feet and hold him against the wall that lined the alley.

'Good,' was all Mr Cotterell said. He wasted no time, but led the way back to Filmore's house.

Georgie persuaded Mr Tully to go down to the kitchen on the promise of a cup of tea and Percy clattered down the stairs in front of them. There they found the housekeeper wringing her hands and alternately sobbing or demanding to know who was going to pay her wages now.

Percy needed no urging to fill the big kettle and put it on to the gas burner.

At that point the housekeeper took over. 'Never let it be said that I can't still make a cup of tea!' she declared, spoiling this by adding, 'And I'm sure I need a cup as much as anyone else does, not to mention a dash of brandy in it for the shock.'

'Good idea!' said Mr Tully enthusiastically.

Georgie went to sit huddled on a chair, feeling suddenly weak and shaky.

When someone came into the house, they all swung round.

'Who's that?' the housekeeper quavered.

Gerald Cotterell followed the sound of voices and stood in the doorway of the kitchen, taking in the scene. His eyes kept going back to his daughter. He would make her feel like his daughter now, show her how he loved her – if that was possible.

He stepped forward. 'Are you all right, Georgie?'

She sighed in relief. 'Yes, Father.'

'Filmore didn't touch you?'

'No. Spencer saved me.'

'I'm glad to hear that he's not completely bad.' Sadness at the thought of his sickly son welled up in him, as it usually did. And his daughter looked so white and upset that for a moment he couldn't speak and had to breathe deeply a couple of times before he could continue.

'Shall we all go into the parlour and you can tell me exactly what happened, Georgie? You don't mind me calling you Georgie? It was my wife who insisted on using your full name always.'

'I prefer it.'

'Good.' He turned to the housekeeper, 'Madam, if you could supply us with tea and something to eat we'd be very grateful. This is for your trouble.' He put a half-crown down on the table in front of her.

The coin quickly vanished. 'I'm happy to help,' the housekeeper said in a calmer voice.

He turned back to Georgie. 'Where's your brother hiding?'

'Spencer's in the bedroom, but I think – no, I'm *sure* he's dead.'

There was utter silence for a moment, then he asked grimly, 'Did Filmore kill him? If so, I'll see him hanged.'

'No. Spencer died in his sleep. He made me share his bedroom so that Francis couldn't hurt me. I didn't hear anything, but when I woke Spencer wasn't moving. I thought he was still asleep, but then Francis tried to get in so I went to wake Spencer, and—and found he was dead.' She shuddered violently.

After a moment's hesitation, he went across and put his arm round his daughter's shoulders. 'Spencer was never in good health, never destined to make old bones. The doctors didn't expect him to live this long. You're safe now, Georgie. I won't let anyone hurt you again. You can come back to London with me, if you like. It's a big house. Not if you don't want to, of course.'

She stared up at him in surprise and he gave her a little hug. It felt so right to have his arm round her without worrying about what Adeline might do in retribution.

'I'd like to come to you. I don't ever want to go back to Westcott.'

'Westcott will change. My wife will be moving out.'

'She won't go. She loves the place.'

'Adeline loves the status it gives her,' he corrected. 'And I doubt I'll have much trouble with her from now on. She cared deeply about Spencer, I'll give her that. If he's dead, she'll fall to pieces.'

There was silence for a moment or two, then he risked giving her another gentle hug and stepped back, feeling as if he'd crossed an important boundary. 'I'd better go and check on Spencer. Mrs Tesworth, could you please take my daughter into the parlour and look after her?'

Isabella turned to Georgie. 'Come on, dear. You're quite safe now.'

'Could you find my daughter something warm to wear, Tez? Maybe there's a coat on the hallstand.'

'Yes, of course.' As Mr Cotterell started up the stairs, Tez exchanged a quick, surprised look with his wife and whispered, 'Never seen him so human.'

'Perhaps he's never dared show it before.'

When they got into the parlour and Isabella would have taken her arm away, Georgie clutched her. 'Please. Can I just . . . hold on to you for a moment? I can't seem to stop shivering.'

'Of course you can. Let's sit together on the sofa.'

Tez came back shortly afterwards and put a man's overcoat round Georgie's shoulders, but though she nodded her thanks, she still clutched Isabella's hand.

'My father seemed . . . different today. More like a father.'

'That's good, isn't it?'

'Yes. Very good. I've felt so alone in the world.'

'You'll have a little niece or nephew too in a few months. I've been trying to keep it quiet, but now your brother and Filmore have been caught, I can tell the world.'

Georgie beamed at her. 'That means something of Philip will continue. And Tez will make a wonderful stepfather.'

'I'm so glad you're happy.'

'I shall absolutely love having a niece or nephew. And a sister-in-law even if you never actually married my brother.'

The two women hugged one another.

When Mr Cotterell rejoined them, he said quietly, 'You were right, Georgie. Your brother is dead.'

'What did he die of?'

'Natural causes, I should think. He was born with various physical weaknesses, including a heart problem. I can't say at this stage which one killed him, but the doctors will no doubt find out. He looked peaceful, at least.'

'Why are Philip and I so different from him? We weren't sickly.'

He hesitated.

'We can leave you alone with your daughter, if you wish to explain privately, sir,' Tez said quietly.

'No. I'm only going to tell this tale once and you two also have a right to hear it since you'll be raising Philip's child, my grandchild.'

He pulled a chair closer to his daughter, speaking to her mainly. 'Spencer was only your half-brother, Georgie. I'm your father but your real mother was . . . someone else. My wife's family carried a fault they'd hidden from the world, one which caused some children to be born with . . . problems. I shall not go into details.'

'I see.'

'I didn't get on with my wife, not at all. And then I met your mother and fell deeply in love for the first time in my life. When I found I'd fathered another child, I was glad.

Only it turned out to be twins and she died birthing you.'

His voice broke and he fell silent for a moment, then stood up again, his face becoming expressionless. 'I didn't expect that, Georgie. I was going to divorce my wife and marry your mother. Only it wasn't to be. I didn't expect Spencer would live this long, either. So I insisted my wife raise you as hers, told her I'd divorce her if she didn't and leave her penniless. I had evidence that she'd been unfaithful to me, you see.

'With your real mother dead, making sure you weren't considered bastards seemed important, the best way to give you a decent start in life. I was too upset to think it through. I no longer let myself be ruled by emotion, not in important matters.' He sighed. 'Once we'd started the charade, it wasn't possible to stop it. Adeline acknowledged that as well as I did.'

He looked across at Isabella. 'Thank you for making my son happy and for giving me a grandchild.'

'I'm not letting you take the baby away from me,' she warned him.

'I wouldn't try, but I hope you'll let me visit him and get to know him.'

'Or her.'

He managed a half-smile. 'Or her. I am not good with children and I have no intention of marrying again, so my wife can stay my wife as long as she moves to her house in Malmesbury and causes no further trouble.'

'Will she do that?'

'Oh, yes. I'll make sure of it. She'll be upset about her son dying. She must be the only person to have loved Spencer. Not an amiable child, even when he was young, and he grew into a nasty human being.'

He turned as one of his men came to the door of the sitting room.

'We've locked him up at the police station, sir.'

'Good. We'll arrange for him to be taken up to London and charged with kidnapping and whatever else the lawyers can throw at him.'

The housekeeper turned up then, pushing a trolley loaded with tea things.

Gerald stayed only long enough to have a cup of tea and something to eat. 'Shall I send a car for you, Georgie? I need to get back immediately, but you'll want to change your clothes, no doubt.'

'I'll find my own way to London. By train, probably.'

'Very well. I'll tell my housekeeper to expect you.'

He left as quietly as he did everything else, but suddenly popped his head back into the doorway to add, 'I'll visit a funeral director on the way out of town and send someone round here. No need for you to have anything further to do with Spencer's body.'

'Why is Cotterell so terrifying?' Tez wondered when the sound of his car had vanished into the distance. 'You wouldn't want to get on his wrong side.'

Isabella considered this, then shrugged. 'I don't find him terrifying, exactly, but then I'm not one of his enemies. I do find him implacable, if that's the word.'

Georgie put her cup down. 'It was the first time he's ever hugged me that I remember. I wonder who my real mother was?'

'I don't think he'll ever tell you. He sounds to have loved her, though.'

'I'll make him tell me. I might have a whole family somewhere to replace the one I've lost.'

'You've got us as well,' Isabella said. 'And you'll have a nephew or niece in a few months. You can come and stay with us for a while, if you like, before you go up to London.'

'Would you mind? I don't really want to go there yet. I'd like some peaceful time first. But I will go and stay with my father in a few days, see how that works out.'

'Of course we don't mind. You can have what used to be Tez's bedroom.' She smiled at her husband and slipped her hand into his. Things would go well for them now, she was sure.

Epilogue

On a snowy morning the following January, Isabella gave birth to a baby boy.

When the midwife had cleaned everything up, Tez came in to sit beside her.

'Mother will need a rest,' the midwife told them severely.

'Mother needs to see Father more than she needs to rest,' Isabella said promptly. She might put up with a domestic tyrant like this woman to guide her through the mysteries of giving birth, but it hadn't been a bad birthing, and she wanted her husband now.

'I'll be back in ten minutes,' the midwife said, giving them a fierce look. 'Then Mother must rest.'

When the woman had grumbled her way down to the kitchen, Tez kissed Isabella's cheek. 'Well done.'

Her eyes were on the tiny body in the cradle. 'I wanted to cuddle him but she insisted on taking him away from me.'

'That's easily solved.' Tez leant across and lifted the squirming infant out of the cradle, giving him a kiss on the forehead before passing him to Isabella.

'Isn't he wonderful?'

'A miracle of beauty,' he said solemnly, eyeing the red squalling face, which looked slightly squashed to him. 'Still want to call him Philip?'

'Yes, of course. Philip Aaron Tesworth after both his fathers.' She gave Tez a glowing smile. 'Thank you for looking after us both so well while I waited for him to emerge.'

'That was my pleasure.'

'You are a lovely man, Tez. And I love you very much.'

His face lit up. 'Darling! That's the first time you've said it.'

'I mean it.'

'I know. You don't pretend about anything.'

To discover more great books and to
place an order visit our website at
allisonandbusby.com

Don't forget to sign up to our free newsletter at
allisonandbusby.com/newsletter
for latest releases, events and exclusive offers

Allison & Busby Books
@AllisonandBusby

You can also call us on
020 7580 1080
for orders, queries
and reading recommendations